Shadow Play

SHADOW PLAY

D.A. Lampi

To Kelli & Mike -
Wonderful friends &
neighbors!
Best always,
Dahlie

North Star Press of St. Cloud, Inc.
Saint Cloud, Minnesota

For my dear friend Ada Cohen,
the strongest woman I know.

Copyright © 2013 D.A. Lampi

ISBN 978-0-87839-689-4

First Edition, June 1, 2012

Printed in the United States of America

Published by
North Star Press of St. Cloud, Inc.
P.O. Box 451
St. Cloud, Minnesota 56302

www.northstarpress.com   Facebook - North Star Press   Twitter - North Star Press

Acknowledgments

I would like to acknowledge the many people who have supported me throughout my writing journey. Thanks to MLO for believing in me. J.E. Nissley, C.E. Jones, Dagnee, Max Keenu, Irene Hamilton, Patti Yaeger, John VanCott, Julianna Drumheller, John Klawitter and John DeBoer, my online writing group friends, all talented writers, gave generously of their time and talents to offer useful insights and suggestions to make *Shadow Play* a better novel.

I would like to thank Paul Negri, who provided valuable assistance at many stages of the manuscript and whose encouragment, thoughtful advice and guidance were invaluable.

I look forward to the first Friday of every month meeting of my in-person writing group. Many thanks to Jeffrey Briggs, Shelley Mahannah, Dan Dietrich and Penelope Duffy, who provide me with thought-provoking discussion, friendship, insight and great coffee. We talk about our characters as if they are real people and no one thinks anything of it. For that I am grateful.

I would also like to thank Mardie Geiser for many years of friendship and laughter and Sylvia DeMott and Bobbi Nicols for their immeasurable support.

And finally, I am grateful for the love and support of my family, who have given me the space and time to see *Shadow Play* to completion.

PROLOGUE

SOMETIMES WHEN IT'S QUIET, I remember what our lives were like before terror hovered over us like a funnel cloud. The abduction occurred on August 26, many years ago and a thousand miles away. A day that still haunts me like an unruly ghost.

My son was six years old then, my daughter, thirteen. The events preceding the abduction have become as smudged as the glasses my son wore as a child, although the memories of the aftermath have never left me.

The months before the abduction were tumultuous. My husband had died of cancer and I grieved his loss. I had left my private practice and worked with inmates at the Rochester Forensic Center so I could have more time with my children. I was a psychiatrist then.

Newspaper pictures taken of me soon after the abduction show a face so deeply etched with grief, I couldn't recognize myself. The Midwest had come to signify treachery and deceit and afterwards I moved to Rhinebeck, a small town nestled on the banks of the Hudson River. Unafraid, I sat on the riverbank and gazed at the water. It was along those banks where I planned a new beginning. These are the events as they occurred.

Grace Rendeau

CHAPTER ONE

THE SMELL OF FALL WAS LIKE WARM rain in the woods. I strode through fluttering gold leaves and waved to inmates dressed in prison-issue khaki uniforms, enjoying a perfect autumn morning. They were on yard detail, hacking at ivy clinging to the razor wire which circled the prison. Uniformed officers stood over them, hands at their holsters.

No matter what their crimes, in the few weeks I had worked in the unit, I had begun to see their humanity and felt a kind of sympathy for them. The barbaric ice baths, insulin shock, and lobotomies my predecessors had once performed on these very grounds still caused me to shudder. I lifted my face to the sun and breathed deeply, enjoying the last warm days before the Minnesota winter swept in once again.

In the late 1800s, patients had worked on the land, growing vegetables, which were preserved in a system of neighboring caves. The food from their labor fed the old state hospital population through the long winters. The grounds now housed the modern Rochester Forensic Center, where I was the newest psychiatrist.

Corrections Officer Bud Anderson fell into step with me halfway to the entrance. At the time, Bud Anderson was forty-three years old, over six feet tall, and as large and gray-headed as a buzzard with a crew cut. "Morning, Doc. What a day, huh?"

I had heard through the prison grapevine he was having marital problems. Word was he had a core made of iron and a life mortgaged to the hilt. He also had a limb length discrepancy resulting from an injury during his service and wore an orthotic shoe with a lift. Even so, his gait was brisk and measured.

"So, how ya doin' Grace?" Anderson asked with a familiarity that set me on edge. He smiled, showing a space the size of a small stream through his front teeth.

I hadn't had time that morning for anything but a slash of lip-gloss and a coat of brown mascara over my nearly invisible lashes. A long

1

lock of coppery hair slipped out from behind my ear. I felt as exposed under his scrutiny as if he'd unzipped my skirt and laid bare all the fears and insecurities I had had since Matt died. "It's a beauty, officer," I said, my eyes drawn to the inmates.

He swaggered through the lot and turned to ask me if I'd care to go out for lunch. I stared ahead, pretending not to notice the narrowing of his eyes and told him I was busy. The look he gave me was brief but I got a glimpse of something dark. To my relief, we reached security before any more could be said. I clipped the heavy key ring the officer at the station issued me to my belt and fled to my office.

The jangling of the keys and the sound of my heels clicking along the cold tiled floor only added to the din in the halls. The smell of disinfectant hovered in the air. I unlocked my door and closed it to the chaos of the psychiatric unit and leaned against the door. I closed my eyes, and for the second time that day, thought of Matt.

Before my husband's death, I couldn't have imagined my patients would be a volatile mix of inmates incarcerated for everything from narcotics to murder. Many were living out sentences here and some were deemed incompetent to stand trial, while others had been transferred from prisons around the country for medical or psychiatric care.

Shortly after he died, I gathered the strength that remained and moved to Rochester. The new job in the forensic center was initially bearable only because I had evenings and weekends free for the children. During my days in private practice, Matt had often been both mother and father to the children. But now I needed this 7:30 a.m. to four o'clock job and the mothering hours it provided.

Beep beep beep . . . Beep beep beep . . . "Paging Dr. Grace Rendeau. Dr. Rendeau please report to the dayroom in Psych West, stat." The sound of the nurse's page echoed through the building.

Jarred into action by the page and the beeper vibrating at my hip, I raced to the dayroom and then stopped stock-still to see two officers restraining my new patient. Emanuel Venegas struggled, his muscles bulging underneath his olive shirt. Blood splattered the walls like a Rorschach. Larry Reynolds, another inmate who had been escorted to the prison by US Air Marshals the previous day, held an icepack to his face and cursed Emanuel. The ebb and flow of aggression in the unit was still new and disturbing to me. Uniformed officers swarmed the dayroom, reminding me of a scene from *A Clockwork Orange,* and my heart beat like a caged bird. As tough as I tried to appear, the continual rage that spilled over on the unit still had the power to upset me.

Warren Hutchings, R.N., a balding, twelve-year veteran of the unit and the size of a minivan, stood in a wide-legged stance. "I gave 'em their meds and as soon as I turned my back, Emanuel punched him in the face. I heard the sound of cracking and turned to see blood spurting out of Reynolds's nose. Then they were on the floor rolling, both of 'em throwing punches."

What a way to start the day. "Emanuel, I'm going to have to put you in the hole. You know the rules. Please escort Mr. Venegas to solitary," I instructed Officer Anderson.

Bud was as firmly in command of the situation as a colonel in charge of an offensive. He clamped cuffs on Emanuel's wrists. "Please escort him to security?" He stifled a laugh. "You're barking up the wrong tree if you think that's gonna work around here. Around here, we say, 'throw him in the hole.' You've gotta learn to toughen up if you wanna survive in this place, Doc."

I despised the smugness with which he expressed his opinions and pulled myself up to my full five feet, eight-inch height. "I'm as capable as anyone else of working here. I'm not going to dehumanize my patients on your advice, officer." So much for having my back. Hutchings handed me a pair of sterile gloves. "Mr. Reynolds, are you okay? Let me take a look at your nose."

Blood dripped from his nostrils and pooled on the floor. "I'm okay, Doc. Just get me outta here. I don't wanna be anywhere near that lunatic." He spit out a mouthful of blood, neatly missing my foot.

"I'm going to have to send you for x-rays. Mr. Hutchings, will you arrange for transport to the ER please?" I should've said, "Get him to the ER STAT," but it was too late. "And get the hazard team to clean up."

"Yeah, no problem," Hutchings said, opening a wad of sterile bandages. "Hold these to your nose, man."

I peeled off the gloves, washed my hands and went to the hole–a seclusion room devoid of everything but a sink, urinal, and a thin mattress on the floor. Emanuel rocked rhythmically in a corner of his cell, with his knees drawn to his chest and his arms clenched around his shins.

Despair oozed from his pores. Thin morning light sifted in from the barred windows, illuminating thick, wormy veins protruding from his hands. He reached his arms toward the window, apparently hallucinating.

The smell of animal fear hovered in the air. "Emanuel, it's Dr. Rendeau. Can you hear me?" I lay my hand on his shoulder and he began to weep. The staff's mission was to staunch the flow of memories, prescribe antipsychotics and occasionally electroconvulsive shock therapy for the severely depressed. But for some patients, time was the only recourse. I asked if he would be willing to take his meds, and he looked at me without recognition.

Risperdol by mouth was what I had decided. If he refused, we'd have to give it to him by injection. He was obviously a danger to others on the unit, possibly even to himself. Hutchings agreed and said he might need some help giving it to him. I did not want a repeat of the earlier scene in the dayroom or to have the team called again unless it was absolutely necessary.

The patient pushed a long, shaggy strand of hair out of his eyes and nodded, almost imperceptibly. He looked like a man buried under an avalanche of pain but somehow still breathing. I waited until the medication subdued him to leave the room.

Before returning to my office, I looked once more through the peephole and watched in horror as Emanuel rose in a frenzy and tore the fabric of his mattress. I was shaking as I pressed a code into my beeper. Within moments, the team barged in, military-style, wearing black facemasks. They took him down, and I witnessed the degradation of a human being sunk to his lowest level.

Emanuel glowered at me. His despair drew him into a dark place far removed from the unit. I ordered him to be restrained and placed under constant observation in order to protect himself, and injected him with four mg of Risperidol–the beginning of a ritual that would repeat itself every four hours.

"Mr. Reynolds, please let me know immediately if there are any changes. I'll see if I can get Josie Garrett to talk to him. Once he's out of restraints, he might open up more to someone who speaks Spanish."

Afterwards, I escaped to the relative calm of my office and sat at my desk, my head cradled in my hands. I had begun to realize working with psychotic inmates was not like my previous psychotherapy with the worried well. Most of my new patients had a very tenuous grasp on reality. If and when they were well enough to begin psychotherapy, it often began with angry protestations of innocence. Paranoid delusions about someone who was out to get them and anger at the raw deal they believed they had gotten followed.

My head throbbed. Still trembling from the scene in the seclusion room, I dug an Aleve tablet out of my purse and sipped cold coffee from a lipstick-stained styrofoam cup. My calendar lay on my desk, Dane's Little League game, highlighted in neon green. I closed my eyes and rubbed both temples. The children and the demands of my days with mentally ill inmates left little time for anything else. If I were lucky, I would find time to fit in a yoga class on the weekend.

The next morning, a band of sunlight sliced through my bedroom window. Jagged lights and a tingling in my right cheek signaled a migraine. I squeezed my eyes tight and gulped an Imitrex from my night table before stumbling to the bathroom.

There was a mandatory inspection at the forensic unit scheduled that day. I trawled through my drawers, with one hand on my forehead, and found a pair of pantyhose without a run. I then rummaged through the closet and found an ironed linen jacket and skirt. I prayed the AC at the prison was working.

The pain began to dissipate, and I mentally viewed the plan for the day. Make breakfast, drop the kids at school, inspection at work, come home, prepare dinner, help with homework, drive the kids to soccer and tee ball, and then baths and bed. I called Caleigh to hurry on my way downstairs. I didn't want to be late.

The sound and smell of coffee perking was as encouraging as a pep squad. Five-year-old Dane sat sleepy-eyed at the table. "Can I have pancakes, Mom?" he lisped. His tongue poked through a checkerboard smile where his two front teeth had fallen out. He had freckled skin and copper-colored hair, similar to mine.

"Sweetie, we don't have time for pancakes. What kind of cereal do you want?" I gave him two choices knowing if it were more, I would be late for work.

"Caleigh? Hurry, honey. I can't be late today!" I called up the stairs again with a tight, fixed smile and then poured two bowls of cereal and a cup of coffee. My superficial temporal artery pulsed under my fingertips, and, still being an anatomy nerd, I was pleased I remembered its name.

The sound of thirteen-year-old Caleigh clomping down the stairs in wedge heels reverberated through the old house. She dropped her backpack onto the kitchen's wide oak planks. "What's the hurry, Mom?" Caleigh was fine-boned and delicate with soft, blond waves. Her eyes were ringed like a badger's. I would have had her wash off the thick black liner if I weren't in such a hurry.

Between Caleigh's adolescent mood swings, the new job, and the constant rush, I ran like an old pair of shoes, wearing away at the edges. "Come on. You know I have an inspection at work today." I poured my coffee into the travel mug. "We need to get out of here now."

The children were quiet and crabby. Dane sat in the backseat with his stegosaurus backpack beside him. I looked at him in the rearview mirror and wished for the thousandth time Matt were here.

The school was twenty minutes away with no traffic. "Have a good day!" I called as Dane climbed out of the car and slung his backpack over his shoulder. "Carry it on both shoulders, sweetie!" He splashed in every puddle on the sidewalk on his way to the entrance. "Bye, Mom!" he turned and yelled, before merging into a throng of children weighed down with backpacks like brightly colored turtle shells. "See you at the game!"

I drove the few blocks to Kellogg Middle School, thinking about the inspection and what it might mean for my career. Hidden somewhere in the corridors of my busy life was a woman who wasn't always rushing.

"Just leave me off. I can walk from here." Caleigh smeared on lipgloss and was out the door.

Sunlight glinted off the car in front of me, directly into my eyes. "Are you sure, honey?" I hated to admit how relieved I was not to have to wait in the line of cars circling around the entrance of the school. I dug in my purse for my sunglasses.

"Yup. See ya, Mom." Caleigh hiked up her skirt and ran her hand through her hair.

The sharp, hammering pain in my temples finally settled behind my right eye and became a mere thud as I drove the short distance to work. I was worried about Caleigh. Ever since Matt died, she had been as angry as a hornet. Dane, who was three when his father died, barely seemed to remember Matt. This, in turn, infuriated Caleigh, who took every opportunity to tell me how differently "Daddy would do things."

CHAPTER TWO

M Y PATIENTS PACED THE HALLS in whitewashed pajamas and flimsy cotton robes. Old Mr. Sandvik scuffled by with the peculiar gait caused by long-term use of anti-psychotic medications. He smiled sadly, his jaw swinging and his tongue lolling like a cow at pasture. *Tardive dyskinesia,* I mentally noted. The balance between a therapeutic dose and the harmful side effects of long-term antipsychotic use was delicate. For my private patients, therapy tranquilizers and anti-depressants had been the more likely course of treatment. The consequences of irreparable neurological side effects in long-term institutionalized patients were not pretty.

The wide set of swinging doors to the dayroom opened to my key. There was a charged air in the room. I knew the inspection team was there before I saw them. The warden introduced me to the five men and women. They asked a few questions about my patients and left to examine medical records. I breathed a sigh of relief and crossed the room to eighty-year-old Finn Koski. After thirteen years in the unit, he had the ghostly pallor of an undertaker. Soft pouches ballooned under his eyes, the saddest eyes I had ever seen.

Finn was slight and stooped with thinning hair and eyes so blue they were the first thing I had noticed about him. His skin was paper thin and creased. An old man. His prison-issue khakis drooped off his slim hips and ballooned around him. His voice still held a twinge of an accent although I knew he had immigrated to Minnesota from his native Finland almost sixty years earlier.

He sat looking out onto the grounds, his thin skin dripping like wax from his jaws. Tyrell Perkins sat next to him. They looked like two elderly men feeding pigeons in the park, just to pass the time, both lost in the magic of the past. Over the last few weeks, not only had I overheard stories about Mr. Koksi's life on the farm and Tyrell's in Chicago, but also about the deep abiding love each had felt for a woman and what they had done for it. They were old men to whom the passage of time had not been kind. I looked at them and wondered what drew me to psychiatry. Most of my current patients, men with less-than-average intelligence and greater-than-average childhood traumas, had been judged criminally insane. Tyrell Perkins had been in prison since the tender age of twenty.

"You know I learned to read by reading the Bible," Tyrell said. In the tiled dayroom, his voice boomed like a church organ. I stood by quietly and listened. "Yep. That's my greatest joy. Reading the Bible and doing an honest day's work. I thank God for these blessings."

Tyrell reminded me of a retired greyhound who had found his calling. He spread the word of the Lord to anyone who would listen. His was a body beginning to bend with age. He had worn prison garb for so long it was doubtful if he even remembered what other fabric felt like against his skin. His joints groaned like creaking lumber as he rose and returned to his mop and bucket. Dragging them behind him, he shuffled to seclusion and peered through the peephole at Emanuel. It was evident he had respect for the intensity of Emanuel's sadness. "Waste of a good man's last years to sit there like that, doin' nothin' at all," he said and then continued his methodical mopping. "It's a world gone wrong but it'll be okay, brother. God is with you," he promised before ambling back into the dayroom.

"Ya know, Finn, I know the power of a human touch," he settled down in a chair to say. "The scorching heat and tenderness of it. The way it sucks a man in. The thrill of those fingers delicately running their nails down my chest and the A-bomb were what I lived for." He paused. "Man-o-man. There's no human touch here. Never dreamed I'd miss it like I do."

Finn looked at him mutely. His eyes were rheumy and lusterless. "My wife was a woman like that," he finally mumbled.

Tyrell nodded. "Early on, I dreamed of a woman's silky smooth skin and way her hips swayed when she walked. No offense, Doc," he said to me, "but I still miss those ladylike moves–a woman combing her hair, reaching her lips up to be kissed, smoothing a wrinkle from a shirt, maybe caressing my cheek. There's nuthin' like it. The love of a good woman can change a man, all right." He shut his eyes and then after a moment, returned to his mopping. His gaze took in the inmates in the room. "My job's to help these guys here now. God and time will slow down the desires of the flesh." He wrung out his mop and it clattered in the pail. The smell of diluted bleach filled the room, and he began the cleansing comfort of back and forth mopping, one foot at a time, as if swathing bandages over burns.

"Good morning, gentlemen. Did you have a good weekend?" I asked, standing next to Finn. A pimple had begun to form on my chin and I forced myself to keep my fingers away from the pre-menstrual breakout. I brought my hands to my lower back and tried to massage the ache away.

"Morning, Doc," Finn stood and shook my hand, his knuckles shifting beneath my grip. "Just thinkin' about what Mr. Perkins had to say. You feelin' okay today?"

My hands dropped to my sides. "Fine. Thanks for asking."

"You're looking fine today," Tyrell said. "You know how it is here. A good weekend is when you see somethin' good on TV, have enough food in your belly, and sweet Jesus watches over you."

"How are you today, Mr. Koski?" I sat down next to him and crossed my legs.

He was a wizened old man, his hands as gnarled as willows. It was painful to watch his gait, stiffened from years of labor and osteoarthritis. His voice dropped to a painful whisper. "Say, you don't know when I'll be leaving here, do you? There's so much to do on the farm at this time of year."

I shook my head. "No, I'm sorry, I don't. Don't worry, the farm will be okay." *Confused and disoriented*, I mentally noted. "How about working with the landscape crew? I bet you could teach them a thing or two about gardening. There is a lot to be harvested this time of year."

"I bet I could teach those young men a thing or two." Something flared briefly in his eyes. Sadness? Relief? Worry? "Just as long as I get out of here in time to plant my fields." He smiled. A smile that reminded me of my father's and broke my heart.

"I'll check with the social worker to see if you can go out with the gardening crew." I would read his chart and find out what really happened. "I'll see you tomorrow, Mr. Koski."

The seclusion room had a mesh-covered peephole in the door. Through it I saw Emanuel lying on his bed staring at the ceiling. His feet hung over the thin mattress. He didn't turn when I entered. Bud Anderson waited outside, his eye glued to the peephole.

"Emanuel, will you take your medication by mouth today? It would be so much easier, and you'll feel better." Another involuntary, court-ordered medication was more than I could bear.

He reached a hand, straddled with ropy veins, for the white medication cup. His hands shook as he put the pill in his mouth, slurped water, and swallowed it.

"I'm going to have to ask you to open your mouth, so I can be sure you have swallowed the medication." He opened his mouth and although the stench was awful, I checked in his cheeks and under his tongue. "Thank you. May I tell the nurses you would be willing to shower and change, maybe brush your teeth?"

He looked at me without comment and then nodded.

"I'll come back later to see how you're doing. I'd like to get you back on the unit as soon as possible." Unsure of how much English Emanuel understood, I continued, "Josie Garrett, our social worker, speaks Spanish. It might be easier for you. What do you think?"

The patient shrugged, his eyes downcast.

"I'll see you before I leave today, okay?" I locked the seclusion room door behind me, entered the nurses' station, and told Hutchings that Emanuel had agreed to take his meds. I asked the nurses to check that he swallowed each dose and the orderlies helped him bathe. I told Hutchings I would talk to Josie Garrett about translating or interviewing Emanuel in Spanish. He gave me a strange look and said, "There are plenty of people around who speak Spanish," but before I could respond, my beeper went off. CONSULT IN MEDICINE. It was turning out to be one of those days when I wouldn't have a moment to sit down. Still curious about Hutchings's reaction to Josie, I followed the jaundiced tile floor to the medical building, reading the consultation notes as I walked.

The subterranean passage was warm that day. Josie Garrett, the unit's social worker, rushed past me in running shoes and turned to wave. Sweat dripped off her wide, dark forehead. My nose wrinkled as she passed—Josie's deodorant must have given out on her. Between the acrid smell, the heat in the tunnel and my lingering headache and cramps, I felt like I was about to be sick.

"Hey, Josie. Training for the marathon? Wait a minute, would you? I just saw Mr. Koski in the dayroom. Do you think you could get him involved in the spring planting with the gardening crew?" I walked faster, wishing I had worn a cool comfortable pair of slacks and flats instead of a skirt and heels. My control top pantyhose chafed at my inner thighs and squeezed my bloated belly.

"Oh, and I was wondering if you could talk to Emanuel Venegas when you have a chance? He hasn't said enough to me so I can't even figure out if he understands me. Maybe he'd do better in Spanish."

"Sure, I'll work on it. I'll be in to see Vengas ASAP. Anyone who was baptized Josefina Antonia Gutierrez Garcia has to be able to speak a little Spanish, huh?" She laughed, her limbs moving with the precision of a marching soldier. "We still have a few months until spring for the gardening. No hurry, right?"

I struggled to keep up. "No. No hurry. He's not going anywhere. Just wanted to give him something to look forward to. Gutierrez Garcia? Where's the Garrett come from?" I asked, wiping the sweat from my forehead.

"Long story. Let's just say I wanted to get rid of Josefina Antonia Gutierrez Garcia, so I married a Garrett. Unfortunately, I fell in love afterwards so I got rid of the man but kept the name. I came out and lost my children. Anyway, I've reinvented myself. Now I'm Josie Garret, LCSW instead of, Sergeant Gutierrez. And I have the woman of my dreams in my life instead of Detective Garrett."

At last I'd found someone who had had more tragedies than I had. Josie was more comfortable in giving out personal information than I was. Fascinated, I took advantage of it by asking more questions. "Josie, slow down! This is a lot to take in. Let me get this straight. You were born Josefina whatever. Got that. Where? You married Detective Garrett and changed your name. You have children? Sergeant Gutierrez? You lost me."

"It was another life. My life was a mess. I was born in San Juan. I was a cop. Moved to Chicago. Sex crimes unit. I was injured and during the recovery and the divorce, I knew I had to make a change so I got my degree in social work, and here I am. It was better for the kids to be with their father. He moved to Wyoming."

"Oh, that's where you get the gorgeous tan and the dark eyes and curls." Josie's hair was almost a purple-black in the sun.

"Yep, I'm a mezcla. In Puerto Rico, it means a mix of Taino Indian, African slaves and white from the Spanish who colonized the island. I probably have some horny Spaniard's golden eyes in my ancestry. Pure Puerto Rican."

"You were a sex crimes investigator? I mean . . . I guess it's a stereotype, but you don't look like one!" Josie had a lean, muscular build and smooth skin in a hue best described as pecan. Her eyes were large and amber-colored. Her dark curls were pulled into a ponytail. "And what about your kids? How old are they?"

"It was easy to blend in. A push-up bra, some cheap makeup and heels and I looked like I belonged on the street. Ten years of seeing young girls return to vicious pimps did a number on me. I got injured and I wanted my daughters to have a nice, safe life with their dad and his new wife in a small town where nothing happens. Then there was the old Catholic guilt trip about being gay. That was ten years ago. They're fifteen and sixteen now. Jade and Kira. Anyway, here's where I get off," she said, unlocking a metal door to the cafeteria. "I wonder what's on the menu for today. Hasta luego." She tipped an imaginary hat as she said goodbye.

Unaccustomed to this much chatter in the prison, I walked slowly to the medical unit, debating whether seclusion and Risperidol were the right choices for Emanuel. I wondered whether Mr. Koski would live out his life on the unit. Both had been sentenced for manslaughter and forgotten like old postcards never mailed.

As the afternoon wore on, the heat refused to budge. Rather than face a hot stove, I called for Chinese takeout from the office. After an eight-hour day, walking out of the prison filled me with gratitude for the simple taste of freedom, even if it was to go home and to do mundane tasks.

I pushed the door open with one foot, juggling my purse, keys and cartons of Chinese with both hands.

"Mommy, you're home!" Dane wrapped his arms around my waist. I dropped the cartons on the table and scooped him in my arms, savoring his little-boy smell and holding him a second too long. "You missed my game!"

I rustled his unruly reddish curls. "I'm so sorry, honey. I had an emergency at work. I promise I'll see the next one, okay?" Our ninety-pound yellow lab bounded toward me, threatening to knock me over, his tail whipping against my legs. "Sketcher, get down! Down, Sketcher!"

"You said that the last time. I'm hungry." He turned away, and I saw Dane had long since outgrown the pudginess of toddlerhood and his jeans were an inch too short again.

I went into the kitchen, washed my hands and became "Mommy" again. I wanted to relish the feel of my arms around him. Since Matthew died, Dane and I had been exceptionally close. "Where's Caleigh?"

"Here," she called from the darkened living room, absorbed in the latest issue of *Teen Magazine*. Backpacks and lunch boxes littered the floor.

The children's homework and notebooks covered the kitchen table. "Come help me clear the table, okay, honey?"

"Mom! Don't put them there! The counter's sticky. Dane spilled the jelly."

I put the books on the floor and brought my hand to my lower belly, cursing under my breath at the painful cramps. Caleigh's indignant whining was more than I could deal with. Once the Chinese take-out was in serving dishes, I had poured a glass of chilled white wine, hoping it wouldn't exacerbate my headache.

Smelling the tangy orange chicken, Dolly, our elderly Persian cat, came into the kitchen and rubbed against my legs. Another reminder of Matt. He had named the cat Doll Face for her sweet nature and flat face but it was quickly shortened to "Dolly" once Dane began to talk and called her something resembling "Dolfae."

The evening became a blur of homework and baths, which led to me being too exhausted to even try to engage Caleigh in conversation. Once the children were asleep and the house silent, I lay in bed with Dolly at my feet. I reached over to Matt's side wondering if anyone would ever take his place. As tired as I was, it took me a long time to fall asleep.

CHAPTER THREE

DECEMBER 3, 2011
OFFICER WALTER (BUD) ANDERSON

THE LACK OF SLEEP LEFT ME bleary eyed. Breathing in the cold air felt like needles hitting my chest. There had been no time to heat up the truck, and my breath condensed in the frigid air. It looked like a damn arctic tundra outside. I strained to focus on the road ahead but my kept eyes drifting. I guess I drifted off because I before I knew it, my head jerked back to the solid white line as I was headed for the ditch.

Pulling over to the roadside, it took a while for my breath to slow. I opened the thermos, gulped a mouthful of steaming coffee and scalded the roof of my mouth. "Shit!" Even that came out in a cloud of fog.

Snow-covered plains and fenced in pastures glistened in the thin, cold light. A smallish ragged-looking coyote scavenged in the field searching for carrion, reminding me of the shaggy cattle of his childhood. They'd stand like that, at dirty feeding troughs, with their eyes glazed over.

Another cup of coffee, but this time I waited while the steamy vapor rose and the coffee cooled. The truck's heater began to wheeze heat into the truck's cabin. I pulled back onto the road, my tires skimming the surface of the slick roadway. It was a delicate balance between traction and torque. I'd seen plenty of violent impacts on icy Minnesota roads and I didn't want to be one of them. I propelled forward trying to remain in control. Christmas lights haphazardly strung on trees and farmhouses cast a neon glow on the snow. Hell, I had barely gotten mine up before the first snow and now I wouldn't even be home to enjoy them. My bags would probably be packed and on the street by the time I got home.

The weather station came in as fuzzy as dust. Most likely, it would be just like it was yesterday and the same way it would be tomorrow. Temperatures below zero and snow flurries likely.

Dunn Brothers' Coffee was on the way so I thought I'd stop for a refill before work. It was busy inside. Rochester's businesswomen were dressed to the nines in suits and scarves that probably cost more than I made in a day, draped around their necks. They issued orders on their smart phones, ordered skim milk lattes and flashed smiles as bright as chrome.

I knew by their looks the circles under my eyes were dark and angry. I flexed my biceps. The elegant, composed types, probably on their way to banks and courthouses, really got under my skin. My medium black coffee ready, I climbed back into the truck. It felt like the day had already kicked me in the teeth.

Ten minutes later, out of habit, I scanned the parking lot hoping to get a glimpse of Grace. Maybe we could walk in together but there was no sign of her or her Jeep.

I clocked in and slid into the morning security meeting. The building was overheated and a circle of perspiration grew under my arms. I imagine it stained my navy uniform black. I stared out the window at the inmates' garden. It was dormant, the annuals long dead and the perennials covered with snow.

Something not only felt wrong, it felt horribly wrong. The walls, a putrid green, had last been painted during Ronald Reagan's administration. My eyes converged on the red-and-white stripes of the flag in the corner of the room. The stripes began to waver. I tried to ignore the dizziness while the drone of words went on and on. My face and hands tingled. The photograph of President Obama on the opposite wall irritated me. I forced myself to take several deep breaths while the pulse in my temple seesawed up and down. It was something I had learned in anger management.

The meeting ended, and I noticed the doctors walking through the parking lot. All that money for doing what? My lips curled as I thought of the team I worked on. I was the one they called when the inmates went berserk. It was the only part of my job I loved. I was part of a team of officers called in to subdue the hell out of the inmates. The docs did the medicating, but without us, they'd be dead. The last psychiatrist got hit over the head with a coffee mug and I had to subdue the inmate. You'd think the guy would've been a little more grateful.

After the meeting, I staggered into the corridor and knew something was wrong. Since my discharge from the Marines and this job in the forensic unit, I had felt a vague sense of restlessness I couldn't put my finger on. Sometimes it was a sick, claustrophobic feeling. The fucking job took so much out of me. Most nights it was all I could do to grab a beer or two, watch TV, and try to get some peace in my own house before the damn kids and the noise drove me nuts.

There she was.

"Morning, Doc." Grace was coming down the hall. She stopped, knowing she couldn't sidestep past me. I stood still and tried to make my voice seem casual. "How are you?"

"I'm fine, thanks," she said, sharp as nails. "Would you please bring Emanuel Venegas for his session?" The door lock clicked behind her.

Bitch.

I imagined her sitting at her desk, readying herself for her session with Venegas, crossing and uncrossing her legs. Sweeping back her thick red hair. Maybe scratching an itch somewhere.

I got the patient and knocked at her door. "Come in," she called. "Please, sit down, Emanuel. How're you feeling today?"

The inmate was new and had to be escorted everywhere he went on the unit. He shuffled slowly into her office, his eyes were downcast and sunken into purple hollows. His head drooped. He looked as limp as an inflatable doll I once loved.

"Officer Anderson, I think you can wait outside if you don't mind," Grace said. She got up and tripped. I leaped across the room and caught her by the elbows before she fell.

"Thanks," she mumbled. "Are you okay? Your hands are clammy." Grace pulled away from my touch as if I had rabies.

"I'm okay." The feel of her in my arms was one I wouldn't forget. "You want me to wait outside?"

"If you don't mind," she replied coolly.

Outside the door, my weight shifted uncomfortably from one leg to the other. I wanted to scratch that itch, and then bang her.

Ten minutes later, Grace opened the door and asked me to escort Emanuel back to his cell. I dug my nails into my palms. A surge of power ripped through me. I was in control here. Emanuel stiffened and stood against the wall.

"Venegas, what're you doin'? Let's go, ya hear me? Shit. That guy gives me the creeps," I muttered under my breath, audibly enough that she heard me. "One sandwich short of a picnic."

"I think that's enough, Officer Anderson." Her voice was terse. "I would appreciate it if you show my patients the respect they deserve and treat them accordingly. This is the second time I've spoken to you about this. If I see you abusing Emanuel again, I'll have no choice but to report you."

"Respect?" I asked. "Sure, I'll show 'em the respect they deserve." The look I gave her made her step back. "Listen, Doc, a correctional facility is no preschool. These guys are here for a reason. People think once they're here, they can't cause any further harm but these are psychopaths we're dealing with. They don't stop being psychopaths just because they're behind bars. You think they wouldn't kill you in cold blood if they had the chance? Corrections officers have been punched, kicked, spit at, and even killed. Fuck, I've had urine and shit thrown at me."

Grace's eyes darkened. "Are you finished?"

"No, I'm not. I run the risk everyday of contracting HIV, hepatitis, and tuberculosis. So don't you tell me about respect, okay, Doc?"

"I think that's enough," she said as I turned to escort Emanuel to the dayroom.

I flashed back to last night as I walked the long cold hall. Stacy's legs wrapped around me, her nails dragging down my back as I pounded away at her. I still had it after all these years. I pictured her begging for more. I imagined Grace and how she would beg me for more. They don't pay me shit to deal with this crap. I unlocked the door to the dayroom and wondered why they didn't send these bastards home where they came from.

Emanuel sat down and stared through the windows outside the prison walls. His sleeves rose as he crossed his arms. He had tattoos of two hearts entwined. MARISOL & EMANUEL FOREVER.

* * *

THE LAST ASSIGNMENT OF MY DAY was to escort the inmates to the chapel. They lumbered in single file to the basement, their identical prison khaki pants and tees were soaked with perspiration. The basement was a good fifteen degrees cooler than the overheated unit was, and my sweaty skin soon felt chilled.

"You may think now this life holds little hope of salvation," Father Tom Schill intoned. "But I'm here to tell you Jesus is the answer to your prayers. Seek forgiveness and it's yours. Repent and you will live in the glory of God forever."

Father Schill was a frail, stooped man with skin as transparent as onion skin. The complexion of a man who had spent much of his life indoors. Once each week he transformed the dank, chilly prison basement into a place of worship. Father Schill had no difficulty believing his flock had been forgiven for the heinous crimes they had committed. I had no such belief. An ex-marine, I was a man who relied not on faith but on myself, my muscles, and my guts. I looked for no forgiveness and offered none. My chest tightened as I sat down and sucked in the smell of despair. Anxiety surged from somewhere inside my gut.

Father Schill blessed the bread and wine, consecrating it according to the mysteries of faith into the body and blood of our Lord, Jesus Christ. "According to the Scriptures, Jesus, on the night before he was betrayed, took bread, and when he had given thanks, he broke it and said, 'This is my body which is for you. Do this in remembrance of me.' He then took the cup, after supper, saying, 'This cup is the new covenant in my blood. Do this, as often as you drink it, in remembrance of me.'"

I was surprised to find my hands clasped in prayer as I listened to the mass. Father Schill placed the Body of Christ on my tongue, absolving me of his sins. I folded onto a wooden pew, my head bowed and my eyelids squeezed tightly together. It had been a long time since I had been in church.

". . . Our Father, who art in heaven, hallowed be thy name. Thy Kingdom come, thy will be done . . ."

When it was over, inmates Venegas, Reynolds, Lawrence, Ramirez, and Isaac shambled back to the unit, with me right behind them. My keys jangled at my waist. It was just before dinner when I unlocked the double doors and sat Emanuel down in front of the television.

Shortly afterwards I gave my report to the evening staff. The unvarying routine of the unit was broken only by the shift changes. The altercations between inmates and the staff entering and leaving were the only real distractions.

As the day drew to a close and shadows deepened, I finished my rounds and clocked out. With nowhere to go, I drove down a long stretch of country road. The snow-covered fields were just like the mood I was in. Dark and empty. Black beady-eyed crows littered the roadsides, searching for road kill. Their cries resonated with my pain. After our lovemaking last night, Stacy had asked me for a divorce. The bitch said she'd done it for old times sake. I attempted to think clearly, to put side my anger and find a space where I could be free of the mind-less agitation.

CHAPTER FOUR

A CREEPING NUMBNESS SPREAD through my fingers. My muffler was wrapped around my mouth, but still, every breath was painful. Caleigh shoveled sullenly alongside me. "Can we go in now, Mom?" she asked. "I can't even feel my feet."

"We're almost done. Next time, I'll call someone to plow." Dane had a growing arsenal of snowballs at his side. He squinted at the slate-gray sky and aimed carefully. "Take that!" One by one, the icy snowballs sailed like missiles causing a flock of geese to flee in an angry squall.

"Dane, what's wrong with you? What if you had hit one of those birds?" I threw a shovel full of snow over my shoulder. The sky looked like matte-gray paint and the children's moods matched it perfectly.

"I don't care. I don't want to go to Grandma's, Mommy." He came to stand by my side and clung like a barnacle to my leg. His breath made tiny clouds in the air. "My face hurts."

"That makes two of us," Caleigh complained. "Everyone's going to Shelby's party tonight. Why do we have to visit Grandma and Grandpa this weekend? And why do I always have to help shovel? I'm cold." As if for special effect, she shivered violently.

"Come on, guys, you'll have fun. The weather's cleared and Grandma and Grandpa are really looking forward to seeing you," I said in the sort of voice a mother uses when she tells her kids everything is going to be all right. It was the first time since Matt's death we would be apart.

Caleigh wiped her nose with the back of a mittened hand. "What about you, Mom? Are you going to be okay?"

"Won't you miss us, Mommy?" Dane asked. "I don't want to go."

Last night's snow clung to the evergreen branches in the yard, weighing them like overweight luggage. "Why don't you bring your sleds?" I suggested. "Maybe Grandpa will take you to Eastwood Park."

An hour later, the Jeep was loaded with sleds, overnight bags, and books. The plows hadn't been out yet on our dirt road. The road could have been a louge track. I put the car in four-wheel-drive and tried to stay in the middle.

At the summit of Pill Hill, in front of my in-law's house, I inched back down the quiet street of stately homes. The neighborhood had been inhabited by doctors beginning with Dr. Will Mayo since the early twentieth century. It was now insulated by a thick blanket of snow. Matt's family's house was designed by Harold Crawford, a local Rochester boy who had returned home from Harvard and designed many of the homes on the hill. My in-laws, Dr. Stan and Dahlia Rendeau's neighborhood was a study in contrasts next to my hometown of Hopewell Junction. My father had barely graduated from high school, and died while I was in college. I missed him still. My mother had remarried and contact with her was fortunately sporadic.

The early cloud cover soon gave way to the possibility of sunshine. I suppressed the urge to turn around and make sure the children were okay and began to anticipate two days of solitude with a degree of pleasure. I had a new mystery I'd been wanting to read. Maybe I'd even have a long, luxurious bubble bath. But that day, the freedom of exchanging my briefcase for a pair of long, shiny skis was first on my list.

* * *

QUARRY HILL NATURE CENTER LOOKED LIKE brilliant strokes of green on a blinding winter canvas. The sky had cleared and the snow reflected a bluish sheen from above.

I wasn't the only one with plans to ski this morning. Standing outside the rustic nature center, once the grounds of the old state hospital, was a tall, lean man strapping his skis on. He had a quick smile and seemingly, an even quicker wit as he bantered with the staff. I busied myself with stepping into my own cross-country skis.

With more enthusiasm than I had felt in months, I attached the bar in the toe of my shoe to the binding plate, fit my shoes into the ridge running along the binding, and then nothing. There was no satisfying click to reassure me my foot was correctly in place. Okay, let's try this again . . . Square toe of the shoe in first, and then . . . Nothing. I smiled sheepishly as the man, now ready to set off, side-stepped over to me. "Can I help you?" he asked.

"No. I can do this." Thankfully, my last attempt ended with my shoes strapped firmly in the binding. He took off ahead of me with a long, athletic stride. I found my own rhythm and soon the weathered cedar nature center became a distant red glow. I skied beyond the pond, gliding easily along the trail running beside it, past black-tailed jackrabbits and flitting red-bellied woodpeckers. I was dressed warmly in black ski pants tucked into cross-country ski boots, an oversize parka, red turtleneck sweater and bright-red woolen mittens. My red hair was pulled into a ponytail. I was glad I had worn a faint coating of lip-gloss to protect my lips from the cold. My skin tingled in the biting chill and perspiration soon dripped from under my arms. The joy of physical exertion and the sound of my skis crunching on the tamped-down snow were exhilarating.

It neared lunchtime, and my calves cramped with the effort of skiing up the incline back to the nature center. I hit a patch of ice and crashed headlong onto the snow, pain bursting like a spigot through my ankle. My left foot was twisted underneath me, still strapped in its ski. It crumpled as soon as I struggled to stand. It was at least three miles to the nature center, but I lifted my skis over my shoulder and began the long trudge back, sinking into icy cold snow with every step. Before long my toes grew numb.

"Hey, do you need some help?" a voice echoed through the chill.

A tall, lithe figure skied toward me, wearing a fitted black jacket, ski pants, and a cranberry-colored knit cap and sunglasses. I wasn't alone. I didn't recognize the man from the nature center until he was almost on me. The cold and exercise had brought out the ruddiness in his cheeks. "You again!" he exclaimed. "Are you okay?"

I squinted and blinked to lubricate my eyes. In the cold, my contact lenses felt glued to my corneas. "I think I twisted my ankle." I grimaced. "I'm having some trouble getting back to the center. If you wouldn't mind carrying my skis back and returning them, I'm sure I can make it."

"How about if I carry you and your skis back? I don't think you should be going anywhere on that foot. I can bring my car to the road just beyond that circle of birches. It won't be nearly as far as going back the way you came."

"Thank you so much, Mr . . ."

"Sawyer. Call me Alex. Not a problem. It's not often I get a chance to practice first aid out here. Did you hurt your eye?"

"Grace," I said, offering my hand. "No. My eyes are fine." I closed them, hoping it would help.

"Here, put your arms around my neck." I reached my arms around his neck, painfully self-conscious as he picked me up and set me on a nearby log. "I guess Grace is not so graceful."

Jerk. I moaned in pain.

"Sorry! I'm going to leave you here for about fifteen minutes while I ski back and get my car. Try to keep moving to stay warm. Here, take my scarf." He removed his thick woolen scarf and handed it to me. "I'll be back to get you, and then we'll see about your ankle."

I tried to keep moving but my contacts felt like they were folded in on themselves and my ankle was swelling rapidly. Once he was out of site, I contemplated taking the contacts out and throwing them away but I wouldn't be able to drive home. It didn't occur to me I might not be going straight home.

Half an hour later, I sank onto a lumpy couch at the center. Pain prodded my ankle like a spur. Alex placed an icepack on it and palpated the lemon-sized lump. He held it up as gently as a newborn, being careful not to move it while he expertly wrapped a bandage around it and secured the icepack in place. "I don't think it's broken but we can stop at the hospital for an x-ray if you'd like. Let's get you some crutches."

I tried not to wince. He had bandaged it expertly. "I think it's a sprain. Luckily or not, I suppose, I have crutches at home. Where'd you learn to do this?"

"Med school. I haven't bandaged many ankles lately but hopefully I haven't lost my touch." His eyes shone like well-polished furniture. "I'm in Infectious Diseases."

"I haven't bandaged many ankles lately either, except in my case it's psychiatry." I thanked him for his help and wondered how I'd make it to the car. He offered his arm. Hobbling to the parking lot with Alex supporting me, I finally realized I was not going to be able to drive. "If I could just get my purse out of the trunk . . ."

He opened the trunk and suggested he bring me to the emergency room.

"I'm sure I'll be fine," I said.

24

"Do you feel well enough to stop for hot chocolate? Maybe we can elevate your foot there. There's a coffee house not far from here."

Why not? Buying hot chocolate for him was the least I could do. I leaned on his arm and we walked or rather he walked and I tottered toward his car. The snow-covered parking lot was blissfully silent. I sat down in the passenger seat, fished for the contact lens solution in my purse and squirted two drops in each eye. Alex's skin glowed and his brown eyes shone when I blinked to look at him.

Minutes later we pulled into the parking lot of the coffee house.

"What'll it be?" he asked shortly afterwards. A fire blazed in the corner fireplace and the air was thick with the smell of cedar and coffee. "Are you hungry?"

"Hot chocolate is perfect. It's so good to be inside." I unwrapped his scarf, and still shivering, handed it to him. There were shoppers coming in out of the cold, and each time the door opened, an arctic blast swept through the coffee shop.

Alex sat back and took a sip of his hot chocolate. "So, you're a shrink? I wouldn't have thought it." He unzipped his jacket and took it off. His hair was longish, the color of wheat on a summer day.

I slurped the cocoa thinking he looked more like a poet than a physician. "I guess I wouldn't have taken you for an infectious diseases doc either." I took my hat off. My shoulder length hair was full of static, crackling like the nearby fireplace.

Alex stirred the dollop of whipped cream into his drink. "So, what were you doing skiing so far out by yourself?"

I know I blushed at the intensity of his gaze. I looked down at my hands and pulled at a hangnail. My torn cuticles and short bitten nails were an embarrassment and I hid them in my lap. I had recently taken off my wedding ring and my hand felt naked without it. A drip of perspiration ran off my forehead. "My children are away for the weekend. I needed some time alone. What better place than the nature center, enjoying the day, and getting some exercise to boot? I guess I forgot how many years it's been since I was on skis. How about you? You were pretty far out too." I couldn't seem to stop talking.

"I try to get out every weekend. It helps to clear my mind." Something flashed in his eyes almost as though he had opened a door and then suddenly shut it. The hands cupping his hot chocolate showed slender, long fingers wrapped around the handle of the signature mug. Where he had rolled up his sleeves, I could see dark curling hair on his forearm. For some reason, the sight of his forearm caused my heart to flutter and my mouth to dry. I hardly recognized the sensation of sexual attraction. It had been years since I had felt the comfort of a man's laughter, or lost myself in eyes like Alex's. "Would you mind driving me home?" I asked. My ankle was aching, but more so, the unwanted sensations made me feel uncomfortable.

"Not at all." Alex stood. "I'm sure there is no skiing in the near future for you. How about coffee next weekend?"

My scalp tingled with the prickly heat as warmth crept from my neck to my head. It had been so long . . . Could there be any harm in that? There was something about him. Images of the children came to my mind and I hesitated. "I'd like that," I finally said.

Alex held the door with one hand and tried to support my weight with his opposite arm and shoulder. I stepped gingerly on the icy sidewalk with my right foot, still keeping weight off the left, and my foot slid out from under me. "Grace! God! Are you okay? I'm so sorry. Here, let me help you."

In a heap on the sidewalk, I was mortified. Tears pricked my eyes at what a klutz I was.

"Hang onto my arm while I open the door. Should we stop at the ER?"

"No. Really. I'm sorry! I think you can put me down now. If you'd bring me home, I'm sure I'll be fine." The sharp sting of embarrassment slapped my cheeks.

"If you're really sure. How about if I give you my number and tomorrow if you're feeling well enough, we can pick up your car?"

"I have my right foot for driving. As long as it's no trouble . . ."

"No trouble at all," he assured me.

We drove in companionable quiet down the snow-covered dirt road to my house. Alex pulled into my driveway and as we said goodbye, I realized I looked forward to seeing him again more than I wanted to admit.

CHAPTER FIVE

ONDAY MORNING. The sun sliced through the small window in my office. Its slanted rays providing a delicious bit of warmth. I rolled up my sleeves, ready to get back to work. My mind wandered to Alex's eyes and the memory of his arms around me, even if it was just to pick me up off the ground. Twice.

Hobbling on crutches to see my first patient was not a good idea. My armpits were sore from the unaccustomed pressure of Matt's old crutches. I was about to call for the patient when the phone rang.

"Hi, Grace, it's me. Alex. Alex Sawyer. Remember?"

"How could I forget?" I tried not to laugh. "My ankle is still throbbing, but I'm getting around okay. How about you?"

"I was calling to see if you . . . if we . . . if you're still up for coffee next weekend?"

Was this a date? "Sure. Saturday? The Canadian Honker? Ten o'clock?"

* * *

FIVE DAYS LATER, I paced nervously in the small entry of the coffee shop. Hot air whistled through the ancient radiators. Canada geese covered the wallpaper. Even the coat hooks were goose heads carved from wood.

A bell jangled each time the glass-paned door opened and a blast of frigid air blew in. There was still a dull ache in my ankle but I had left the crutches home, determined not to hobble. I checked my watch more often than necessary and my skin prickled with the embarrassment of my adolescent behavior. My reflection in the plate glass window of the entry showed a woman with rows of freckles on the wintry pallor of her face despite the foundation I had smoothed over my skin. It occurred to me I might leave and make up an excuse for not being able to come. As I read the posted specials for the third time, I heard his voice. So cliché that old expression, music to my ears, but there really was no other way to describe it.

It was evident he had walked there. His cheeks and nose were red and he was bundled in a North Face parka, knitted hat, boots, and, what seemed to me, an air of anticipation. I wiped my sweating palms on my pants and extended a hand.

He took off his hat and said, "I'm glad you could make it." Static electricity caused his hair to stand on end and reassured me that maybe he wasn't perfect after all.

"Me too. It looks like snow, doesn't it?" Why had I thought this would be a good idea?

We found a table near the fire. The dining room was cozy and warm, decorated with a Minnesota cabin motif. A smooth stone fire-place, maroon-and-forest green-patterned furniture, and a scattering of "Up North" moose décor added to the backwoods feel. No one seemed to be in a rush to do anything but enjoy the morning. Alex removed his coat and we sat down to face one another over the green-checked tablecloth. Our knees touched and we quickly apologized. I fought the impulse to bite my lip. "How's work going?" I asked.

"Good. How are things at the prison?"

"Good." I cast a glance around the room and busied myself with stirring my coffee. Each awkward question fell like clanging silverware to the floor.

"Sorry, Grace whenever I think of that place I think of Nurse Ratched in *One Flew Over the Cuckoo's Nest*. I really can't picture you there," he said.

He was funny. "It's not as bad as all that. We try to weed out the malingerers. The closest we have to Nurse Ratched is probably Bud Anderson, a corrections officer. Everyone else is pretty harmless. Really professional and caring, actually. But I suppose transference issues must develop there as anywhere. I don't know why it surprised me when I began working there."

"Whoa! Malingering? Transference issues? Sorry, Grace, I don't speak your language!"

"Oops! Sorry . . . Malingerers are, you know, those people who fake symptoms to stay in treatment or in the hospital. They're getting some kind of gain by pretending to be sick. And transference is, uh, when you're in a therapist/client relationship and during the course of therapy . . . Alex, am I boring you?"

"No! Not at all. What's the matter with this guy Anderson?" Alex leaned forward.

"I don't know. There's just something about him. He's a loose cannon. I may be imagining things but I could swear he's leering at me in a way that makes me really uncomfortable." I was boring him and on our first date too, and now I was telling him about Anderson. I had really lost the art of conversation.

Alex cut into his blueberry muffin. "I'd think it'd take a lot to make your skin crawl. I imagine you've seen and heard everything there. Why don't you report him?"

I dropped my spoon on the floor and bent over to pick it up. "For what? Leering at the new psychiatrist? Come on, it's a beautiful Saturday morning. Let's talk about something else, okay?"

The coffee shop was full that wintry Saturday morning. A line of people wound into the entry. Mayo Clinic visitors stopped in for mid-morning coffee and pie. A couple of lavender-haired elderly women sat at a corner table, and I wondered if they retreated to the loneliness of their solitary lives afterwards.

The tension soon drifted away, and we began to relax in the smell of wet wool and freshly baked muffins. There was just something so Norman Rockwell-wholesome about the place. Maybe it was the homey gingham-covered tables and the smells of good food cooking. From the corner, a whiff of Bengay almost overpowered the smells of bacon sizzling and coffee brewing. It smelled like Sunday mornings at home. Matt had been a weekend warrior sort-of-athlete and the smell of Bengay always reminded me of a muscle pull or strain.

An hour later, with two empty mugs in front of us and no desire for another refill, it was time to go. I pulled on my coat and Alex asked, "Do you feel well enough to take a short walk at Silver Lake?" making no move to put his jacket on.

I didn't want the morning to end with me boring Alex with my psychiatric jargon. I had worn my rubber-soled boots. Hopefully I could stay upright. Between the cold air and the touch of his hand on my back, I felt as electric as Alex's flyaway hair. Silly as it sounded, each touch caused a moth-like fluttering in my chest. We walked along tamped down paths, a smooth blanket of cold air enveloping us and snow swirling around our legs like leaves in autumn. We were surprisingly comfortable in our silence.

Alex must have noticed my ankle was starting to ache because he stopped and said, "Why don't we stop so you can rest your ankle?" supporting me with his arm. "Here's a bench. It looks like you're still limping."

His arm around my shoulder felt as odd as slipping on a new pair of shoes. Not uncomfortable, but strange. We turned to read the inscription engraved into the bench. Donated to the memory of "Tootsie" Abrahamson. I wondered what kind of woman was named "Tootsie." "I knew someone with a dog named Tootsie once, and I don't have fond associations with the name! She was a mean, snippy little dog," Alex said, and I laughed.

We watched tow-headed children in bright parkas make snow angels and the chronic knot in my shoulder melted. The park looked like a sugary frost. Their exuberance reminded me of Caleigh and Dane at that age. For a few moments, I enjoyed an exhilarating sense of freedom from the cares and responsibilities which normally spun around my days. The sun was piercingly bright and an unaccustomed joyfulness jostled for a place inside me.

Morning wore on to noon, and as I shifted in the cold, Alex turned, tilted my chin and kissed me. His lips barely grazed mine but the tenderness brought a stab of pain. I was breathing hard, barely able to let him go before I pulled away.

"Can I see you again sometime?" he asked, his voice reverberating with emotion.

I was dumbfounded at what had just happened. "What?" I asked, startled by the question. "Alex, I'd better go. The kids are home, and I promised my son I'd watch a movie with him. I really don't like to leave the kids home alone," I babbled. Poised somewhere between still feeling married and being free, I found it hard to take the leap. A shadow passed over his face and I wondered what it meant.

Later that afternoon, I sat on the sofa in the drafty living room and stared vacantly at the TV. I tried to feign interest in the video I had promised to watch with Dane.

"Mom! You're not watching!" I had missed the last fifteen minutes of the movie. "Can we watch the movie about Daddy?" he asked, plaintively.

"Not again, Dane! We've seen it like a hundred times. What's up with you, Mom?" Caleigh glanced up from texting. "You look weird. Where were you all morning anyway?"

The DVD I had made of our lives with Matt shortly after Matt's death was Dane's favorite. Caleigh was right—we had watched it countless times. Now the mention of it burned my cheeks with shame as I replayed the kiss in my mind and waves of longing coursed through my body. "I met a friend for coffee. Who wants popcorn?"

The buttered popcorn sat between us on the sofa. Dane dug in with both hands while Caleigh delicately picked out one kernel at a time.

CHAPTER SIX

THE BLACK SLACKS AND IVORY silk shirt I had put on for work that morning were as crisp as soggy vegetables. The table for two at Chester's, Rochester's newest restaurant was covered with a snow-white cloth and a candle. As I waited, I spritzed my wrists with perfume and nervously smeared on lipstick, and then puckered my lips and blotted it off. I checked my phone for messages. Maddy, the sixteen-year-old girl next door, had been happy to stay with the children for a few more hours and twenty dollars more when I had impulsively called her that afternoon.

Alex entered in a well-cut charcoal suit and crisp white shirt and tie. Michael Jordan-kind-of-tall, he captured the attention of every woman in the room. He came to the table, kissed my cheek and said, "I'm so glad you called. This is such a nice surprise. How's your ankle?"

My mouth was a river run dry. Damp watery stains were developing under the arms of my blouse. "I wanted to thank you for picking me up. What I mean is . . ." I stammered. "I wanted to thank you for helping me when I fell. I wanted to thank you for the coffee." *Jesus, Grace, get a grip!*

"Well. You're welcome. Is that why you asked me to meet you here?"

The hum of quiet conversation filled the air. There would be time enough to tell him the knot in my shoulder had returned and about the stress of my day on the unit. The continued uneasiness I felt whenever I saw Officer Anderson. How much the kids still missed Matt. How hard it was to be both mother and father to them. Instead, I looked at him across the table and smiled. His eyes were the color of cool, sweet waters. The tension seeped from my shoulders, beginning to loosen the painful knot. An old Shirley Johnson blues song played in the background. "Unchain My Heart."

He took off his jacket and hung it over his chair. "Is everything all right?" he asked. A table full of elderly women at the table next to ours shrieked, "Surprise! Happy Birthday!" as the waiter brought out a large chocolate cake covered with what looked like dozens of candles.

The birthday girl blew out the candles in four stages. "Come on, Betty, you can do it!" they screeched.

"Sorry I'm late. I was arranging for a medical mission trip in Indonesia when you called. I'm planning to attend next summer. What's wrong?" He glanced sideways at the raucous birthday celebration. Betty was cutting the cake. After the first slice, the waiter took over and passed thick slices of chocolate cake around the table.

Maybe it would be a relief to talk to another man. "My husband died almost two years ago. It still seems strange to think of myself as a widow. There's something so dark and old about that. Women my age aren't widows. I've had a hard time with the kids lately. And I wanted to apologize for my adolescent behavior the other day."

Alex took my hand across the table and the candlelight flickered. "I'm glad you called me, and I have to agree. You hardly fit the stereotype of a widow." He motioned the waiter over. "Would you like a drink?"

Matt's face flickered before me. Along with an image of Alex's hands on my body. So now, Matt's face and Alex's hands were on me. "Pinot noir, for me." I hoped a glass of wine would smooth the jagged edges of guilt.

"I'll have the same," Alex said.

"I shouldn't have called you," I said as soon as the waiter left with the drink orders. There were more screams from the table next door. Betty opened her gifts and passed them around the table while the ladies oohed and ahhhed and Alex's brows knit.

"I mean, I'm not sure I'm ready to be in a relationship." A filmy web of contrition engulfed my heart. What was I doing? Was it crazy to become even remotely emotionally intimate with someone new, no matter how kind he was? "Forget I said anything. Tell me about you," I stammered.

"Well, I'm divorced. No kids. I'm an infectious disease doc, as you know. I do a lot of traveling. I guess too much traveling. I worked with local clergy in Tanzania to denounce the practice of murdering people with albinism for their body parts. The dehumanization of Africa's albinos and the superstitions regarding the potions made from their body parts are unconscionable. And the fact those body parts are sold on the black market for profit . . . I had to do something about it, so I wrote a book to try to expose these practices. All proceeds will go to helping these poor people." More noise erupted from Betty's table. They were busy dividing the check.

"My God, I had no idea." What a wonderful, selfless thing to do. I allowed myself a moment to imagine the feel of Alex's body next to mine, imagining the warmth of his body and the feel of his breath in my hair.

The waiter arrived to take our orders. The birthday crowd left and the after-work crowd poured in and filled it with an air of *joie de vivre*. Alex and I breathed a collective sigh of relief. Well-modulated laughter floated through the air. I was still discomfited about my fantasies of Alex. My heart beat faster—my attraction to him was growing like wild-fire tickling the edges of my life. "The butternut squash ravioli with sage brown butter sauce sounds good," I said.

"Were you married long?" Alex asked after the waiter left. "Can you believe it's finally quiet in here?" His eyes were as warm as caramel.

"Twelve years. Matt died two years ago." Each time I said it, I still managed to choke up.

Alex met my gaze. The sound of silverware clattering sliced the air. "I'm sorry. That must have been very painful for you. How old were your children?"

"I guess somebody dropped something in the kitchen, huh?" I tried to laugh. I felt sheepish. "This was not the quietest place to come. Anyway, Caleigh was eleven at the time and Dane was three. Oh, let's change the subject. I don't mean to pry but what about you? Did your wife have a problem with the traveling?"

He looked away. "Yes. She did," he said quietly. "With that and other things." The hint of a shadow crossed his face. His jaw tightened almost imperceptibly.

"Is this something recent?" I asked cautiously, taking a bite of the entrè.

"It's been a year. Angela can't seem to get over it. I wish she'd talk to a therapist about this. That looks good," he pointed to the ravioli. "How is it?"

"Delicious. How do you feel about that?" *Come on, Grace, get over yourself. He doesn't need a therapist. You're having dinner, for God's sake. Relax.* I saw it again–the slight tensing of the muscles in his jaw.

He loosened his shirt collar. "Angela still calls and texts. I've asked her to stop–there's nothing to be gained by it. I'm afraid she's losing it. Our marriage was rocky from the beginning. I was a last-year resident and Angela had just gotten her MBA. You know what a resident's life is like. Angela was finished with school and working normal hours as an investment analyst. She had a hard time understanding I wasn't always available for drinks and parties with her new group of friends."

My fork was halfway to my mouth when I stopped and said, "It must have been hard for you to divide your time like that." The din in the restaurant rose to a new high. Happy Hour was in full swing.

"The worst was when she began to insist we have a baby. By then I knew that was the last thing I wanted with her. She became obsessed with the idea. I don't know–maybe it was a means to try to save what was obviously a failing marriage."

"Did you try counseling?" *Grace! You're not on call here!* Why did I feel obligated to plumb the depths of everything he said?

"For a while. She just wouldn't give up on the idea of getting pregnant. Towards the end, I discovered she'd stopped taking the pill without telling me and that was the last straw. I asked for a divorce. and she refused. I moved out and was granted a divorce by the court a year later."

"And she still calls and texts?" Maybe he wasn't perfect. At least he had some unwanted baggage.

"Yup. I've tried changing my number but she somehow manages to get it. Wow, this beef bourguignon is outta this world."

"Maybe there are some legal ramifications." I don't know why I kept pressing. Before I could ask any more questions, I took a sip of wine to shut myself up.

"I haven't wanted to go there yet. Let's talk about something else, okay? Would you like dessert? The raspberry cheesecake is supposed to be good."

The waiter edged closer. "Will there be anything else?" A line of would-be patrons snaked around the lobby.

"I'm fine. How about you?" Alex asked.

"Nothing for me, thanks."

Afterwards, we walked to my car and he took my hand. "This has been great. Can I call you sometime?"

I wanted to melt into him and hold him tight but Caleigh and Dane were home, waiting for mommy to help with homework and tuck them into bed. He pulled me close and kissed me as I closed my eyes and gave him a quick hug. "Alex, I just don't know." He did have an ex-wife who still called him.

"Grace, I . . ." I heard him say but I had already turned and kept walking before he had a chance to finish.

Only the thin beams of my headlights and the stars lit the night on the drive home. It wasn't late but it was a lonely country road. Jesus! What was wrong with me? He was wonderful. He must have thought I was crazy. I stopped in the garage, took out my cell phone and dialed Alex's number. I trembled and dropped the phone. Fuck. Alex's voice sounded from the floor. "Hello? Hello? Grace, is that you?" I grabbed the phone and said, "You must think I'm crazy, but yes. Yes, I want to see you again."

CHAPTER SEVEN

T HE YELLOW LEGAL PAD WAS COVERED with what looked like a seven-year-old's handwriting. Uncomfortable fantasies of Alex persisted in jabbing at me but I put on my glasses and determined to ignore them. I began to read, "Marisol. Mi amor. Mar y sol. Sea and sun. Mar y sol. You open yourself to me and I am filled with you. A rose with moist petals unfolding only for me . . ."

Why had I gone into psychiatry when I could have gone into dermatology or pediatrics or any other specialty where I wouldn't be sitting at my desk reading the ravings of a psychotic patient? My choice of psychiatry as a specialty wasn't about the money or the prestige I might have found elsewhere. It was about delving into the lives of people and uncovering their darkest dreams and innermost secrets and setting them free. Known to be a good listener, the choice had not been a difficult one to make.

There was a knock at the door. The first session of the day. Officer Anderson and Emanuel ambled into the room. "Thanks, officer," I said curtly. "Would you mind waiting outside? I'll let you know when we're done."

After he left the room, it was time to sit back and switch into the professional Dr. Rendeau persona. The thought of Alex's arms around me had caused me to toss in bed much of the night, and I was certain I looked as drained as I felt. Struggling to remain focused on Emanuel, I tried to keep the images of Alex's lips on mine at bay. In the last session, Emanuel had made some progress and seemed to remember what had brought him here. I asked how he was feeling and he looked at me blankly. The room felt airless and I wondered if our tenuous connection had been lost. "The last time we met, you were telling me about the house you and Marisol bought. And you were going to the beach with your family. What else do you remember about that day?"

Emanuel had showered before coming to my office. His dark, still-wet hair fell in ringlets around his face. He was twenty-five years old—still a young man. It was difficult to understand what a man in his position might feel. Memory can be such an unmerciful thing. Was this escape his response to the hurt, the anger, the trauma of what had happened? Possibly the effects of drug use as well. So many things went through my mind that morning. Unwrapping Emanuel's secrets was just one of them.

"She was pregnant," he finally said. His mouth was dry, a side effect of the medications and he puckered over his words. "Her skin was stretched over her belly, with a deep purple line from her navel to her pubis. During the pregnancy, her thighs spread. She wrapped them around my waist and held my shoulders, scraping her nails along the length of my spine. She was as fleshy and sweet as an over ripe mango."

Patient exhibits possible sexual preoccupation, I scribbled in my notes.

"Eventually we got the house. I gathered Marisol in my arms and carried her over the threshold. There was a back yard for the baby, an extra bedroom and a park nearby. You didn't even have to water the grass." He stopped abruptly, his eyes clouding.

I had learned to be patient and wait during the stop-and-go sessions I had with most patients unaccustomed to dealing with psychic pain. "Would you like to continue tomorrow?"

He nodded and I opened the door. "Officer Anderson, would you please escort Emanuel to the dayroom?"

"Sure, Doc. Anything for you." He smirked at me, his lips stretched over his smallish teeth. "You limping, Doc? Let me know if you need any help. If there's anything I can do for you—"

I turned on my heel, revulsion creeping along my spine, and pulled the door shut behind me. I made a note to see if it was possible to have another officer escort patients to my office but really, what would I say? I don't like the way he smiles at me?

After a few phone calls, Finn Koski came to my office, shuffling in, unescorted by security. There was a stack of records on my desk going back to 1999. It was difficult to believe this mild-mannered, polite little man had caused the death of his wife of fifty years. It brought Matt back to mind again.

The memories I had so desperately clung to were beginning to fade. It was more difficult to conjure up the slope of his cheek or the feel of the stubble on his jaw when he went a day without shaving. It was difficult to imagine how people could take the life of someone they loved.

"Mr. Koski. I'm sorry it has taken me a while to see you again. I'm still fairly new and it's been a bit of a challenge to see all of my patients in as timely a manner as I would've liked. How are you doing?"

Finn looked at me expectantly. "Fine, just fine." The slight Scandinavian inflection was apparent in the long drawn out vowels.

"Would you like to take up where we left off last time? You were found guilty of the charge of manslaughter . . ."

"I killed her. She was in pain, Doc, and I couldn't take it any longer. I did it and I'm glad she's not suffering any longer."

I closed my eyes and visualized the scene. "Do you want to tell me what happened?" It was the first time I had dealt with someone who willfully caused the death of his spouse. I almost didn't want to know the details of what had happened. "Your wife had breast cancer?"

His expression provoked a flare of sympathy in me and I nodded encouragement, hoping this would help Finn continue what was obviously as painful as a mule kick to the gut to discuss. I waited for him to speak. The muted sounds of an argument between inmates somewhere on the unit reverberated through the room. "Would you excuse me for a moment, Mr. Koski?"

Moments later, I returned to my desk. The commotion was an argument between two elderly men with dementia who were harmless but often antagonized each other on the ward. "What happened after that?" I asked, back in my chair.

"It was impossible for me to sit there, useless. All that talk about urinary catheters and IVs. I tried to think about all there was to do on the farm that spring, but I finally got up and walked out," Finn said, looking as though he had been beaten with a stick.

"That must have been very difficult." The voices outside the door escalated and I wondered if I should call security. I turned my attention back to Finn and finally the voices drifted away.

Finn braced himself. "Eva was wheeled into the operating room on a what-cha-ma-call-it . . . a gurney. Three hours later, the surgeon came in and told me Eva was stable. He had to do the radical mastectomy. I was with her in the recovery room when she brought her hand to her right breast and realized it was gone. Not only the lump, but her whole right breast. The smell of the flowers I brought made her sick. She tried to smile but instead, cried and apologized. As if any of what had happened was her fault."

He blew his nose and threw the balled up tissue in the wastebasket. "Three days after surgery, I packed Eva's belongings and brought her home. Later, we met with the oncologist and he said he took out the breast and ten lymph nodes. It was a stage-three cancer, you know."

I nodded reflexively, remembering Matt's chemo sessions. He had lost forty pounds. I knew that chill, saw the bright lighting and false optimism in the room and smelled the vomit and disinfectant. It was a smell I would never forget. "I'm so sorry, Finn. I've been through this," I told him. "I know how this feels."

Finn coughed a loose phlegmy cough. A scintilla of understanding seemed to pass between us. "I tied the laces on her shoes and helped her put on an old sweater that still fit. I sprayed a little perfume on her so she wouldn't smell like moth balls and brought the car around to the front door. I got her in, covered her with a blanket and buckled her seat belt across her knitting. That was the last time we went to chemo."

It was surprising that this elderly man had been so sensitive to the nuances of his wife's appearance and how it affected her. I could almost smell the sickly-sweet odor of mothballs tumbling into the room. "Why was that?" I asked, thinking I already knew the answer.

Finn remained mute. The hour drew to a close and I said, "Well, thank you, Mr. Koski. I'd like to continue on Monday, if it's okay with you." I knew exactly what Finn had gone through. After Matt's diagnosis of esophageal cancer, our future had been cut short too.

It would soon be Christmas season again. I was sure Finn dreaded it as much as I did.

* * *

I'LL BE HOME EARLY," I said to Dane and Caleigh, who had already settled in to watch *Diary of a Wimpy Kid* with Madeleine. It was negative eight degrees outside and I sorely regretted agreeing to accompany Josie to the staff Christmas party.

It was the kind of Minnesota cold that made it hurt to breathe. Too cold to snow even. Everything seemed to crystallize—my breath, the air, the snow banks lining the driveway. The world outside looked like a black and white photo—all inky sky with a white-gold moon hanging in the distance. I started the car with my remote charger and, five minutes later, braved the elements.

It was a short drive through mostly deserted streets to Dr. Regina Stafford's neighborhood. I parked a few blocks away and as I walked to Regina's house, Josie drove up and parallel parked behind my car. "Hey, girl! Wait up."

My heels sank into the snow-covered street. "Hey there, yourself. Ah! Shit!" I had slipped and lost my balance again. Josie grabbed my arm before I fell. "Those are some quick reflexes you have. It was stupid of me to wear these shoes. My ankle must still be weak from the last time I fell."

Josie wore military style boots, not very fashionable, but practical in the snow. "No problem. We're almost there." She made no move to release my arm as we arrived in front of Regina's house, and I was grateful for the support. Regina's house was a white colonial, as cheerfully decorated as a Hallmark card. The party was already underway—silvery laughter and strains of music filled the night air like stars. It had been a while since I had felt any joy at Christmas. Since Matthew's death, I had observed the holidays quietly at home with the children.

"Thanks for coming," Josie said. "Melanie had an activity at our daughter's school tonight but I wanted to make an appearance here. It's only once a year and I like Regina."

"It's okay. I really need to make an effort to get out more." The door opened and Regina hugged us and took our coats. She pointed the way to the buffet where a mouth-watering spiral cut ham, several glazed platters of hor d'oeuvres and an enticing array of salads and desserts on the table resembled a beautifully painted still life. Josie stared at the tree in awe. It was so enormous it reached the high vaulted ceilings of Regina's house. "Are you seeing your kids this Christmas?" I asked softly.

"Nah. They're with their dad and the woman they call, 'Mom.' It's been like this since Kira turned eleven." Her eyes blazed. "I'm not 'Mommy' anymore. I'm 'Josie.'"

"I'm sorry," I said, my eyes tearing.

"After all those years of working the night shift so my babies could have someone at home at all times. My husband worked days, and I was home baking brownies, going on fieldtrips, you know, all the mommy stuff. Now it's Marcus's new wife doing all that. Guess two mothers are one too many. Whatever. He's a *come mierda*."

"Josie, I'm really sorry. That must be so painful for you." We loaded our plates and looked around the crowded room for seats. "I don't think I know that expression, but my Spanish wouldn't get me from here to the city."

"I'm surprised you haven't heard it at the prison. '*Come mierda*' is someone who eats shit. Anyway, it is harder around holidays. I'm lucky to have Melanie and her kids. It still feels like Christmas with them around."

"When am I going to get to meet the mysterious Melanie?"

"She's pretty busy, but one day we'll get together."

"You never really talked about the divorce and how you feel about it," I said. The first sip of wine went right to my head. "It's fine if you don't want to talk about it."

"Do you want the short version or the long version?" Josie asked warily before taking a sip of her vodka and cranberry.

We shifted to a quiet corner where we sat at a corner table, the party noise mere muzak in the background. "Whatever you want to share."

"I guess I always knew," Josie said softly and I fell silent, feeling as though we were insulated in a bubble of pain in the midst of so much good cheer. "I always knew I was gay. Gays had a tough time in Puerto Rico. Between the cultural taboos and the rigid gender roles, it was a wonder anyone survived. Women were meant to have children, be subservient, take care of their children, keep house and keep their man happy, overlooking everything he did. I left as soon as I could but I guess not soon enough."

"What do you mean?"

"I had already accepted those gender roles and got married faster than flies flock to shit. I met Marcus as soon as I enrolled in the police academy, got knocked up and did the good-girl Catholic thing. It only lasted a few years. But, hey, that's water under the bridge."

"I'm sorry, Josie. Does your family know?"

"Yeah. Marcus and the girls at least. My mother still has no idea. He came home one day and found me in bed with a woman I'd met at work. It had taken an instant for me to be swept off my feet. The shit

hit the fan and that was the end. I was head-over-heels in love with Alicia and didn't contest the divorce. God, I loved that woman. I was literally drowning in love. We lasted a year. The day I realized she didn't love me anymore I couldn't breathe. I had given up everything for her, including my kids, and she threw me away like yesterday's paper."

"Oh, Josie, I'm sorry." I hugged her tightly. "I'm glad you found Melanie."

Josie stood and said, "I'm gonna get another drink. Want something?"

"No, I'm good." Bud Anderson stood in the corner talking to another officer I recognized from the medical unit. Antonio Alvarez. Another military man who looked as though he was trying to make his way to the bar, escaping Bud. The atmosphere was loud and feverish, carnival-like. I barely recognized Bud without his uniform but felt his gaze on my body, making me feel as though I were standing in my bra and panties. I wished I hadn't worn such a clingy red dress or the strappy high heels.

I sensed him behind me as I refilled my wine. "Hi, Doc." Bud smirked and slurred his words. "Merry Christmas." He leaned in. The room was beginning to blur at the edges. I smelled alcohol on his breath. Peals of laughter hurtled around the kitchen. I nodded and turned away. He put a hand on my shoulder.

"Thanks, officer. You too." I stepped away, as brittle as the first freeze.

He took a step closer. "Call me Bud."

My eyes scanned the kitchen looking for Josie, but she was deep in conversation with another social worker. "Bud, if you'll excuse me, I was just getting a drink."

"Bitch," he muttered.

Trembling, I walked across the floor to where Josie sat. Wine sloshed from my glass onto the wooden floor. I sat on the sofa next to Josie and kept an eye on Bud across the room. His gaze was still locked on me. "Josie, do you know Bud Anderson?"

"Sure, he's hard to miss. He's a bastard. All six-foot-three of him lurking around every corner."

"That's just the feeling I've had about him." I finished the wine and waited until he left the kitchen to go back for another glass, wishing

I had invited Alex. I took a sip, put my glass down and walked down the hallway to the guest bathroom thinking I would call him later to see if he had plans for tomorrow.

The mirror reflected the glittery ornaments Regina had hung in the bathroom. I washed my face, reapplied lipstick and opened the door. "Oh, Officer Anderson. Excuse me. Did you need to use the restroom?" I felt uneasy in his presence. How long had he been standing outside that door?

"Yeah. I mean, no." His tongue flicked snake-like around his lips. The metallic glint in his eyes repulsed me. His nostrils were flared and his breath was ragged. I had had enough experience with dangerous men to listen to my sixth sense. Something was about to happen. Anderson leaned in closer. "I told you to call me Bud," he said, his alcohol-laced breath heavy in the air. He backed me against the bathroom door and pulled me to him so that my breasts were pressed against his chest and his erection was hard against my pelvis. He gripped my shoulders so hard I winced.

"Let go of me."

"Hold on there, Doc." His hard pinkish mouth was fixed on my lips. His breath was hot and sour. I gagged as he thrust his tongue in my mouth and then grabbed him by the hair and squirmed. He held me tight and pushed me against the door. The room spun and the carols grew louder as his mouth pressed harder against mine. I bit down on his lip and tasted the coppery taste of blood. He pressed his pelvis into mine. With all the strength I could muster, I raised my knee, hard, between his legs. He cried out in pain and something dark flashed across his face.

"If you ever touch me again, I will kill you."

"What is it? What's wrong?" Josie asked when I returned. "I was just about to come looking for you."

"That bastard Anderson grabbed me and tried to kiss me."

"What the fuck? You want me to do something to him? I know some nasty little tricks that'll make him think twice about ever touching you again," Josie said in a way that surprised me.

"No, I think I'd rather just forget about it. I don't think he'll be bothering me again."

"Jesus. That makes me wish I hadn't given up smoking," she said angrily.

CHAPTER EIGHT

BUD ANDERSON

I WAS TIRED AS HELL, thinking about heading home but the neon sign in the window beckoned me in. There's something about a neon sign with your favorite beer and a hammock under the palm trees in the dead of winter that's hard to resist.

The light inside was so dim I could hardly make out the regulars or make my way to my duct-tape patched barstool. The high school hockey game was on and I was looking forward to some decent checking when the refs' backs were turned. I ordered a Bud and a crepe. Not what I'd try anyplace else but the owner's wife was a French woman who made damn good salmon-filled crepes. Nobody in Douglas had ever tasted a crepe like this before she moved to town.

Stacy threw me out a couple of months ago and the beer was tasting better all the time. With the first, long, cold slug, I drifted into the promise of a quiet evening, undisturbed by thoughts of Stacy or the kids or Grace. With each sip, Stacy's bitching about child support and the kids' attitudes seemed farther away.

I have to admit a beer or two after work had become a six-pack or two, but it was my reward at the end of a long hard day. A couple of beers couldn't hurt. It helped me forget about Stacy and the little incident at the police academy with the rookie who kept coming onto me. Helped me not get all worked up about that bitch Garrett threatening me with sexual harassment, as if it was any of her business. She had no idea what I was capable of.

A couple of hours later, I stumbled back to the truck, sagging like a curtain. The sky was leaden and it took me a while to find the keys. The cold was freakin' alive. I should've covered my nose and mouth with a scarf or a ski mask. The engine grumbled twice before I got it started.

The small bungalow I rented was at the end of a long winding drive. A remote place, but I liked it for that reason. I liked the isolated lives Minnesotans lead. As isolated as the state itself. After I got outta the service, I never wanted to live in a sardine can again. I wasn't a reader but I once picked up one of Stacy's books. It said something about desire and secrecy slithering like bull snakes through the isolated prairie. It made me smile. Most of the time, I felt like a bullsnake slithering through the prairie.

The garage light had gone out and I tripped over the step leading into the house. The first thing I noticed was the formaldehyde scent of the damn carpet the landlord installed just before I rented the dump. That and the seam between the living room and the hallway. I don't like the guy but he forked out some dough for this shitty carpet. The least they could've done was line up the pieces right.

The cold air slapping my face had given me a second wind. I kicked off my boots and sank onto the kitchen chair to log in. One stroke on the keyboard and the messy complications of my life were behind me. My favorite porn site showed a naked woman tied to a bed. The guy standing over her was muscular and easily overpowered her. I unzipped my pants and tried to get it going. Damn it. Nothing. Again.

At 4:00 a.m. I had tossed and turned for a couple of hours but now I could smell the snow. Four or five inches already on the ground. The snowfall meant I'd have to plow the drive before clocking in at seven.

I had put on my long johns, jeans, and a flannel shirt and headed to the kitchen, swaying, a little unsteady on my feet. I'd been drinking a little more than I used to, but I was a big guy and it took a lot to get me drunk. I pressed my palms against the wall and went back to the bathroom for a bottle of aspirin.

I looked pretty bad that morning. The bathroom mirror showed blood shot eyes and broken red blood vessels criss-crossing my cheeks. I needed to cut back but life took so much out of me lately. My mood felt like the color of the garage floor. A dreary slate gray.

The garage was unheated and I expected a helluva time getting the John Deere going, but it roared to life despite the negative-twenty-degree temperature outside. I wanted to see how that bitch cleared her driveway now that I had the John Deere. The wind whipped my face but I felt calmer plowing those long, meticulous straight rows down the drive. It was as comforting as opening the first beer. The moon broke the darkness of night. With that and the tractor headlights illuminating the snow-covered road, I could get it done quick. A large deer leapt into the drive and was caught in the headlights. The buck stood in the middle of the road trying to make up its mind which way to go. I blasted the horn, shattering the early morning peace.

If it kept snowing at this rate, I'd have to plow again when I got off of work. By the time I finished, it was 6:00 a.m. so I drove into town for coffee. Main Street looked like a curtain had been drawn around it. The wind still lambasted the swirling masses of snow with vengeance.

With the fresh, hot coffee in hand, I headed to the prison, my neck in gridlock. My fingers found the knot in my shoulder, and massaged it as I rotated my neck in small half circles. The closer I got to town, the more my shoulder hurt.

The snow banks along the road brought a flash of memory I'd just as soon forgotten.

I was an eight-year-old kid excitedly preparing breakfast, full of joy. "It's a snow day!" I yelled. Cereal overflowed into a chipped blue and white enamel bowl and I spooned sugar and poured milk on top of it. I can still hear the clang of my spoon against the metal bowl. In my excitement, I spilled the sugar and stood numb, watching it cascade to the linoleum-made-to-look-like-flagstone floor. I took a step and my slippers crunched on Mom's freshly mopped floor. Fear rose in my chest and migrated to my throat.

"Look what you did, Buddy!" Sis taunted me. "I'm telling Mom!"

"I'll clean it up," I muttered, frantically searching the closet for the dented, metal dustpan and broom. The joy of the snow day was over. The sugar was a minefield waiting to explode. The lines between the sham stones moved in worm-like waves. My mother came down in her flowered housecoat and defeated eyes. "Buddy, you know I can't stand stepping on sugar. It's like nails on a chalkboard. Are you stupid? Go to your room and stay there."

Later, I heard heavy clomping up the stairs. "Whoever spares the rod hates their children, but the one who loves their children is careful to discipline them," she said, the belt lashing against my bare skin. "That's Proverbs, Buddy. You're to stay home today and think about what you'd done. One day you'll thank me for this, son."

For some reason, that reminded me of the freakin' Christmas party. I don't know what came over me, coming onto the doc like that. It'll be a while before I'd forget the way her face looked when she kneed me.

There was a spot for the pickup in the West parking lot. The eight-foot cyclone fence topped with razor wire made me feel as trapped as the inmates. It continued to snow. I stuffed my hands into the pockets of an old army surplus jacket, and walked as quick as I could to the entrance. No sign of Grace in the parking lot.

The snow was deep and I kicked at a rust-flecked pick-up to loosen the snow off my boots. Ever since our little misunderstanding, Grace had been avoiding me, turning her head when I passed her in the unit. I liked 'em a little spunky though. I had seen her around with that guy, and I had a pretty good idea of where he lived.

It was another gray morning, with a metallic sky and the smell of snow in the air. Hunched over against the wind, I didn't see Warden Briscoe until he was right by my side.

"Cold enough for you?" the warden, one of the few African Americans who worked at the prison, joked. There was a bitch of a northwesterly wind. Only the warden's reddened eyes were visible above his muffler.

A rolling wave of moist heat sucked us in through the revolving door into the sallyport along with everybody else trying to get out of the bone cold. It felt like Hawaii calling me.

"Mornin', Bud," Officer Stephen Christie said. "Helluva snow last night. It's so damn cold this morning, my Siberian husky was shivering."

I laughed, thinking it was a joke, and then placed my shoes, belt, and wallet on the conveyor belt to be x-rayed. I emptied out my pockets, and fingered my new cell phone. *Shit.* We had a strict no cell phones rule. Now I'd have to walk back to the truck with it. It felt like I was working at the fucking White House.

CHAPTER NINE

MONDAY MORNING. I woke up jittery and ill tempered, as if I had a hangover. The look on Anderson's face and his body pressed against mine was enough to make my temples throb. It was still Christmas vacation and Madeleine would be coming over soon to stay with the kids. I dressed quickly, kissed the children good-bye and left early for work hoping to miss him during the morning shift change. My plan was to see Finn that morning. We had made such headway last week.

I shook the snow off my boots and changed into low heels. Josie was in the sallyport going through security. "That fucking bastard," she said, balling her hands into a fist when she saw me. "I couldn't stop thinking about what you told me at the party. You should've let me take care of him. Given him a kick right where it hurts. I was a cop re-member? Had to learn how to defend myself. Are you gonna report him to the warden? Maybe I can threaten him with sexual harassment."

Her monologue made my head ache more. "Josie, no. It didn't hap-pen at work. He probably just had too much to drink. What would I say, he tried to kiss me?" It occurred to me Josie was taking this too much to heart. "Why does this bother you so much?"

"Because he's a fuckin' *bendejo*, that's why! A real *jodon*."

"I don't know what those words mean, Josie." I tried to make light of it. "Let's just forget about it. I kneed him pretty well. That'll give him something to remember me by." The officers were looking at us and I laughed self-consciously. "Thank God I have an ex-cop who was a sex crimes investigator on my side. I gotta get back to work. I'm seeing Mr. Koski this morning. I heard from the warden that he'll complete his sentence soon."

"Just remember, if you want me to do something about it, I will, okay?" Josie said as we parted. "I don't want anybody messin' with you."

I wouldn't want to be on Josie's bad side, I thought as I said good-bye and headed to my office for my session with Finn.

Stillness on my part usually made the patient uncomfortable enough to start talking but a full minute went by before Finn said any-thing. His shoulders shook under his prison-issued shirt. "You shoulda seen her, Doc," he finally said, his eyes widening as though he were seeing his wife again. "Eva looked like a newly hatched robin. Cold and blue, her skin stretched across her bones like a drum. I tried to make her drink the Ensure the hospital gave us, but she hated it."

The way he described her, I understood they were, neither of them, any longer the dewy young man and woman they had once been. They had almost become redundant. That's what happened when you got old. One day you woke to find yourself extraneous, hidden in the body of an old woman. A caricature of your former self, with something about the eyes remaining. I remembered it from my own grandmother.

"After the last chemo, we went home and she collapsed on the sofa. She tried not to cry. After almost fifty years of marriage . . ." He took out a handkerchief and blew his nose. His sobs wracked his slender body. "You know what she said to me?" he asked without waiting for an answer. "She said, 'Finn, you've been a good man. I know I shouldn't ask you to help me, but I can't do this alone. Will you help me put an end to this?' She begged me, Doc! After that, I paced all night. I couldn't lose her after a lifetime together. Finally, I lay in bed beside her. I didn't know if I could do it."

I nodded encouragingly. Time seemed to stand still

"I pleaded with her to drink some water but she refused. She let me wipe her lips with a wet washcloth wrapped around ice chips. I crushed her pills into applesauce, but Eva couldn't swallow the mixture. I raised her head to help her breathing. She used to stop breathing and it scared me half out of my wits.

"One day she said, 'Now, Finn. I'm ready now.' She had suffered so much. I kissed her on her lips and picked up the pillow. I told her I loved her and then I pressed the pillow over her face."

I reached for a tissue and dabbed at my eyes. The silence in the room lay as thick as smoke. "What happened next?" I whispered.

"Eh?"

"What happened next?" I spoke louder and unconsciously pressed my ballpoint pen hard enough to tear the yellow legal pad. I could barely breathe.

"The visiting nurse rang the doorbell and looked through the glass door. She ran in screaming, asking what I was doin'. I told her I was doin' what Eva asked me to do."

"Oh, my god." I brought my hand up to my mouth.

"She pushed me aside and ripped the pillow away from Eva's face. Eva was as white as a ghost. Already on her way to Heaven. Mrs. Jacobson pressed her hands into the center of Eva's chest, leaned in and began pushin.' She screamed, 'Call 911' but I wouldn't do it. Eva was gone. She wouldn't have wanted to be brought back again to suffer."

I remembered a baby bird I'd once crushed in my sleep and a vision of that lifeless body crept across my brain.

"She kept pressin' down on Eva's chest. One-one thousand, two-one thousand, three-one thousand. I yelled at her to stop. Her weight would crush Eva's rib cage. I still see those blood-red fingers of hers pressing into Eva's chest."

I pictured Mrs. Jacobson crushing Eva's fragile ribs, the bones cracking and splintering into sharp, jagged spears, and Finn helpless to stop her.

"I sat and stared out the window. The first yellow leaves were flutterin' to the ground. Fall was Eva's favorite season. Mrs. Jacobson finally gave up, too exhausted to continue. She closed Eva's eyes and covered her with her sheet. She told me she had to call the sheriff and that what I had done was wrong. I waited for the sheriff and told her it may be the only thing I'd ever done that was right. I think that's about all I can say right now."

Finn's face was as dark and overcast as the day. The phone buzzed in the mole-sized office. "I'm so sorry. Will you excuse me for just a moment?" I said, frowning under my professional facade.

"Dr. Rendeau speaking." I picked up my pen and tapped it against my desk.

"Grace? It's me."

"Alex! What a surprise. How are you?" I should have sent the call to voicemail. I tried to keep my private life completely separate from my job with inmates but just one brief conversation couldn't hurt.

"I was wondering if we could get together sometime this week."

"Can I call you back? I'm in the middle of something right now. Okay. Talk to you later." I smoothed my skirt and turned toward Finn. "Now . . . where were we?"

Finn sat perched on the edge of his seat, his hands burrowed in his pockets. He had been listening intently, I was sure of it.

"I was saying that's about all I can say about it." Finn stood. "I think I'd better get back to the unit now."

I thanked him and told him I appreciated how difficult it must have been for him to tell me this. He left the office like a wind-driven cloud.

As medicine struggled to pull people away from the edge of death, it could do little to alleviate intractable suffering in terminal conditions. Did society have a moral right to protect and preserve all life? As I pondered Mr. Koski's tragic situation, there was a knock at the door. It was Emanuel. I had been so deep in thought about Mr. Koski's dilemma of ending his wife's suffering, that I had forgotten it was my day to see Emanuel Venegas.

CHAPTER TEN

I WAS REALLY NERVOUS," Emanuel said, tucking his hands under his armpits. There was a smell resembling a mixture of ammonia and vinegar in the small office, and I wondered if it was coming from him. "I was pacing back and forth in the living room. It was hot and still. I tried to stay cool, ya know? I dunno, maybe it would work out. We'd go to the beach, maybe stop at a restaurant on the way home. I could get out and make the call, pick up the stuff and be back before they realized I was gone. It was the last time, I swear."

"Go on." His eyes bore in to mine. Every breath he took appeared labored.

"Mariangelie was already packing her beach toys. She was so excited. I told Marisol I had business that I didn't want to mix with pleasure." He looked away. "No real Puerto Rican goes to the beach in any month with an 'r' in it, but Mariangelie kept pestering me. Begging to go to the beach. Then Marisol got in on it. I didn't want to bring them but they wouldn't take no for an answer."

He began to drum his fingers on the oak grain surface of my desk. "He called my cell phone and asked me if I was ready. He said not to screw it up. My heart almost jumped out of my chest."

"Who called your cell phone?" I scribbled a couple of notes in his chart. The drumming had begun to annoy me but I hesitated to say anything.

"That bastard, del Toro." His eyes flashed. There was something dark and tormented behind them. "I drove down to the beach at Boqueron with Marisol and our little girl. The heat and the smell reminded me of being down by the docks when I was a kid. Mari was tired and fell asleep in the car sucking her thumb. Marisol asked how far it was to Cabo Rojo and it pissed me off. The highway winds through the mountains like a corkscrew and it was hard driving."

I had been to Puerto Rico. The image of skinny, flea-bitten dogs lying in the shade of coconut palms at the beach barged into my mind as he spoke. Matt and I had gone when Dane was a baby. Matt's parents had watched the kids. Now I'm glad we had a second honeymoon.

Besides the unwanted and abandoned animals I'd cried over, it was a perfect trip. With a start, I realized Emanuel had been talking while I'd been lost in the memories of moonlit walks and making love during the hot tropical nights.

" . . . I told her it was another hour and drove faster. Then she asked what we were really doing there. I didn't want to talk about it. I never wanted her and Mari to come that day. It was something I had to do and then I was gonna be through." He stared into the distance. "The road continued to the coast, where it ended on this sandy road at a desalinization plant. I was supposed to be at the plant at eight. I had a bad feeling and wished we hadn't come. Then I turned left and headed toward Boqueron Beach."

I closed my eyes and visualized the scene. "What happened when you got to the beach?" The tension in my office rose quickly as Emanuel described that day.

"Boqueron Beach stretched for miles. We found a spot under a palm and Mari jumped up and down, grabbing my hand, wanting me to take her to the water. Marisol smeared sunscreen on her and I held out my hand. Mari wrapped her fingers around my pinky." Emanuel paused to wipe his eyes. "I kept looking at my watch and Marisol asked me again what I was so uptight about. She told me to relax. It was a gorgeous day. She just wanted to have some fun, ya know?"

I remembered Caleigh at that age and the trips to the lake Matt and I had taken with her when she was a small girl. It was hard to hear Emanuel's story, knowing its tragic end.

"I raced Marianglie and held her hand while she dipped her toes in the water." His eyes softened and he laughed a small self-conscious chuckle. "The water came up to her shoulders and she shrieked each time a wave lapped her. She grabbed my hand, and yelled to Marisol to look at her."

"What else do you remember?" Although it was late and I was scheduled to see another patient, I pressed on, wanting Emanuel to keep going.

His eyes clouded. "I wanted to leave them at a restaurant to wait for me but they wouldn't stay behind. Mariangelie was worn out and fell asleep in the back seat. Salt-water lagoons and lime cliffs with a two hundred foot drop into the ocean surrounded the lighthouse. It got dark as we got closer. Again, Marisol asked me what we were doing there. I yelled at her to shut up and told her to just stay low and keep quiet. I told her I was meeting someone and we couldn't leave. I was picking up something for del Toro. She said she didn't trust him." He put his head in his hands. "Ay, *Dios mio*, I wish I had listened to her."

The room grew silent. It was that critical moment in therapy where the patient confronted his deepest fear and darkest memory. I cleared my throat and said, "Sometimes the scariest moment is just before you say it. After that, things can only get better."

"Huh?" Emanuel shook his head, looking everywhere but at me. "I parked the car, killed the engine. Opened the window. We heard the sound of waves crashing against the rocky coast. Mariangelie stirred in the back and headlights rounded the bend, coming toward us. Marisol told her to go back to sleep. I almost jumped out of my skin when I heard a voice at the window asking me, 'Manny, you ready man?' He was wearing a black tee shirt and jeans and came up to the driver's side. I didn't know him. He said, 'Let's go, man. I want to get out of here.' Then, I followed him."

Emanuel's eyes were glassy. Sweat beaded on his forehead. His breath came in gasps. "I told Marisol I'd be right back and to stay in the car. I got what I needed and ran back to the car, popped open the trunk, got in the driver's seat and started the engine."

My office was the size of a walk-in closet in some of Rochester's new subdivisions. It was so still that the fluttering of a wilted leaf falling from the ivy plant on my windowsill drew both our attention.

"She kept bugging me about what I was doing and I yelled at her to shut up. The other guy ran across the road and got into his car. His tires peeled as he turned his car around, one hundred and eighty degrees. I turned around on the narrow road and followed. There was a roadblock ahead of us. The guy had been pulled over to the side, and the fuckin' D.E.A. agents surrounded his car. I don't know how they knew. I pressed on the gas and plowed through the roadblock. Marisol screamed when they fired at us. *Cabrones*." He slammed his hand on my desk. "When I get outta here, I'm gonna kill that guy."

"Who would you kill?" I sat on the edge of my seat and held my breath. It was still disconcerting to be in such a small space with someone who had just said 'I'm gonna kill somebody' in his previous breath.

"Anybody who gets in my way." He knew enough not to threaten the FBI agent by name. "They're gonna pay."

He stared out the window and I had the sensation he was so tightly wound, he could have sprung forth at any moment. My autonomic nervous system kicked in, flooding my body with adrenaline. My face and hands flushed a prickly red. The radiator wheezed, making the room uncomfortably warm. "You know I have to report that you have made a threat against someone's life," I said in measured tones. "We'll talk more tomorrow." I'd asked the nursing staff to keep a close eye on him for the remainder of the day.

"I haven't heard a thing from Marisol." He wrung his hands as if he hadn't heard me. As if he hadn't just mentioned murder. "Even though I've written her every day."

I took a moment, framing my thoughts before I asked, "What were you expecting to hear?"

"Anything. I just want to know they're okay. I want to know she still loves me."

I wasn't sure this was the time to tell him what happened or even if he knew what had happened. Afraid he would lapse into another catatonic state, I said I wanted to increase his medication and he nodded as tears rolled down his cheeks. I winced at his unwavering despair. The first stanza of "Invictus," a poem I loved, came to mind:

Out of the night that covers me,
Black as the pit from pole to pole,
I thank whatever gods may be
For my unconquerable soul.

It had been a bad morning. I was exhausted by the depth of his emotion and still disturbed by Finn's sad story and Bud's simmering anger. And about the way he had groped me at the party. Several scalding showers later I still couldn't get rid of the feeling of his hands on my body. I noted Emanuel's homicidal ideation in his chart and called the warden.

CHAPTER ELEVEN

THE NICKEL-SIZED BLOB of clear, viscous blue gel in the palm of my hand wasn't going to do it. My hair was as electric as a cat's fur in a warm house in winter. I brushed the gel through, put on a coat of mascara and pulled on high-heeled boots.

"What are you all dressed up for?" Caleigh asked when I came down the stairs.

"I told you guys I'm going to the movies with Alex tonight. Do I look okay? Do you think these pants are too long?"

"You're going to the movies? But what about Daddy?" Dane asked.

My heart sank. Dane's reaction was a complete surprise. I had actually begun to flirt with the idea that my children were on board about me seeing Alex.

"What about Daddy, sweetheart?" I put my arm around his bony shoulders. Caleigh glared at me. Dane squeezed his eyes to slits that eked out a spotty trail of tears, mixing with the lump of mashed potatoes on his plate. "Can you turn the TV off for a minute? I want to talk to you."

"Don't you love him anymore, Mommy?" Dane ran to the sofa and burrowed into the pillows before I could respond.

"Dane, look at me. I loved your father very much and some part of me always will, but he's gone and our lives have to move on." After several months, I was falling in love with Alex. It was time for Caleigh and Dane to meet him.

"Yeah, right. You mean *your* life has to move on, right, Mom?" Caleigh snarled.

"No, I mean *our* lives have to move on. I know this is hard for you. It's hard for me too. But please, couldn't you try to give Alex a chance? Try to get to know him? I'd like to invite him here to meet you."

"Seriously? That's the last thing I want to do." Caleigh sunk deeper into the overstuffed chair and opened the latest issue of *Teen Magazine*.

"I want to watch the movie about Daddy again," Dane said. He began rummaging through the wooden chest where Grace kept DVDs. "Mommy, where is it?"

Caleigh refused to meet my eye. I walked over to her and swept her bangs away from her face. "Look at me, Caleigh."

"Where's your wedding ring, Mom?"

There was a knock at the door at precisely that moment and Madeline soldiered in with an armful of books. "Maddy!" Dane yelled. "Can you read my new Harry Potter to me tonight?"

A hot flush of shame surged in me. I was relieved Dane had changed his mind about watching the video clips of our lives with Matt again. Caleigh mumbled something unintelligible and ran up the stairs. The sound of her bedroom door slamming shook the house. Dane covered his ears and gave a philosophical shrug.

Maddy asked, "Do you want me to try to talk to her, Dr. Rendeau?"

"I'm afraid you won't get very far, but sure. Maybe after I'm gone you can have some dessert and play a game or watch TV together. Something to get her out of her room, okay?"

* * *

THE THICK, PLUM COLORED CARPET was as spongy as new grass. The smell of hot buttered popcorn made me feel like a teenager on a first date again. I was ridiculously early, and I began to feel something between concern and insecurity. I tried to smooth my hair down and looked at my watch again.

A few minutes later Alex came in through the plate glass doors. He looked distracted as he searched the lobby, but my smile, when he saw me, lit up his face. His arm around me felt so matter-of-fact. "I've been looking forward to this all day," he said.

"Me too." I tried to put aside the children's reaction to my date as we eased into the stadium seating and he reached for my hand. I wanted to bottle the moment and savor it. The film was a typical boy meets girl movie. Boy falls in love with girl. Boy and girl fight insurmountable odds to be together. I wondered whether the parallels between the film and my own life were as clear to Alex as they were to me.

After the movie, the lights came on and I checked my phone for messages. "Expecting a call?" Alex slipped on his coat and picked up mine.

"I guess not. The kids seemed to have a hard time when I left and I just wondered . . . It's nothing. It's fine. I want you to meet them."

"I don't know. Are you sure that's a good idea?"

That seemed like an odd question. "I thought it was." The theater was empty. I hadn't realized everyone else had left. "I guess I'd better get home and see how they're doing." I wondered what he meant by whether meeting Caleigh and Dane was a good idea.

The next morning, breakfast was a quiet affair. It was my weekend on call. "It's getting easier," I said, pouring pancake batter onto the griddle, as much to myself as to the kids. "Did you have a good time with Maddy?"

Caleigh removed her headphones. "Did you say something?"

"She asked if we had a good time with Maddy and she said it's getting easier!" Dane yelled. He obviously had the ears of an elephant.

Caleigh shrugged. "Great," she said. "It's getting easier for you, Mom, not for me." She put the headphones back on.

"I know, honey. It'll get better. I promise. What about you, Dane?"

"Huh?"

"I asked you if it's getting easier to think of me seeing someone." The smell of burnt pancakes hung on the air. I had left them on a moment too long. "Shit!"

"Mommy! You said a bad word," Dane put his index finger to my lips. "That's okay, I wasn't very hungry anyway."

"I know, sweetheart. I'm sorry."

The telephone rang, destroying any hopes I had for an uneventful weekend. "Dr. Rendeau? Mr. Venegas has been refusing food and meds again," Warren Hutchings, the weekend charge nurse said.

"I'm on my way." I told the kids I wanted to continue our discussion later. I wanted to talk to them about Alex. "Stay inside, okay? Don't use the oven. Don't open the door to strangers. I'll call you in a couple of hours to make sure you're okay, all right?"

"Mom! I'm thirteen. We'll be fine." Caleigh rolled her eyes and sighed in the way teenage girls everywhere had perfected. The number of times I would see that expression made me shudder.

Half an hour later, I was in my office. I asked to see Emanuel, not wanting to lose the gains we had made in yesterday's session. We had been at a stalemate for so many months. "Mr. Hutchings called to say you refused food and meds this morning. Can we start where we left off yesterday? You were telling me about the day at the beach."

The quiet heaved in waves around the office. "Do you think you can tell me about it? Emanuel?"

He covered his face with his hands. "I dunno."

There was something sensual about probing the depths of a human psyche—of being a voyeur to the darkness and despair, the desperately suppressed fantasies and the hint of memory that threatened to burst forth. That moment. The moment just before the expulsion of repressed desire into conscious thought was a delivery of sorts, as painful as a birth. I dug deeper. Emanuel hedged and relented, hedged and relented. It was a seductive dance, one in which he breathed deeply, panting almost, culminating in an emotional release as cathartic as sex.

I glanced at his chart and he began to talk. "We were in the car, and she screamed. We sped through the stop sign on Route 301 and I saw the oncoming pickup coming at us, fast. I hear the sound of his brakes screeching over and over again. It sounded like something living." He was almost mechanical in his recitation of the events of that day. His eyes looked dead. I jotted, *flat affect* in my notes.

"The pickup struck Marisol's door and the door folded around her. We went airborne. It looked like we were flying toward the stars. Streaks of blood and light everywhere. The car kept spinning. It reminded me of a carnival. Like the dizzy feel of being on a roller coaster. We flipped over and over again and then we landed. A while after that there were sirens. The fuckin' D.E.A agents swarmed like flies over a dead dog. Cabrones. I heard 'em say the other driver never had a chance. They checked us all for a pulse. Marisol had blood running down her face, pooling at her throat. Marianglie was thrown from the car. She had a pink backpack with a princess on it and her name at the top. I heard somebody yell they found it. Ay, Dios, mio. We were loaded into the ambulance, and brought to Ponce's Distrito Hospital emergency room. I don't know where Marisol and Mariangelie went after that." Emanuel looked at me and I looked away.

* * *

I WALKED IN THE DOOR shortly afterwards. Sometimes it was extremely difficult to go from a session to my family and this was one of those times. "What'd you guys do while I was gone?"

"Not much. I tried to play a board game with the little broski but every time I sat down, the phone rang," Caleigh complained. "It was, like, really annoying."

I sifted through the morning mail. "Oh, yeah? Who called?"

"No idea. They just called and hung up."

"That's strange. Unknown caller. Three calls. Was it a man or a woman?"

"Mom! How would I know? They hung up! I can't tell by their breathing if it's a man or a woman."

"Next time, check the caller ID and don't answer if it's an unknown caller, okay, Caleigh?"

"What's the big deal? It was probably just some little kids playing a prank," Caleigh muttered.

* * *

ON MONDAY MORNING, I presented Emanuel's case in the morning rounds. All staff was present. I cleared my throat. I knew there were things in life that could make a person snap.

"Emmanuel Venegas Torres is a twenty-four-year-old Hispanic male admitted on June 19, 2011. He was in handcuffs, escorted by two federal marshals, dressed in prison garb. He's been here for almost seven months. He's five feet, ten inches tall, weighs one hundred and sixty pounds, is well nourished, clean shaven, has short dark brown hair and brown eyes, and a heart shaped tattoo with the words 'EMMANUEL AND MARISOL' on his left bicep. We had a breakthrough last week but since then he has reverted back into psychosis. He shows no interest in unit activities besides writing to Marisol."

There were quiet murmurs among the staff who had looked at me expectantly.

"I remember reading his writing, fragmented as it was during his first acute psychosis," I said calmly. "He wrote of his love for Marisol coherently at times. I have never seen anyone more anguished." I paused. "He has relapsed. Comments?"

Bud stood up. "He may be psychotic, but he's no security risk. Not anymore." He began to sit down but stopped. "What about his wife? Would it kill her to answer a letter? Maybe it would do some good. Fuckin' wives," he muttered under his breath.

"Officer Anderson," I said. "Marisol is dead. And so is his daughter."

Bud stared at me.

"Emanuel was charged with their deaths and couldn't accept the reality of what happened. That's why he's here . . . indefinitely."

Bud fell back into his chair. "Sorry, I didn't know," he whispered.

CHAPTER TWELVE

"MR. KOSKI, I HAVE GOOD NEWS for you," I told him first thing in the morning. "The board has reviewed your records and you are eligible for parole. You're eighty-one years old now. Is that correct? You've served your sentence. If we can find placement for you, you'll be able to leave within a few days."

Finn's face crumpled. He ran his hands through his thinning hair. "Within a few days?"

I took off my glasses and looked at him. "I thought you'd be pleased that you'll be able to go home and garden, maybe spend some time with your children and grandchildren." The end of my pencil was missing its eraser from my chewing on it. This was my first release. I wanted him to be as elated as I was.

"My children don't want me," he grunted. "They think I killed their mother. I haven't seen my grandchildren since their grandma died."

I leaned forward in my chair until we were an arm's length distance apart. "Mr. Koski, I don't know what to say. Josie, our social worker, will arrange for a meeting with your children and perhaps your grandchildren, who must also be adults by now."

"I'm not gonna be a burden to 'em." Finn crossed his arms over his chest. "They have their own lives." His breathing had become audible.

I nodded noncommittally and crossed my right leg over my left. "I understand how you might feel this way, but let's try to see it from their point of view. It's possible they would welcome you home and enjoy time spent with their father and grandfather."

Our eyes met and Finn looked away. "You don't know that."

"No, I don't know that," I admitted, "but isn't it worth the chance to find out?"

The corner of Finn's mouth twitched and he attempted a tight-lipped smile. "What if you're wrong?"

"If I'm wrong, Josie Garrett, our social worker, will find housing for you. It's a new beginning, Mr. Koski."

Finn traced figure eights on the desk. "I'm too old for a new start. What I had with Eva was all I ever wanted. Without her, there's no home to go back to. There's no new beginning."

"I'll have Josie call your family and then we'll take it from there, okay?" My stomach began to rumble. It was getting close to lunchtime. *Come on, Mr. Koski. I have enough to worry about*, I thought.

"I tell you, I'm not going anywhere," he said as he got up to leave.

I hadn't anticipated Mr. Koski might not want to leave the unit. Josie had to have dealt with this issue in her ten years with the bureau. I gave her a call and asked if she'd had lunch yet.

An hour later, we were sharing sandwiches and Josie's homemade oatmeal cookies. "Can you believe it? Every single patient in this place is dying to get out of here, and the one who's eligible doesn't want to leave!"

"You're new here. It's not so surprising, really." Josie brought a lunch that could feed three people, but she was still as slim as a twelve-year-old-boy. She brushed dark curls out of her eyes. "It's pretty common actually. Not everyone has a place to go, sad as it may seem."

"Josie, how many ear piercings do you have?" I was counting the rows of gold rings climbing the cartilage of both of Josie's ears.

"Twelve. Shhhhh. Let's not mention a word of it, okay? Warden Briscoe doesn't seem the type who would appreciate piercings, even those you can't see." She winked. "I try to keep them covered."

"Anyway . . . what do you think about Mr. Koski? Do you suppose his family will take him in?"

"I wish they would but it's not likely. He was ill a few years ago and I called his daughter to let them know, but she wanted nothing to do with him. They've never even come to visit."

I swallowed the cheese along with a lump in my throat. "That's just heartbreaking," I said and got up to throw the plastic wrap from my sandwich away. "Really? So, where does a person like Mr. Koski go if his family doesn't want him?"

"We'll probably send him to a half-way house or a nursing home somewhere where they'll take him. Elderly men with a record are hard to place, even if they've served their sentence with no incidents. I'll have to start looking."

"But even under extenuating circumstances? How many half-way houses are there in Minnesota?"

"Not necessarily here, Grace. I've placed patients all over the country and escorted them there personally. Could be anywhere. Wanna cookie?"

"Sure." I reached across the desk. "Don't tell me that. Mr. Koski is always talking about his farm. Didn't one of his kids stay there? I don't know if he could live anywhere else. Yumm. These are delicious, by the way. Did you make them?"

"Nah, Melanie's the baker in our house. I'll see what I can do. In some ways, he really might be better off staying here, but I know how that'll go. The warden will want him outta here ASAP. Well, back to work! Let's do lunch again sometime." Josie smiled. "I'm glad we're getting close."

"Me too. I'm still waiting to get together with Melanie and the kids," I said on my way out. I thought about Josie's comment on my way to the dayroom. I'd missed having female friends and was grateful to have met her.

The day crawled by. When it was finally time to go home, I poked my head into the dayroom. Mr. Koski was seated next to Tyrell, staring out the window. Under the thin veil of dry, wrinkled skin, his face was tight with anxiety. Tyrell's voice boomed, "Now, that's just fine, Finn. Just fine! Praise the Lord."

I'd never imagined leaving here could be an adjustment in itself. That someone might actually want to die here. I hoped Josie could find him a place to stay where he didn't have a curfew and could sit at his wife's grave once in a while.

* * *

THE NEXT MORNING THE DREARY wintry weather made a return visit. "Hey, Josie? I'm swamped with meetings today but I wanted to ask how it's going with finding Mr. Koski a placement."

"Good news and bad news," Josie said. "His release is set for next week . . . that's the good news."

"And the bad news?"

"The bad news is I told his daughter he was being released and she went ballistic. She says she's in poor health and can't take care of her father. She blames him for her mother's death. The grandchildren are in college so they're out of the picture and there's really no one else."

"Shit. That's crazy. From what I've read and what he's told me, his wife was terminally ill and it was her last request that he help her die. He's served his time. Now what?"

"I've found him a placement in a halfway house in town, so more good news. At least he'll be in familiar surroundings," Josie said.

The radiator blasted dry heat into my office. I took off my sweater and stretched. "I guess I'll have to tell him today, huh?"

"Yup, I guess you will. Talk to you soon, okay? I have a conference call in a few minutes."

"Thanks, Josie. Let's get together with the kids soon, okay?"

"Will do," she said before hanging up.

Not long afterwards, there was a knock at my door. "Good morning, Mr. Koski. Come on in." I had kicked my shoes off earlier and hoped he wouldn't notice I was in my stocking feet behind the desk.

Mr. Koski's thin-lipped smile stretched across his wizened cheeks. His joints creaked audibly as he lowered himself into the chair across from my desk and waited for me to speak.

"The good news is you'll be released within a few days," I told him, still hoping he would be pleased to hear the news.

His smile faded instantly. His speckled hands flew to his forehead. "What if I don't want to go?"

"Josie Garrett, our social worker, has found a halfway house for you."

"A halfway house?" He folded both arms across his chest.

"Yes. It's here, in Rochester. You'll be able to come and go, walk to town if you'd like. It looks like she might even have a job lined up for you at a plant nursery nearby. I think you'll really like it, Mr. Koski."

"What about going back home to live?"

"I'm afraid that's no longer a possibility. Josie contacted your daughter and she seems to be too ill herself to assume responsibility for you. I think this is the best option. What do you think?"

"I think if the best option is to die alone in a halfway house, I'd rather die here where everyone knows my story and I don't have to tell it again."

Shadows shifted and obscured his face as I phrased my words as appealingly as a perfectly wrapped gift. "I'm afraid this is the only option available to us, Mr. Koski."

"I could stay here, couldn't I? Like Tyrell and Emanuel and the other guys. At least the ones who aren't on drugs, you know? They know me. I don't have to prove anything to nobody here. They know I did what I did 'cause I loved Eva."

"Mr. Koski, you don't have to mention anything about your background when you go to Oakwood Manor. Josie knows the social worker there. You'll be another patient to them. Like everyone else."

"But I'm not like everyone else, Doc. Don't you get it? I did something that no one but these guys here will ever understand. Not mentioning it's like losing Eva again. I already made my peace with the fact I'd die here."

The sky darkened to a faint violet. Shadows lengthened and I switched on the light. "I know how difficult these transitions are, but you've served your sentence and you'll be discharged next week. Josie will be bringing you to Oakwood Manor since your daughter is not able to assume responsibility for you. I'm sorry. Perhaps you can contact your daughter from there and see if reconciliation is possible."

"I don't think so, Doc. I'm an old man. If she hasn't seen me in the thirteen years I've been here I don't know why she would change her mind now."

"Our time is up, Mr. Koski. I wish you the best."

Mr. Koski gripped his armrests to propel himself out of the chair. "I wish you hadn't done this, young lady."

I looked at him questioningly. No sooner had he left, the phone rang.

"Dr. Rendeau?" a woman's voice asked. "This is Kirsti Niemi, Finn Koski's daughter."

Maybe she's changed her mind. "Yes, Mrs. Niemi? This is Dr. Rendeau. I was just speaking to your father."

"Dr. Rendeau, I want to know just what you think you're doing releasing the man who killed my mother," she said in a venomous voice.

My heart thumped in my chest as I fought for the appropriate response.

"What's a matter? Cat got your tongue?" Mrs. Niemi hissed. "My mother was a good woman. She didn't deserve to die that way."

I silently counted to three. "Mrs. Niemi, I understand the social worker contacted you to tell you your father was being released. As his psychiatrist, I can assure you he's served his sentence and is no longer a threat to anyone."

"Yeah, well, he was a threat to my mother wasn't he?"

"I'm sorry I can't get into the specifics of why he did what he did. I understand your mother was terminally ill."

"He didn't have the right to take her life into his own hands." Her voice was bitter. "Who knows how long my mother might have had? He became unbalanced when my mother got sick and finally took leave of his senses and smothered her," she said with a sob.

"Mrs. Niemi, there are often extenuating circumstances you may not understand. Why don't you talk to your father and give him a chance to explain?"

"I never want to see or talk to that man again, you hear me? And if you know what's good for you, you won't let him out on the street. Understand?"

"Are you threatening me?" This day was going from bad to worse. "I'm sorry if you don't understand that your father has served his sentence and is in need of some family support right now, but I think this conversation is over."

"Maybe you don't know that my mother and father had a very stormy relationship," Mrs. Niemi said.

"What?" I massaged my temples.

"That's right. Whatever he has told you about killing my mother out of mercy, is really because he never forgave her for not being the wife he wanted. They separated once."

"When was this?" I asked, looking at my watch.

"Twenty years ago."

"Mrs. Niemi, I hardly think a separation that happened twenty years ago would be motive enough to kill someone. Your father has served the sentence for the crime he was found guilty of. No matter what so called 'evidence' you might want to bring forth now, he cannot be tried again."

Finn's daughter slammed the phone down. Could the separation have played any role in Finn suffocating his wife? The office was shrouded in a blanket of darkness. The jarring zig-zag lights in the periphery of my vision signaled a migraine. A roar sounded behind my eyes. I wished I could go home and crawl into bed. What a way to end the day. It could only get better.

* * *

A WEEK LATER, I GOT THE NEWS. Josie called me to say, "There's a bed for Mr. Koski at Oakwood Manor."

"What? So soon?"

"It's available now. Mr. Koski will be transferred today. They've agreed to take him, and I don't want to waste any time."

"Oh, Josie, no!"

"Grace, what's wrong with you? He's getting out of prison, for God's sake."

"I know, but it seems like this place has come to be his home. Do I at least have time to say good-bye? I've grown kind of attached to him."

"If you hurry. I have a car and an officer outside now to escort him to the half-way house with me," Josie answered.

I flew to the dayroom, expecting to see Finn in his usual spot by the window. "Mr. Perkins, have you seen Finn?" I deliberately took slow, deep breaths.

"Yes, ma'am, he's in his room packing now, praise the Lord."

"Thanks, I'll catch him there."

"Mr. Koski?" I knocked on his door.

Finn turned, looking older and more defeated than I had ever seen him look. He wore ill-fitting civilian clothes and shiny new shoes. "They're kickin' me outta here, today, ya know."

"I wanted to come and wish you the best, Mr. Koski. Congratulations on your release."

"Congratulations? You must not know anything about halfway houses, young lady. Or about being unwanted. I'm sorry, but this is not the last you'll hear of me."

There was nothing more to say. "Well, good-bye, Finn." I wanted to talk to Alex although it was hard to verbalize to anyone who didn't work in a prison how attached I had become to certain patients. Even though they were seen as monsters, they were, after all, human.

CHAPTER THIRTEEN

BUD ANDERSON

AFTER WORK, I DROVE DOWN West River Road along the Zumbro River. It wasn't late but the sky glowed like an ember, gray and red. The news was out that Koski was being released and I felt kinda bad for the schmuck. Tough break but he brought it on himself.

A bald eagle soared over the river and I watched as she flew over her nest. Her nest was the freakin' Taj Mahal of nests, high in the fork of a tree over the water. The biggest fuckin' nest I had ever seen. She scanned the river, swooped down, came back up clutching a fish in her talons and then glided back to the Taj Mahal, the fish flopping in the air.

It was early for eaglets but they'd hatch soon in the order they were laid. I read once the oldest eaglet killed its siblings. Survival of the fittest. Nature knows best. It had always been my philosophy too. That and a woman's place was at home in the nest.

It was Saturday and I didn't have much going on. I started up the truck and headed around to the prison. She was on call that day so I parked across the street, under the pines, and waited for her to leave.

Bingo. There she was. I stayed a good distance behind Grace's car. She had an unlisted number. I hadn't been able to find her address. This was my chance. It was easy to slip into Saturday traffic, sparse as it was and follow her. Since she went to Garrett with that ridiculous story about me assaulting her, I'd been meaning to talk to her about it. Garrett told the captain but lucky for me, I was able to apologize and explain that it was a misunderstanding. I was a man and misread the signals, that's all. Thanks to Garret, I was on probation. Prison policy. Captain told me he'd better not even see me looking at Grace at work. Ever.

Damn it. She was turning up ahead. The light turned yellow and I wasn't sure I'd make it. I sped up a little and was right behind her. She was in the right turn lane. I put my signal on and let another car in front of me. She turned at the next light into Trader Joe's.

I parked several cars spaces away and watched her in the rearview mirror. She was laughing. The guy was waiting for her outside the store. They walked into the supermarket with his arm around her shoulders. For some reason it pissed me off.

I pictured the grocery cart's rubber wheels squeaking as they maneuvered through Trader Joe's, hand in hand. Grace probably picked ripe tomatoes from the bin and held them to her nose. Maybe bought some fresh asparagus, corn, baking potatoes, and filet mignon. Some wine for dinner. Chocolate dipped strawberries for dessert. She seemed the type who had to have everything perfect.

They came out of the store smiling. I felt sick. It was kind of a hopeless feeling in the pit of my stomach, like when something bad's about to happen and there's nothing you can do to stop it. You just have to stand by and watch. "I'll follow you to your house, okay?" I heard her call after they loaded the groceries in her trunk. She was unaware that I sat a few cars away in my truck, watching.

They took a route I had never driven. At the next light, there was a dilapidated wooden sign in front of an equally dilapidated-looking one-story yellow brick building. The sign read OAKWOOD MANOR. So that's where Koski went.

A few minutes later, she parked her car behind Alex in the driveway of his two-story cedar shingled townhouse. I knew Garrett's address and I was surprised to see the building sat back on a quiet tree-lined street, a few doors away from Josie's house. A bunch of children played across the street. I parked across the street and saw Grace blot her eyes like she'd been crying. The guy opened her door and hugged her before they carried the groceries into his house.

There was nothing to do but turn around. I wasn't ready to go home yet so I drove to Silver Lake Park. The waning light shimmered through the branches. A sharp pang of longing, almost a twinge of pain, shot through my belly as I remembered what it was like to return to a home. The sky turned orange and ignited a desire in me for a real home with a wife and kids. A day I hadn't thought about in years came back to me as if it had happened yesterday.

Nineteen ninety-nine. The shockingly cold water was a welcome relief from the rising heat wave. The scorching sun and haze had held Rochester in its grip for several days. Tornado weather. We went to Chester Woods. The Twins cap I wore that day was still around somewhere.

The kids were laid out like pork sausages on a red plaid blanket. Side by side they sunned themselves, their bodies oiled and slick, and squinted in the sun. Sharon was five. She wore a pink one-piece bathing suit with a little ruffle around the top. She was a serious little girl with gray eyes and a somber manner. Kristen had huge round eyes the color of cornflowers with a faint eclipse of golden lashes. Her silky, fine platinum hair was caught up in a baby's pigtails. Sunscreen covered her chubby folds, the insides of her elbows and the tops of her pink thighs.

The tops of her ears were burned bright red. Kristen was a baby then and she laughed, a high-pitched little girl laugh, with the exhilaration of a summer afternoon in her eyes. We ran into Chester Lake, Krissie perched like a princess on my shoulders, in her bright orange flowered swimsuit. She held onto the top of my head and I bent to dip her toes in the water while she squealed.

The icy water sent shock waves through my nervous system. Danny laughed and ran to us with big exaggerated strides. His stubby legs struggled against the weight of water. "My turn. It's my turn. Carry me, Daddy!" he cried. I taught Danny to swim that day. At first, he clung to my leg but he picked it up quick.

Day turned to dusk. We grilled hot dogs and roasted marshmallows on a coal-filled pit. Stacy set up lawn chairs and wrapped the children in blankets. I wondered if we had any pictures of that day. To tell the truth, I hadn't thought about that day in years but now that the kids were grown, it'd be nice to have a memento.

I got to Silver Lake and parked, hoping to avoid another long night at home. I thought about what Grace and that guy were doing and felt a hard-on straining against my pants. Grace jogged here once in a while but there was no chance she'd be here today. I got out of the truck and stood in the parking lot. It was cold for April and I stuffed my hands into the pants pockets. I got soft again—I wasn't into playing with it. The lake was nice. Quiet. The geese honked plaintively. A light snow began to fall as I sat on an empty bench facing the water and thought about Grace. Even tonight, there were joggers out. Why the fuck do they always run in pairs? I guess I had forgotten what it was like to feel like part of a couple.

Trees curled toward one another against the flinty sky. Giant Canada Geese surrounded me. Their webbed feet were caked with oozing green shit. I threw a stone at them and they scattered. They had a history in these parts, older than my own. They had a steady supply of bread and no natural predators or hunters and Silver Lake had become home for them.

The temperature began to fall. It hurt like hell to breathe. An arctic air mass was shifting south from Canada. It was almost spring and it was still freakin' cold. I tugged up the woolen scarf Sharon knitted me for Christmas to cover my nose and mouth. A bunch of homeless people warmed their hands over a small trash can fire and I yelled at them to get a move on.

I stayed there for a while, rubbing my hands together to stay warm, while images of Grace floated through my mind. Not the ones of her lying on the floor with that asshole but images of her trudging through the parking lot in the blue light of winter, wrapped in her red scarf. Grace standing in her office, bathed in sunlight. Grace laughing on her phone as she walked into the supermarket. Grace lying next to me as I held her close, firelight flickering in her eyes. Grace taking my hand and holding it to her cheek. Grace's eyes when her back was arched with passion. Grace's soft touch on my bare back.

Half an hour later, a coppery sun skimmed the horizon, and I climbed into my truck, ready to go home and determined to find out where she lived.

CHAPTER FOURTEEN

ALEX CAME TO UNLOAD THE GROCERIES, a smile skidding across his features. "Sweetie, what's wrong? Have you been crying?" "I passed my patient's new home. Oakwood Manor. Somehow from the sound of it, I had imagined a much nicer place than what I saw on my way here."

"Who's the patient?"

"A very dear old man, by the name of Finn, who served his time and whose family wouldn't take him. He lives there now. I just can't see him fitting in with all those addicts hanging out in front of the building."

"Tough break, huh, hon?" Alex said, and kissed my nose. "I love you for being so caring."

The merlot we bought was perfect. We listened to Adele and I tried to put Finn out of my mind. Alex pierced the potatoes and wrapped them in foil. He paused and turned to kiss me. I trembled and forgot all about Finn as I fantasized about unbuttoning Alex's shirt and unzipping his pants.

"Grace? Sweetheart? Earth to Grace," I finally heard him say.

"What? Oh. Sorry! What were you saying?"

We lingered over dinner and sipped wine while soft jazz played in the background. Afterwards, I fed him chocolate-dipped strawberries. The kitchen clock ticked slowly, the sound echoing through the condo.

"Hmmmm . . ." Alex murmured. "Why don't we go into the living room? I'll clean up later." He looked into my eyes a little bit longer than usual, put his arm around my waist and led me to the couch. The feel of his arm around me as we walked together was as fluid and effortless as swimming in a two-person school of fish. I closed my eyes, breathed in his musky scent, and put my hand out to feel the curve of his cheek. It had been so long since I had been with a man.

"I can't believe you might actually go on the mission trip to Indonesia with me," he said. "A few days together in Bali afterwards is just what we need. Just the two of us."

"Thank God for Matt's parents. They've agreed to stay with the kids for the week. Not that they wouldn't love it anyway." A deep sexual thrill surged through me at the prospect of going away with Alex. I twined my fingers through his.

"You're beautiful when you smile, you know that?"

I felt younger than I had in years. "I think it'll be good for all of them to spend this time together. They'll stay at the house with the kids so they'll be in their own routine. I am a little worried about it though."

"You're a wonderful mother." He nuzzled my neck. "A whole week together. I know you're going to love it. I'm going to love it with you there."

Something dark flashed through my mind. I wondered if it might be too soon for the children. Alex tried to reassure me, telling me he wanted to be part of my life and wanted to know my children. "I'm looking forward to working side by side with you in Indonesia. And being alone together in Bali. But if not this time, there'll be other opportunities," he promised.

I curled into the promise of him next to me and said, "I just need to do what's best for the kids."

"I know. Just give it some thought, okay?"

I put my hands on his chest and felt Alex's chest rise and fall with each breath. He pulled me toward him and found his way underneath my shirt, touching my skin so softly it was almost painful. The telephone rang, piercing the silence. "Just ignore it," he whispered and then kissed me again, parting my lips with his tongue.

My hands moved to his shoulders. Already, it felt like home when I was with him. I wanted his hands on my body, although I wasn't sure where. I needed to have him touching me.

Alex stroked my hair and kissed my cheek and my neck. I was desperate for him to kiss me. He got up and spread a blanket down in front of the fire, threw another log on the fire and pulled me down next to him. The light from the fireplace cast a warm yellow glow in the room. I felt as luminous as the candles he had lit. He turned to me and traced the outline of my cheeks and jaw, again kissing my neck. I ran my hands along his back and gathered him closer as his hands slid underneath my skirt. "You are so beautiful. God, I want you," he murmured.

I grabbed him, kissing him hard, impatient in my need for him. As our eyes met, the urge to melt into him was irresistible. He tilted my head back with one hand under my chin and brought his lips to mine, very gently, cautiously. I kissed him, arching my back so he might kiss me more deeply. Intoxicated with desire, I caressed him and told him with my body that I was ready. He touched every part of me as we made love. There was nothing like being in his arms and connecting with him with such love and tenderness and passion.

Afterwards, we sat on Alex's all-season porch and looked at the stars. My cell phone vibrated. It was Josie. "That's strange," Alex said at the same time. "There's somebody on the street looking this way. It looks like he's looking at us."

"Josie, hey! Can you hold on just a second?" I asked. "Alex! That guy in the dark jacket and hat? You're right."

I picked up the phone and Josie asked, "Grace, where are you?"

"I'm at Alex's. Why? Ya wanna stop by or something?"

"No, I wanted to warn you. I wasn't sure if you were there or not, but I saw Bud Anderson's truck parked outside the building. I went down to have a word with him and it looked like he had a camera with a zoom lens or something in his hands. He put it away when he saw me coming but I could've sworn he had a perfect view of Alex's window. He said he was waiting for somebody."

"Oh, God. Alex, go check if the curtains are drawn in the living room, okay?"

Alex came back and said, "No, they're not, why?"

"Shit. Gotta go, Josie. Thanks for telling me." I hung up. "Alex, Josie just told me she saw Bud Anderson parked out in front of your townhouse with a camera or something in his hand. She went out to ask what he was doing and he played dumb."

"Is she sure it was him?"

"Yeah, she knows him, all right. She had a word with him and the captain after that incident at the Christmas party I told you about."

"I think we ought to call the police, Grace. I'm worried about you."

I hated to make things worse. He was probably just a harmless jerk with nothing better to do on a Saturday night. Besides, it was getting late. The children were with their grandparents but I needed to go home go to take Sketcher out. I asked Alex to walk me out, just in case.

"Damn it!" I kicked the rear driver's side tire. "I have a flat!"

"Here, let me take a look at that. Grace, this isn't a flat. Your tires have been slashed!"

"My tires?"

"The back tire is flat too!" Alex exclaimed, walking around the car.

"Why would anyone slash my tire? Do you think it was Anderson? This hasn't happened before in this neighborhood has it?"

"Not that I know of. I don't think this can be repaired. How about we buy you new tires tomorrow? I'll call and report it to the police. I don't think you should be home alone. I want you to stay here tonight."

"I'm gonna call Josie . . ." As soon as I said it, I heard Josie's voice. She was walking quickly toward us. "Grace! Is everything okay? Bud got me so riled I couldn't sleep and I saw you out here," she said looking at my flat tires. "What happened?"

"I think Anderson slashed my tires. That bastard."

"Whoa! After I came down to pay our peeping tom a little social call, he sped off like a bat outta hell. I'm sorry, I didn't notice the tires. *Que cojones!*"

"Great. I have four flat tires and a lunatic out to get me." I tried to laugh it off. "What else could go wrong? Shit. Alex, can you give me a ride home so I can let Sketcher out?"

"Sure, let's go. We can see about your car tomorrow. But I want you to come back with me, Grace. I don't like you being home alone."

The moon cast a bright light on the narrow road in front of us. I lowered my window and the air was ripe with the smell of manure and mud. Cornfields surrounded by barbed wire flanked both sides of the road.

"I forgot how far out in the country you live," Alex said. "Do you remember the first time I brought you home?" He chuckled and stole a sideways glance at me.

I could feel my cheeks reddening. "Yup. That was an auspicious beginning. What a klutz you must have thought I was!"

"I did wonder if you had a flask of something stronger than hot chocolate with you that day."

"You did not! Tell me you don't remember how icy it was. You didn't think I was drinking, did you?"

"No, no. I'm kidding!" Alex laughed a deep belly laugh which made me smile every time I heard it, no matter what the circumstances.

"Anyway, it's not that far. It takes about twenty minutes to get to work. As you can see, there's not much traffic out here. I like it. The drive gives me time to think and be alone for a little while each day. Know what I mean?"

"Yeah, I do. You don't have much time for yourself, do you?" His face grew serious. "Do you have any idea who else might have slashed your tires?"

It was quiet, except for the sound of Alex's tires crunching the gravel road. I was pensive. "No, I really don't. When I lived in Minneapolis, I knew to avoid certain areas at certain times of day, just like anybody in a big city would. I felt safe though, even though there was evil out there, because I knew to mind my own business. I don't know. This feels different. I guess there's violence in the suburbs as well, it just seems more hidden. Everybody here looks like a soccer mom or a gym teacher. So, it's really shocking to think someone would slash my stupid tires."

"There's someone else out on this road," Alex said, looking in his rearview mirror. A car was barreling down the road behind us. "And they're coming awfully close."

A set of bright headlights, shining like cat's eyes, hurtled in our direction. "Alex, why don't you pull over and let them by? I'm already on edge from the whole tire thing. Let's just drive slowly. No use in speeding up just because some idiot wants to get somewhere fast."

Before Alex could put his turn signal on and pull over to the side of the road, the small dark compact car passed us and cut back into the lane with inches to spare. Alex slammed on the brakes and the car skidded several yards along the pebbly road. We both lurched forward but the shoulder harness and lap belts of the Volvo held us in our seats. "What the fuck?" he yelled. "Grace, are you okay?" He yanked his phone out of his pocket.

"I'm fine," I said although I felt like crying. The shadows cast by the moon seemed to shift, turning the dark into something malevolent closing in on us. I tried to take a deep breath and noticed Alex taking out his phone.

"I'm calling the police," he said angrily. The near collision with another car served as a warning. Something was going on here.

"Alex, don't. It's late. By the time the police get here that idiot will be in the next county. I didn't even get a glimpse of the driver, did you?"

"No, but the car was a dark-colored Civic or Sonata. He almost ran us off the road."

"A lotta help that is. A car just like that cut in front of me the other day. Forget it. Let's just go home, okay?" I wished I could pick up the kids and we could cocoon ourselves in our house, lock the doors and forget tonight had ever happened. I was still shaken when we pulled into the driveway.

"I'm sorry this evening turned out to be such a disaster!" Alex leaned over to kiss me. "Are you sure you're okay?"

"I'm fine. I'm just gonna feed Sketcher and let him out and then we'll leave, okay? I think I'll take you up on that offer. I don't want to be here alone. I'm ready for a good night's sleep."

An hour later, we arrived back at Alex's. As we made small talk and got ready for bed, there was a loud creaking noise outside, and I jumped. The color drained from Alex's face. I reached for his hand and gripped it so tightly he winced. He got up slowly and walked around to the window. "I'm going out to see if anyone's out there."

"Alex! No! Are you crazy? What if it's some lunatic?"

"Sweetheart, it was probably a tree branch. The wind has really picked up. I'll be back in a minute," he said, slipping on a sweatshirt and jeans. I followed him into the kitchen and gasped when he grabbed a kitchen knife and a flashlight. "You're not going out there," I said, but he had already opened the front door. The door creaked on its hinges. I could hardly bear the sound.

I stood at the window, behind the floor-length drapes. The beam from his flashlight shone around the bushes in the yard. I breathed a sigh of relief when he entered the house and locked the door. The dinner we had so happily shared was churning its way up my esophagus, my throat felt as though it were on fire.

"The street's deserted. Let's try to get some sleep, okay? There's nobody out there." Alex attempted half-heatedly to reassure me.

I hovered in the half-state between waking and dreaming for most of the night. It seemed as though I had barely closed my eyes when I woke at six to a chill in the room.

CHAPTER FIFTEEN

THE BEEF STROGANOFF NEEDED TO SIMMER just a bit longer. I turned down the flame and sent Alex a text. PLEASE DON'T MENTION THE TIRES IN FRONT OF THE KIDS. THE CHILDREN DON'T KNOW ANYTHING ABOUT MY TIRES BEING SLASHED AND I WANT TO KEEP IT THAT WAY.

Dane came into the kitchen, a dinosaur in each hand. "When's dinner, Mom? I'm a t-rex and I'm hungry!"

Determined to put what had happened behind me, I kissed the top of his head. "Soon. Go wash up, okay? And tell Caleigh to come down. Alex will be here soon."

Dane skipped out of the room, his jeans an inch too short again and called, "Caaaaleigh . . ."

The ensuing argument drifted down the stairs. "Tell Mom I'm not coming down!"

"Mommmmy! Caleigh says she's not coming down," Dane hollered from the top of the stairs.

I threw down the dishtowel and marched upstairs. "Listen to me, young lady, we're having a guest for dinner and you are to be washed and presentable. Wash that eyeliner off your face. And take off the black nail polish."

"And what if I don't want to, Mom? What're you gonna do then?" The defiance in her eyes sliced at me. Caleigh had never spoken to me like this before.

Dane stood at the door, all ears.

"Come on, honey. Do it for me. As soon as dinner is over, excuse yourself and come back up to your room. Would it kill you to do that?"

"Yeah, Caleigh, would it kill you to be nice to Mom for once?" Dane parroted.

My daughter thundered into the bathroom and my anger simmered. At least she'll come down without the black eyeliner. *Oh, Alex, you don't know what you're in for with a thirteen-year-old girl in the house,* I thought.

The doorbell sounded through the house. Shit. I wasn't even ready yet. This was not the ideal first meeting I had envisioned between Alex and the kids. "Dane, would you get it, honey?" I called down the stairs. "I'll be right there."

I stepped into my room, shut the door, and stood with my head against the wall. I hoped the meeting between Dane and Alex wouldn't be too awkward. The bathroom mirror showed there was flour in my hair and the eye makeup I had applied earlier in the morning had long since worn away. I tossed my jeans and tee shirt into the laundry basket and pulled several outfits from the closet. After three changes of clothes, I finally settled on a pair of pressed black jeans and an emerald cashmere sweater. I tugged a brush through my hair and slicked the frizz down with a squirt of gel. A smear of lip-gloss and I was as ready as I was ever going to be.

The smile I presented when I entered the living room was as fake as the potted plant on the shelf, but within minutes, the grin was real. Dane had not wasted any time in getting out his dinosaur collection. Alex sat cross-legged next to him on the floor doing his best imitation of a tyrannosaurus rex. There was a new addition to Dane's collection.

"Mom! Look what Alex brought me!" Dane beamed as he held up a life-like dinosaur. "It's a triceratops! Alex says he's the biggest and heaviest horned dinosaur ever!"

"I see that." I looked at Alex and tried to thank him with my smile.

"And, he has batteries and walks and his eyes light up and he makes noise! Wanna see?"

"I sure do!" Alex and Dane seemed to have hit it off well. Caleigh sat in the reclining chair with a sketchpad propped up against her knees. "What're you doing, honey?" I asked.

"Alex brought her an art kit!" Dane exclaimed. "With tubes of paint and charcoal pencils and brushes and everything! And flowers for you, Mom!"

Alex shrugged, clearly pleased that his gifts had been well received. I winked at him before going to the stove to boil water for the noodles and putting the spring bouquet in water.

"Dinner's almost ready. Caleigh, will you set the dining room table?" Prepared for complaints, I was pleasantly surprised when Caleigh got up without a word and pulled four dinner plates, glasses, silverware and napkins out of the cabinets.

Alex came into the kitchen and squeezed my arm. "Is it okay if you and I have wine? Where's your corkscrew?"

"I'd love some. Corkscrew's in the top drawer on the left." My choice of sweater and jeans had been a poor one in the overheated kitchen. I felt as soggy as overcooked noodles.

Alex uncorked a bottle of what appeared to be very expensive red wine, set it on the table and said, "I didn't know if you'd have time to make dessert so I stopped and bought a blueberry cheesecake on my way over."

"Cheesecake?!" Dane yelled from across the room. "That's my favorite!"

"You're a hit," I whispered and then kissed him before pouring the stroganoff into a serving dish. The noodles were done. A tossed salad and homemade dressing and we were all set. I wiped my brow with the back of my hand and called everyone in to eat, pleased the evening might turn out all right after all.

"Can I light the candles, Mom? Please, Mom!" Dane jumped up and down. "I'll get the lighter!"

"Just be careful, okay?"

Dane flicked the lighter on. "Ouch!"

"Let me do it!" Caleigh muttered.

"No! Mommy said I could do it!" Dane said defiantly.

"Here, buddy, how about if I help?" Alex asked holding the candle close to Dane's quivering thumb. They finally lit the long white taper candles as I spooned fresh spinach and mushrooms and sliced kiwi onto his salad plate. "Ranch or blue cheese?" I asked, flashing Alex a smile.

"Ranch!" Dane said, a little too loudly.

"Me, too, Mom." Caleigh reached for the water pitcher.

"Make that three. Everything looks delicious." The candlelight flared showing Alex's smile. His compliments sent a shiver of pleasure through me. The stroganoff simmered on the stove and filled the kitchen with a homey smell. Just like a home should smell, taste and feel. I'd been so focused on making this evening perfect I was glad for an opportunity to step into the kitchen to savor the moment. "Be right there," I called, before adding mushrooms and a dash of red wine to the stroganoff.

"So what do you guys like to do?" Alex asked the children.

He didn't have to ask Dane twice. "I play basketball and football and baseball and I like dinosaurs and movies and Harry Potter." Dane pulled the dinosaur Alex had given him from his lap and put it on the table. Thank God, they were on their best behavior. When I returned to the table, even Caleigh had a hint of sparkle in her eyes.

"I like roller blading and drawing and reading and I love horses. May I be excused, Mom?" she asked unexpectedly.

"Sure, hon. Are you sure you're done?"

"Yeah, I'm not hungry anymore."

After dinner, as we cleared the table, Alex asked, "Did I say something wrong?"

"No! Sweetheart, she's an adolescent. This is par for the course."

We brought our glasses to the living room to find Caleigh sitting in her favorite chair by the window. "Can I see what you've drawn?" Alex asked, standing next to her.

It was as though I were watching a play unfold. I crossed my fingers, and prayed Caleigh would be civil. She opened the sketchpad and spoke in barely audible sentences. "Sure, I'm not very good. You can look if you want." Quiet fell over the living room.

"This is beautiful. Where'd you learn to draw like this?" he asked.

"My dad taught me," Caleigh said after a moment's hesitation. "He was really good at drawing." Caleigh blushed. The sun's last rays streamed through the slatted bamboo blinds, and filtered the spring light through the living room.

"You're really talented. You said you like horses? Do you ride much?"

"I love horses. I've been dying to get one forever, but I don't get much of a chance to ride. My dad always promised we'd get a horse when I was old enough to take care of it." She looked pointedly in my direction with a look that said, I'm still waiting.

"You really got the musculature down and the shading is perfect. I imagine you miss your dad, huh?"

Caleigh nodded and I cringed, hoping the defiant and angry adolescent wouldn't return. The phone shrilled sharply, further jangling my nerves. I rose and glanced at the Caller ID. UNKNOWN CALLER, it read.

"Do they have art at school?" I heard Alex ask Caleigh.

"Hello?" I said. The line went dead.

Caleigh's laughter floated across the room. "Art's an elective for half the year. It's better than FACS!"

That's odd. I hung up the phone and went into the living room. I sat down next to Alex, thankful my qualms about the children meeting him seemed to be for nothing.

"I'm really behind the times," Alex laughed. "FACS? Anything important?" he turned to me and asked.

"Family and Consumer Science," Caleigh continued. "You know, cooking and sewing. Everybody takes it. It's the pits!" She rolled her eyes as she spoke.

"No. It was nothing." I was determined not to let anything stop me from enjoying the evening. "I still remember the awful peasant blouse I made when I was in middle school. I loved it and made at least four more! One for every day . . ."

"Mom! You didn't." Caleigh laughed.

"You'll find this hard to believe but a hundred years ago when I was in seventh grade, girls took what was then called Home Economics and boys took Industrial Tech. Now, that was fun. I made a lamp out of a bottle. I still have it somewhere," Alex said.

Matt had made the same wobbly lamp and had it in his first apartment when we met.

"I used to ride when I was a kid. Maybe we could all go out to the stables some weekend and go on a trail ride," Alex continued.

"I'd love that!" Caleigh was more animated than I had seen her in weeks. It looked like he had made strides with both kids. Caleigh was actually laughing.

Dane climbed into my lap and closed his eyes. I smoothed his hair away from his face before he jumped up and asked if Alex wanted to see the rest of his dinosaur collection.

"Sure, I do! But, call me Alex, okay, buddy?"

"And then it's bed time for you, young man," I told him. Dane would soon collapse and have to be carried up to bed.

"Mom! No! Alex just got here."

"Come on, kiddo. I'll go up with you and look at your dinosaur collection," Alex said. "I bet it's a good one."

Nothing had felt so right in a very long time. I was humming a popular song from the radio when Alex's phone vibrated on the kitchen counter. He had already gone upstairs with Dane. I glanced at the caller ID, thinking it might be the hospital and wondered if I should answer. ANGELA SAWYER. Angela Sawyer? Wasn't that Alex's ex-wife's name?

A few minutes later, he came into the kitchen. "He's all tucked in. As soon as his head hit the pillow he was out like a light. You should've waited, I would've helped you clean up. I guess Caleigh went to bed too, huh?"

I turned on the dishwasher and ran a sponge over the countertop. "Hmmm. What?"

"I asked if Caleigh went to bed. I think it went pretty well. How about you? Dinner was delicious, by the way."

"Uhm. Yeah. Thanks. They seemed to like you. It was huge for Caleigh to sit around after dinner with us."

Alex picked up his phone and looked at his missed calls.

"Is something wrong?" I stood facing him, tugging at my ear-lobe. *What is that look that flickered across his face?* I wondered. Guilt? Irritation?

Alex was silent. His left eye twitched. Apparently, he didn't intend to tell me Angela had called. "I hope whatever it is this hasn't ruined your evening. By the looks of it, something has," I said pointedly.

"No, it's been a wonderful evening." He poured himself another glass of wine and asked if I wanted more. "What makes you think anything is wrong?"

I suddenly felt sick. "Alex, you were upstairs when I heard your phone and I picked it up thinking it might be the hospital. I'm sorry. I know it's none of my business, but why is your ex-wife calling you? You're in my house, you met my kids. I wouldn't have brought you into their lives if I knew you had this 'unresolved' thing going on with Angela."

"Grace, sweetheart, is that what you're worried about? Come here." Alex put his arms around me. "You have absolutely nothing to worry about. Do you remember I told you Angela was having trouble accepting the end of our relationship? It's been over two years, and I guess she still hasn't given up. She wouldn't agree to the divorce and I was only able to get it after moving out and being separated for a year. She still calls and texts."

I suddenly felt terrifyingly vulnerable. "Why don't you change your phone number?"

"I have. Twice! Now I just try to ignore her and hope she'll eventually get the message and move on with her life. Let's forget about it. I know you have to get up early, but let's sit and relax for a while, okay? Angela is ancient history."

I pulled away. "You think if you ignore her she'll get the message? It's been two years! If she hasn't gotten the message by now . . ."

"What do you want me to do?" He flushed.

It was the first time I'd seen him angry. "I don't know. I guess I'm just on edge after everything that's happened." I hadn't slept well since the tire incident. I knew I had shadows the color of the spring flowers Alex had brought under my eyes. "Get her to stop."

"I told you I've tried. Short of getting a restraining order against her, I really don't know what to do."

"I don't know. Is she mentally unbalanced or what?"

"I don't know," he admitted. "She wasn't when we first got married, but then she did become pretty obsessed with the idea of having a baby."

"Well, I hope she gets some help. You don't think she's dangerous, do you?"

"No," he said slowly. "I'll have a talk with her, okay?" He kissed the tip of my nose and I couldn't resist being a little petulant. "What's she look like?"

"Who, Angela? Well, let's see, she has horns growing out of her head, and warts on her nose, and she wears black capes. Believe me, baby, she's got nothing on you." He laughed almost bitterly. "I know what happened last week is upsetting you . . ."

"Alex! Seriously, how old is she? This is kind of frightening."

"Why is it that women always want to know what their lover's ex looked like?" Alex shook his head. "Okay, she's a few years older than I am. That would make her about thirty-eight. She's got, WANT TO GET MARRIED AND HAVE A BABY written all over her forehead. Does that answer your question?"

CHAPTER SIXTEEN

THE DREGS OF MY MORNING COFFEE were there, waiting to be read. If only it were so easy to know the future, I thought that morning, pulling my hair back. Alex would be here any minute so I hurried. I squeezed a half-dollar size amount of sunscreen into my palm and rubbed the SPF 50 on my face and neck. My skin had already begun to freckle, even though it was a mild May morning.

"Caleigh, it's warm out. Do you really think you need to wear a sweatshirt?" I asked when she came downstairs.

"What's it to you, Mom? At least I'm going."

So much for that. Alex arrived a few minutes later. He opened the doors of the Volvo and the kids climbed in the back. It truly was a beautiful day. And for me, full of promise.

Caleigh got in the car and put on her headphones. Alex looked at me skeptically. "Caleigh, take those out right now! This is a family outing and I expect you to participate." I had enough of Caleigh's attitude.

"Mom, can we learn to geocache?" Dane asked twenty minutes later, when we arrived at Quarry Hill Nature Center. Caleigh sighed loudly.

"I'm ready for a little bit of bush whacking." Alex parked in the shade of a centuries-old oak and laughed. "You know they hide the geo-caches pretty well, right?"

"Ugh," Caleigh groaned. "I am not walking around the pond. The last time we were here, I almost stepped on a snake!"

"That was just a garter snake," Dane said. "I wanna see a timbler rattler!"

"Luckily, those are pretty rare around here," Alex explained.

We got out of the car and as we walked along the trail, he jumped, pretending to see a rattler. Caleigh screamed. Alex laughed and said, "More likely we'll see mud turtles," and then proceeded to point to several turtles sunning themselves on logs submerged in the pond. Velvety green algae floated on the surface, making the southern end of the pond look like pea soup.

"I learned about those." Dane grinned. "They're called painted turtles! Look at 'em, Alex! Their heads are black with yellow stripes! Their shells are green and orange! Look! There's a baby woodpecker!" They turned to see a canary-size woodpecker pecking at an oak branch. "He's trying out his little pecker!" Dane shouted.

"Oh, my god, shut up!" Caleigh yelled and burst out laughing. "Do you know what you just said?"

Caleigh was about to explain Dane's faux pas with sadistic pleasure so I interrupted. "Hey, look guys, you can see where I work, just over there beyond that oak savanna." The Rochester Center for Forensic Psychiatry was just beyond the grove of trees. The grounds were as pristine as a child's first communion.

"What'd I say?" Dane asked. "Mom, what's Caleigh laughing about?"

"Never mind, sweetheart." I glared at Caleigh, daring her to laugh at Dane again. "I want to show you the cemetery near the prison building. There are supposed to be graves from the early 1900s there. The grounds of the nature center were once part of the state hospital."

Caleigh rolled her eyes. "Sounds like fun, Mom." She stuffed her hands in her pockets. "You said he's trying out his little dick, dummy," she whispered to Dane.

"Did not! I didn't say anything about a dick. Tell her, Mom!"

"Oh, come on. Aren't you at all interested in history? How about you guys take the cave tour?"

"Yay! I want to! I want to!" Dane skipped ahead.

Alex shrugged. "See what you're getting into?" I whispered. He laughed but I wondered if he really knew what it was to raise children. "Look, that's a restored prairie. Maybe we can find some fossils around the limestone quarry. Did you know you can see rock layers and sink holes there? A shallow sea once covered this whole area. Maybe we'll even find some sea shell fossils."

"The data is in the strata," Alex joked. "Each rock layer tells its own story. Did you know that, buddy?" he asked Dane.

"I wanna climb the rock wall!" Dane clamored. "And see the cave!"

"The cave sounds cool," Caleigh admitted. "I'll go with you."

"The cave it is then. Do you guys mind if I wait outside? You know I hate tight places."

"Mom, you're not claustrophobic, are you?" Caleigh nudged me. "What about all that 'face your fears' and 'deal with your feelings' crap you're always giving us? A few bats won't hurt you."

"Yeah, Mom. Come on. I want you to come in too!" Dane pulled me by the hand along the trail to the cave. "Please!"

"Come on," Alex said, putting his arm around me. "If you get scared, I'll walk out with you."

A trim, bearded, blue-jeaned naturalist led the way and Dane followed closely behind. I kept his faded jeans and red sweater within sight. Plunged into the darkness of the sandstone cave, I shined my flashlight on the damp cave walls, dreading what I might see. The air was as foreboding and cold as a mausoleum. Dane turned and flashed a crooked grin at me.

Caleigh was so close I could hear her breath. Maybe this wasn't such a good idea after all. Tendrils of fear curled along my spine. I struggled to maintain normal respirations. Every step I took plunged me nearer panic.

"Can we go now?" Caleigh asked. "It's cold in here!"

"You think you're cold? Now I wish I had worn a long-sleeved sweatshirt. Let's get out of here! Alex, Caleigh and I are going to wait outside, okay? I'm cold and this place gives me the creeps. Would you mind staying with Dane?"

"Sure, sweetheart, we'll be right out. You okay?" He squeezed my arm.

I tried to meet Alex's eyes and fought the urge to run. I wanted to keep my voice steady for the children's sake. "Yeah, but I really need to get out of here."

"I'll tell you if we see any bats, Mommy!" Dane charged ahead.

Caleigh and I backtracked cautiously, with only the thin beam from my flashlight to guide us through the narrow halls. The close, narrow passages felt like large, cold hands squeezing the breath out of me. Suddenly the mouth of the cave gaped open before us. Open space and blue skies had never looked so good. Caleigh turned to whisper in my ear. "Mom, I think that woman is watching us! I kind of noticed her around earlier too."

A slim, dark-haired woman dressed in dark-wash jeans, a red jacket and blue baseball cap walked away. I tried to shake off the chill that wrapped around me and fleetingly wondered if I was becoming paranoid after all that had had happened lately.

Caleigh and I hiked to the top of the ridge while we waited for Alex and Dane to exit the cave and the woman was forgotten. "How about we take a walk through the cemetery?" I asked, taking comfort in Alex's hand holding mine. "I think we can just make it before it rains." The sky had changed to a denim blue as a river of clouds rolled in.

"Oh, Mom, you and your cemetery." Dane, already ten steps ahead glanced over his shoulder and grinned. "Is it creepy?"

We hiked uphill to a large, irregularly shaped hole in the ground surrounded by dull, tawny layers of rock formation. "That's the old quarry, Dane," Alex said. "They had the biggest stone crusher in all of Minnesota here at one time."

"Was it big enough to crush anything?" Dane asked before running off to skip around the quarry.

"Dane! Be careful. You'll fall in!" I still felt as jumpy as a fly escaping a frog.

Alex let go of my hand and went after Dane. "Come on, Buddy," he called. "Let's see if we find some fossils."

He was wonderful with Dane. I had worried about nothing. Caleigh would be a tougher nut to crack. "The state hospital bought the property in the 1870s," I read from the pamphlet I had purchased. "The old quarry was used in the 1870s to 1880s. Oh, look at this. The cemetery was used from 1886 to 1965! The state hospital stopped using the cave in the 1940s. They must have gotten refrigeration then."

"I see 'em!" Dane yelled, skipping ahead through the cemetery. "Look! This one's from 1918! What's his name?"

"Matthea Ballerud, died November fifteenth, 1918," I read. "The crumbling grave markers mark the final resting places of scores of Scandinavian immigrants looking for a new life, and finding it in the state insane asylum."

"And here's another old one. Andrew Bergstrom, 1911. Wow! He's like a hundred years old, huh, Mom?" Caleigh said. "Here's a new one. Elsie Block, 1961. And look at this one. Margaret Broe, 1965. That wasn't so long ago."

"Two thousand nineteen people were buried here. The older ones from the 1800s are in unmarked graves on the grounds," I said.

"You mean we could be walking on them right now?" Dane's eyes gleamed.

"From 1886 to 1965 some of the graves just had a wooden cross or number stamped into a concrete marker molded from a coffee can. There was a committee of citizens who took over the restoration of the cemetery and had headstones made for these poor people."

"It's kind of like they're talking to us from beyond the grave, isn't it, Mom?" Caleigh asked. "It's sad that their secrets are buried with them and no one even knows who they are anymore."

"Yeah, I guess it is." I was surprised by my daughter's insight. As we stood reading headstones, a greenish gold darkness descended. Thick clouds scudded across the sky. Dane ran over to another grave under a willow tree. "Dane, come back!" I called.

The first drops of rain begin to pelt. "I'll get him," Alex said, taking off in a slow jog.

"Look, Mom! There she is again!" Caeligh pointed.

The dense, chilly rain fell in big fat droplets. "Hmmm? Who?"

"That woman! The one with the red jacket and the baseball cap!"

Caleigh was right. Again, I saw only the woman's back as she walked quickly toward the nature center. "Let's get going, okay? Alex and Dane are on their way back," I said. Lightning streaked across sky and a shudder slammed through me. I had a premonition of someone walking over my grave, as my grandmother used to say. Not wanting to worry the children, I put the woman out of my mind just as thunder sliced the sky open.

CHAPTER SEVENTEEN

I'M GOING TO TELL THEM before you come over, okay? I think it's been long enough. They're ready. I love you, sweetheart." I hung up the phone and heard a knock at the door. Josie stood there in her running shoes.

"What's up with you? No one should look this happy in prison," she said and plopped down onto the metal, straight-backed chair in my office. "Ouch! Not much padding on Uncle Sam's furnishings, is there?"

I buzzed with excitement. "Can you keep a secret, Josie?" There was nothing that could disturb my peace of mind that day.

"You know it. What's up? You look like the cat that ate the canary. Ya know, I've always wanted to say that!"

I grinned. "Do you or don't you want to hear the big news?"

Josie sat on the edge of her seat. "Of course I do! Tell me already."

"Well, you know I've been seeing Alex . . ."

"Yeah, yeah . . . Prince Charming carried you through the snow like a damsel in distress. I never thought you were the helpless sort, but whatever . . ." She shrugged.

"Josie, you know that's not me! Anyway, we've gotten really close. In love kind of close. It's been about nine months now, and I don't know. It just feels right. Even the kids are crazy about him. So, the big news is that Alex and I have decided to move in together."

Josie looked at me quizzically. The room seemed to grow smaller. "You're kidding, right?"

"No . . . You're not happy for me?" I couldn't quite decipher the expression on Josie's face.

"Sure I am, girl." Josie's eyes grew dark. "But don't you think it's a little soon to have the guy move in with you? I mean, how long have you even known him?"

"Long enough to know he's perfect. I know what you're thinking, but you're wrong. I've given this a lot of thought. The kids have gotten to know Alex and so have I. I think we could be a family."

"Me thinks she doth protest too much. But, congrats! Reminds me of when I moved in with Melanie. It was rough in the beginning with her kids, but it all worked out. I just don't wanna see you hurt. Just call me overly protective, that's all." Josie stood up to hug me. "Of course, I'm happy for you."

For some reason I didn't believe her. "Let's talk about this, okay? Meet me for lunch? Did you bring yours today? Maybe we can go to the park to eat."

"Yeah, I did. Meet you at twelve?"

"Sounds good. See you then."

* * *

WHAT'S UP? You look so serious. Is something wrong?" I asked a couple of hours later, as we followed the paved path to Eastwood Park.

A single shaft of sunlight spotlighted the picnic table where Josie sat down and took out her sandwich. "Grace, I've never told you this but . . ." she began, shielding her eyes from the sun's glare.

"What's going on?" There was something in Josie's voice that made me stop and put my sandwich down.

"I really don't know. It's probably just fuckin' PMS, but lately I've been thinking a lot about my brother."

"I didn't know you have a brother." I was hungry and took a bite of the sandwich I held in mid-air.

It was like pulling her metaphorical teeth for her to say, "He died when I was eighteen." She stared off into the distance.

"Oh, my God, Josie! What happened?"

"He was murdered," she said. Her voice was venomous. "I woke up early that morning. The apartment was stifling. The standing fan in my room circulated hot stale air. That was also the day I first realized I was gay. I had dreamed of Naomi Alvarez again and woke up in a sweat."

"I'm so sorry. I had no idea about your brother. And, I can imagine that's a difficult realization, especially in the Hispanic culture."

"Yeah, tell me about it. I got up and there was a note on the table. It said, 'At work. Be a good girl. Take care of your brothers. Get down on your knees and pray. *Te quiero mucho.* Mami.' I remember thinking maybe I'd go to La Igleisa de San Jose for mass that day. Partake in the Sacrament of Reconciliation. That's how desperate I was."

"Were you brought up a strict Catholic?"

"Oh, yeah. Mass on Sundays, prayers at night. Confession whenever I committed a mortal sin, which seemed to be pretty often after I stopped trying to deny my feelings for Naomi." She laughed bitterly.

I took a sip of bottled iced tea and felt a well of sympathy rush up for her.

"Anyway, that morning, my brothers were still asleep in the next room. We lived in La Perla, kind of a notorious barrio most people stayed away from. All I wanted was to get out of there. No, that's not true. All I wanted was to be a normal girl."

"Josie, you can't really believe you weren't a normal girl, whatever that means, can you?" I interrupted.

Josie shrugged. "A few blocks away from La Perla, the rich Sanjuaneros, dressed in these starched white guayabera shirts went to work. I would sometimes go out just to watch the women, all made up, walk to work in tight skirts and high heels, wishing I was one of them."

I didn't know what to say.

"My mother left early for work that morning. She must have forced herself out of bed, numb with exhaustion. But she'd always kneel and say her morning prayers, no matter what. It's one of my most vivid memories . . . her hands reddened and rough, clasped together in prayer. Danny was nineteen. He woke up late. I heated the milk for *café con leche*. I still can't stand the smell of coffee." Her eyes dimmed and she shuddered. "Danny worked as a day laborer, doing yard work or painting but there was nothing that day. He showered and got dressed and I told him we didn't have eggs for breakfast."

I had a bad feeling about where this was leading and I thought about changing the subject, but I just couldn't.

"I remember the sound of a baby crying and a mother screaming in the apartment directly above us. It was so hot my brother's white shirt clung to his back. He flipped through the morning talk shows growing more and more agitated. 'Danny, we need eggs,' I said again. I offered to go with him. We went downstairs and Danny unlocked the rusted patio gate. The smell of rotting fish made my stomach turn. The dogs had scavenged through the garbage can and the trash was strewn in front of the gate. Fucking dogs. We finished picking it up and heard a voice. It was Luis del Toro. Bendejo."

"Who was he?" I sat back and let Josie talk, noticing by the size of her pupils she was becoming angrier.

"A fuckin' drug dealer. 'Hey! Danny, man, over here,' he called. 'What's up, man?' I told Danny we had to get out of there but he wouldn't listen so I went inside and hid in the entryway. I saw del Toro as he approached, but he didn't see me. Shit, I still see his small eyes narrowed into slits. His sleeves were rolled up to show this huge fuckin' gold watch. I leaned against the wall in the only shade the courtyard offered. I turned away for a second and then heard a shot ring out and Danny fell to the ground."

"Oh, Josie, no!" I stood and knelt beside her, taking her in my arms, but Josie pulled away. "What did you do?"

"I ran inside and told Roberto. He came down with me but Danny was already gone." Josie stared stonily ahead. "We called the police but there was no possibility of testifying. That *hijo de gran puta* would've killed us." Josie clenched her soda can and banged it on the table. "Fuckin' *bendejo*."

"Oh, Josie, how horrible for you." My own suburban childhood had been as safe as a cocoon.

"I'm fine really. That was a long time ago," she said angrily. "After that, I went to community college and became a cop. Sex crimes unit. A few years later, I left La Perla behind forever. My mother hugged me in the airport, took off her silver crucifix and hung it around my neck. She told me she was proud of me and gave me her Bible. I took it and left behind the ten-pound rock I'd carried in my chest since Danny was killed. My older brother, Roberto was sentenced to federal prison for conspiracy to distribute cocaine. Sad story, huh?"

I nodded silently in agreement. No wonder Josie had fled to a new life where she'd become Josie Garrett.

* * *

THAT AFTERNOON, clouds swirled like gauzy curtains in the sky. It was spring and I sang along with the radio. What a difference daylight savings time and a few weeks made. Daylight at 5:00 a.m. was as welcome as the first tulips of spring. Maybe Caleigh and I would shop for new spring clothes that weekend. It was a thrill Minnesotans eagerly anticipated each year—putting the dark days of winter away along with their winter wardrobes.

There were empty juice packs and cookie wrappers strewn from one end of the kitchen table to the other when I walked in. "Can you believe how much homework I have?" Caleigh complained. "Look at this," she said thrusting her required daily planner at me.

I turned off the TV to Dane's complaints.

"You know the rules. No TV before your homework is done." I picked up the juice packs and wrappers. "Jeez, could you guys learn to be a little neater? Alex is coming over for dinner tonight. I don't want him to walk into a pigsty."

"What's wrong with you, Mom?" Caleigh looked up from her Earth Science textbook. "You're acting weird."

"There's nothing wrong. We had a really great day at Quarry Hill, didn't we? Can't I just be happy without everybody thinking I look weird? Anyway, come here. There's something I want to tell you first." I stood at the sink washing mushrooms, and green peppers and cherry tomatoes for Alex to grill. The steak was marinating. Caleigh and I had dragged the grill from the garage back onto the porch as soon as the snow had melted. "You guys know Alex and I have been seeing each other for a while now, and it's pretty serious, right?" Dane nodded solemnly and Caleigh lifted her plucked brows.

I put down the kitchen knife and wiped my hands. "We've decided we'd like for us to be a family. Alex knows he can never take your dad's place but he wants to be part of our lives. I want him to be part of our lives."

Dane's eyes grew wide. Caleigh squinted. "You're kidding, right?"

"Everything else will stay the same. You'll go to the same schools, we'll still live here with Sketcher, you'll have the same friends, you'll even have the same bedtime," I joked. "Alex will be moving here to live with us in a couple of weeks. The other news is that we'll be going on a medical mission trip at the end of the summer. Grandma and Grandpa will come to stay with you for the week we're away."

"Can I go?" Dane asked, picking up a rubber band and shooting it across the kitchen.

"Why would they take you along? It's supposed to be romantic." Caleigh rolled her eyes. "They want to be alone. Get it?"

"Is it, Mom? Is it supposed to be romantic? Yuck. Why can't I go?"

"Ow, stop it! Mom, he just shot a rubber band at me!" Caleigh picked it up and aimed for Dane.

"It's a medical trip, Caleigh. Not a romantic rendezvous. I'm sorry, sweetheart. Dane, stop that! It's a very poor country and we'll be busy the entire time. There won't be anyone to watch you. Grandma and Grandpa are very excited about coming here to spend time with you."

"Figures," Dane muttered. "I never get to have any fun."

There. It was out. "What do you think about Alex living with us?" I asked.

"I guess it's okay. Where's he gonna sleep?" Dane asked.

"Oh, my god, are you stupid!" Caleigh said. "He's gonna sleep with Mom! Right?" She gave me a dirty look and I flushed.

"Yes, that's right. Are you guys okay with that?"

"I guess so. Can I still come in when I can't sleep?" Dane asked, his hands knotted in front of him.

"Of course you can, sweetie. Come on, guys. It's a beautiful day. There's plenty of time before dinner to take Sketcher on a nice long walk. We can talk more about this later."

"Is this how I'm going to spend my summer vacation, Mom? Walking Sketcher and taking care of the broski?" Caleigh mumbled. "I guess Alex living here is okay with me."

I had an urge to laugh, jump up and down and to hug my children.

"Mom!" Dane squirmed as I wrapped my arms around him. "What are you doing?"

"I love you guys so much. Can't I give you a hug now and then?"

"Whatever, Mom," Caleigh said.

"All right. Come on! Get going." Sketcher came into the room carrying his leash between his teeth. "See? He wants to go out."

I returned to dinner preparations with a smile, washing egg-sized red potatoes and crushing garlic for fresh garlic bread. The doorbell soon chimed. "Hey, sweetheart, I ran into the kids walking Sketcher on my way over," Alex said, kissing me. "Did you tell them?"

"I did. Dane wants to know if he can still come into our room if he can't sleep."

He nuzzled my neck. "Our room . . . I like the sound of that."

"And Caleigh said, 'I guess it's okay if Alex lives with us,' and for her, that's pretty amazing." Alex picked me up and spun me like a puppet, my feet dangling in the air. "So, tell me about the trip. How long's it for?" I asked. "I'm still kind of worried about the kids and how they'll manage while we're gone."

"We don't have to decide about the trip yet. Why don't we just take it a day at a time? The trip is not for a couple of months. Who knows what might happen by then? Let's get me moved in first," he said happily. "I can't wait!"

"You're right. Me either." We sat on the couch and I kissed him.

"What's this all about? Maybe I ought to come for dinner more often."

"I just love you like crazy, that's all." I kissed him again. The air smelled of his cologne and the baking garlic bread. I felt the vibration of his phone before he did. "What now? Can't we ever have a romantic moment? I think it's a conspiracy!" he said. "Who the hell is calling me now?" He dug the phone out of his pocket. "Dr. Sawyer here. Hello? Hello?"

"Who is it?" I took the bread out of the oven and savored the scent of fresh, hot bread.

Alex looked at the caller I.D. "Unknown caller. I don't know. Must not have been too important. Now where were we?" He came into the kitchen and put his arms around me. "When did you say I could move in?"

"Soon. Very soon."

CHAPTER EIGHTEEN

THE AIR CONDITIONING WAS DOWN that morning, the air close and fetid. Inmates on cleaning detail took their time sweeping and mopping the corridors while Emanuel paced. Even Finn and Tyrell Perkins, normally the best of friends, bickered.

Josie and I walked down the corridor to our offices. "Josie, just cut the therapeutic head nodding, would you?" Her curls were damp and as springy as a head full of slinky toys in the humidity, reminding me of how much I'd loved my slinky as a child. I would edge it down the stairs, watching the helical springs bouncing up and down as it stretched and reformed itself with the aid of gravity. A scientist even then. "I'm sorry for snapping," I apologized. "I just thought you'd be happy about my news."

"You're really serious about this guy, aren't you? I'm not, 'not happy' for you. You haven't known him very long, that's all. I just went through this and I know it's hard for kids to accept another person in their lives. I'm sure Alex is a great guy, okay? I'm great too but it still took a while for Melanie's kids to adjust."

"You've said this before. Is it because you're gay?" I unlocked my door and breathed in air as warm and thick as stew.

Josie followed me in. "No! They've known their mom was gay since they were young. They really loved her ex. Shelby was another mother to them. After the split, they only saw her like every other weekend or something. So when I came along, it was really tough to get anything but a scowl or a grunt out of them. Whatever. I thought maybe I just wasn't meant to be a mother but after a while they came around and it was really great."

"So it really had nothing to do with you." Was that a tear in Josie's eye? "The kids really like Alex. Thank God, there's no problem there. How long did you say it took for Melanie's kids to come around?"

"Oh, probably a few months. It helped that I'm good at Spanish. Every time they had problems with their Spanish homework, they came to me, and it sort of developed from there. It's fine now. Hey, I inherited two great kids I might not have had otherwise." She wiped her eyes with the back of her hand. "Damn allergies. We have a girl and a boy. Ashlyn is fourteen and Max is twelve."

"Caleigh is thirteen and Dane is six. He'd be thrilled to hang out with an older kid. I'd love for you to meet them."

I wondered again if those were tears glistening in Josie's eyes. "What school do they go to?"

"Um, Willow Creek. That sounds great. I just want you to be prepared for the possibility they may not take it as well as you think. And Alex may not be the man you think he is."

"I'll keep it in mind, but I think you're wrong. Really? Your kids go to Willow Creek? I thought you lived in the Kellogg district. That's where Caleigh goes."

"Nope. They go to Willow Creek," Josie said.

"Hmmm. That's strange. Well, I guess they have changed the boundaries this year. Anyway, I couldn't help but notice you teared up a little when you talked about Melanie's kids."

"Fuck you, Grace. Why would you say that? I told you I have allergies. Anyway, I gotta go. I've got to get some work done."

Josie had a reputation for biting people's heads off, but I couldn't help but be hurt by her outburst. Something smelled fishy. Josie was lying.

* * *

A FEW DAYS LATER, I fed the kids veggie pizza for dinner and then went to my room to dress. I was tired but not unpleasantly so. After a dab of moisturizer and foundation, I brushed on a new apricot eye shadow. A thin line of charcoal liner, two coats of brown-black mascara, a dab of raspberry lip-gloss and I was ready to slip into a new sleeveless black dress, pantyhose, and heels.

"Mom! Maddy's here!" Dane's voice carried up the stairs.

"I'll be right down!"

"Wow, Mom. You look nice. Where are you going?" Dane asked as I teetered down the stairs in my new three-inch heels.

"I told you, sweetie. Alex and I are going out to dinner tonight."

"But it's a school night," Dane whined. "Is he coming here? Who's gonna tuck me in?"

"I will," Madeleine chirped. I cast a thankful glance in her direction.

"Alex is working late so I'm meeting him at the restaurant. I won't be late, sweetheart. Go to bed when Maddy tells you it's bedtime, okay? I'll come in and kiss you goodnight when I get home." I gave him a quick hug. "Be good. Bye, Caleigh."

A muffled, "Bye, Mom," floated down from Caleigh's room.

"Call my cell if you have any problems. You have my number, right, Maddy?"

"Yup. Don't worry, we'll be just fine."

I gave Dane one last hug and grabbed my purse and coat. "I'll be home early."

* * *

THE MAITRE D' LED ME to the table where Alex sat at a table for two. He'd chosen Pescara, Rochester's chic new seafood restaurant inside the Doubletree Hotel, for what he said was a special dinner.

"You look beautiful," he said, pulling my chair out for me.

The restaurant's candles and twinkling lights reminded me of Van Gogh's *Starry Night Over the Rhone*. "What's the occasion? This is kind of a fancy place for a Thursday-night dinner."

"I ordered champagne," Alex said, his features suffused with anxiety. His light-blue shirt had circles of perspiration under his arms.

"Champagne? Alex, is something wrong? You look kind of nervous."

The waiter brought a bottle of Dom Perignon Rose and poured the bubbly drink into champagne flutes. "To us," Alex toasted.

"To us." The first sip tickled my nose and I sneezed.

Alex laughed. "I'm trying for a romantic evening here! Can you just play along, Grace?"

"I guess you don't want to hear about how the candlelight in here reminded me of Van Gogh, huh?"

He put his flute down, looked into my eyes and took my hand. "Grace, listen. I love you. You and Dane and Caleigh. All of you. You know that, don't you?"

An image of Matt asking me to marry him flickered across my brain. It had been after his graduation from medical school when I was still a fourth-year med student. I realized with a start I still thought of Matt as my husband. I needed to move on. That part of my life was over.

"Grace, will you marry me?"

"What? What did you say?" I looked at the face I had grown to love and tears sprang to my eyes. I nodded, not trusting myself to say anything.

Alex pulled a jeweler's box from his pocket and opened it. He reached across the table and squeezed my hand. It was an understatement to say that I was happy. "Oh, Alex. It's beautiful. Yes! I'll marry you." He slid the ring over my knuckle. A perfect antique diamond, surrounded by sapphires in a white gold setting.

"It was my mother's," he said. "She would have been so happy to see you wear it."

Nothing had ever felt so right. "It's beautiful. I'm honored to wear it. I love you, Alex Sawyer."

Alex wiped his forehead theatrically. "Whew. That was nerve racking. I'm hungry! What would you like to eat?"

My eyes drawn to the sparkle of the diamond on my left hand. "Mahi-mahi. I'm starved!" The waiter took our order and I stupidly said, "Alex, I don't want this to sound petty, but Angela didn't wear this ring did she? I mean since it was your mother's and Angela was your first wife and all . . ." As happy as I was, I still couldn't get her out of my mind.

"Is that what you're worried about? No, my mother was still alive when Angela and I married and she never offered the ring to her. There wasn't much love lost between Angela and Mom. I should have listened to her. I know she would've loved you though. Mom told me after Angela and I were divorced that she would leave me the ring because she knew I would find the right woman one day. We can get you another ring, if you'd rather."

I held my hand up to the candlelight and admired the ring. "No! I love the ring. It was silly of me to ask. I can't wait to show it off."

We finished dessert, a Blanc de piore so sweet, it made my teeth ache. Alex paid the bill. "How long do you have the sitter?" He smiled seductively.

"Any particular reason you're asking?"

He drew me close. His breath tickled my neck. I knew exactly why he was asking.

The short drive to Alex's townhouse was electric with anticipation. We entered through the mudroom. He turned on the light and I breathed in his male smell—a combination of musky cologne and freshly shaven skin. I responded to his smell, to his arms around me, to his kiss and arched my back as I pressed my body to his, my breasts against his chest. The only thing that mattered was having his bare skin next to mine. I unbuttoned his shirt and he pressed himself against the warmth in my pelvis. My hands went to where they had wanted to go the entire ride—underneath his clothes.

"Upstairs." A guttural sound escaped from his mouth. "I want you upstairs, Grace."

He led the way through the darkened living room, up the stairs and down the hall. I ached with desire for him. Nothing in the world had ever mattered more than having Alex inside me. He flipped the night light on his room. The thick, dark comforter, the cherry wood bedroom furniture, the coffee-colored walls all screamed sex! Before we got to the bed, he pulled my dress over my head and tore off my pantyhose and thong. My bra was next. I stood naked in front of him and he began at my mouth and then kissed my breasts, made his way to my abdomen, taking particular care to kiss the pearly white stretch marks from my pregnancies. He dropped to his knees and made his way lower.

I began to moan a deep, throaty sound. A mix of pleasure and need. My hips swayed until I finally released everything I had held back for so long. He stood and kissed my lips so I could taste my own sweet, salty taste. "I love you," he said. "I love you so much."

CHAPTER NINETEEN

THE NEXT MORNING the children's silence cast a shadow over what I had hoped would be happiness at being a family with Alex.

"May I be excused? I'm not so hungry anymore," Dane finally said after pushing his eggs around on his plate for the better part of fifteen minutes.

"Sure, Dane, are you sure you don't want to finish your breakfast? What's wrong, sweetie?" I asked but Dane was already clomping with his cowboy boots on every single tread of the stairs.

"How about you, Caleigh? Are you okay?"

Caleigh scowled and left to follow her brother. "What do you think, Mom? I guess it's gonna happen, whether I am or I'm not, right? When did I ever have any say in what happens around here? Are you guys going to Indonesia on your honeymoon?"

Against my better judgment, I yelled, "We're going to Indonesia," wondering if it was too much too soon, "on a medical mission. We haven't even talked about a honeymoon," but I was talking to the wall.

That evening, the doorbell rang. Alex stood on the porch with a bouquet of flowers wrapped in cellophane. "Hi, baby. What's wrong?"

I attempted to smile, torn between not wanting to hurt Alex with the children's reaction to our news and my own worries. He sat down while I found a vase and arranged the bouquet of irises, daisies, and tulips and placed it on the table. We sat across from one another and Alex took my hand. "I told them we're getting married and I showed them the ring. I thought maybe when they saw how beautiful it was, they'd be excited about it, but it's been like a morgue around here ever since."

Alex opened his mouth, as if to respond and then closed it again.

"I don't know. I know they like you, Alex. Maybe it's just too soon. Maybe it was just too much."

"How about we try talking to them together?" The look on his face was enough to make me cry.

Upstairs, Dane sat on the carpeted floor of his bedroom, surrounded by his dinosaur collection. An image of Matt painting Dane's room sky blue and putting up dinosaur wallpaper borders scampered across my mind.

Alex sat down next to Dane. "Hey, buddy, what's up? You okay?"

"Yeah, I'm okay," Dane said before staging an attack with his T-Rex. "Grrrrrrrrrrrrr. Take that! Arrrrrrrrrrrrr. And that!" he said to his toy dinosaur trainer, Captain Livingstone, toppling the plastic figure over.

I smoothed back his hair and tried to be therapeutic. "Hey! Why are you so mad at Captain Livingstone, buddy?"

"I just hate him, that's all, Mommy."

I raised my eyebrows and shot Alex the look. "I think I'll talk to Caleigh alone," I said. "Why don't you stay here with Dane and play? Would you like if Alex plays dinosaurs with you, Dane?"

He nodded and handed a dinosaur to Alex. "Here, you can be the T-Rex, okay?"

I knocked on Caleigh's door. "Come in," she said, sounding as if she had a clothespin clamped to her nose. Caleigh was lying on her bed, her eyes rimmed with red, clutching Flop, her faded purple bunny. She sat up and yanked her robe on when I entered.

"What's going on, Caleigh? Can I come in? Are you cold?"

Caleigh nodded. Her face was tear-stained. I sat next to her on the double bed. She pulled an old quilt around her.

"I know it's hard for you to think of me marrying another man after your dad, but Alex loves me and you and Dane too," I began. "And I love him."

"I know." She bit her lip and sniffled as tears spilled down her cheeks. "It's not that."

My eyes drawn to the framed photo of Caleigh and Matt on her night table. "I know it sounds really stupid, but it feels like it means that Dad is really gone. Like you won't even remember him anymore. Like he'll just be forgotten like those people at the cemetery." She reached for a tissue.

"Oh, sweetheart." I hugged her. For a thirteen-year-old-girl, she was the most fragile thing I'd ever seen. "We'll never forget Dad. He'll always be your father, but life has to go on even after we lose someone we love."

"I know, Mom. I'll be down for dinner in a few minutes, okay? I just want to think about Dad for a while."

"Sure, sweetie, take your time. Alex and I will be downstairs waiting."

Alex sat on the sofa, checking his phone when I came downstairs and sat down next to him. I began to worry that this parenting thing was not what he had bargained for. "What happened? Weren't you two going to play dinosaurs? What's up?"

"I got a phone call." He put the phone in his pocket and kissed my brow, smoothing my hair from my forehead.

I pushed him away. "Not now, silly. I'm making dinner. Who called?"

"Oh, it was no one. Did you say dinner?" He asked, his smile not entirely convincing.

"Yeah, you know, dinner. Is something wrong? You looked kind of funny when I walked in." I rose to set the table on the deck with blue woven placemats and napkins.

"Nope, nothing at all. Here, let me help you."

The barbecued chicken and pasta salad, normally the kids' favorite, went untouched by them. They came down, finished their milk, asked to be excused and marched upstairs. "I was sure they'd be thrilled about us getting married. They seemed to be fine with you moving in and with the trip. Welcome to parenting," I said to Alex.

"I hope it's not too soon. I know they've been through a lot, but so have we. I'm not good alone, Grace. I like being married, and the thought of a family with you thrills me."

His words sent a shiver through me. "I know. I love being married too. Just sitting around at night, reading and watching TV, cooking together, waking up together in the morning. You know, all the dull things married people do. I love you. I could use some help with the kids, if you feel you're up for it."

"Don't worry, sweetheart, we'll be fine." He kissed me again.

I hadn't wanted to ask him before but I asked now why he never wanted kids with Angela. He seemed like he would be the perfect father.

"Soon after we were married, I just knew it was a mistake."

I cleared the table and scraped the spaghetti into the garbage. "How long has it been since you heard from her? You think she's met anyone else?"

"No idea. I don't keep track. Hey, I forgot to tell you earlier. A colleague of mine has offered me one of his dog's puppies. I told him I'd ask you what you thought of getting a puppy for the kids."

"Are you trying to change the subject or what?"

"Grace, I just don't want to ruin our day talking about Angela, okay?"

"Okay. Me either. What kind of dog is it?"

"A King Charles spaniel. Very cute."

"Sketcher is getting on in years. And it would give the kids something to do over the summer."

"Do you want to surprise them? Stephen said the pups are ready to go now. We could go over and get the pick of the litter. Maybe tomorrow?"

"The kids will love you forever. No doubt about it. Tomorrow after work sounds perfect. Hey, you never told me what was bothering you."

"Nothing at all," Alex said. "It's nothing for you to worry about."

* * *

LATE MAY 2013

KIDS! BREAKFAST!" The sun refracted into soft turquoise and coral on the kitchen walls. They came in, doe-eyed and sleepy. "I'll be a little late tonight. I've asked Maddy to stay a bit longer. I want you to have all your homework done. Alex will be coming home with me tonight. Maybe you could set the table and make a salad, okay, Caleigh?" I had to bite my lip to keep from telling them where Alex and I would be going after work.

Caleigh looked at me quizzically. "What's the big deal? It's Monday night. Isn't it like, left-overs night or something?"

"I want to make something a little nicer for Alex than left-over meatloaf. Can you just try to help when you get home?"

"Whatever, Mom. Why do you always have to make things so nice for Alex?"

"Come on! It's time to go." It was harder everyday to deal with Caleigh's moods. "You really have no idea of what I've gone through, Caleigh." Before the words were out of my mouth, I felt the pangs of guilt pulling me in like fly lines.

"Whatever, Mom. You have no idea of what I've gone through. Can we just go?" Caleigh opened the door to the garage and threw her backpack in the car. "At least there's someone who understands me."

I was too angry to rise to the bait and ask who might understand Caleigh better than her own mother.

On the way to Dane's school, we passed Oakwood Manor. Still angry, I barely noticed the sign. I turned to look at the old man standing on the corner. "Mom! Stop!" Caleigh pressed her hands against the dashboard. I slammed the brakes and the squeal of tires filled the air.

"Didn't you see that car?" A small blue car had pulled out in front of us and sped away. She looked at me angrily. "Mom, what's up with you? Seriously."

"I'm sorry. I was distracted." I willed my heart rate to slow. "See that old man?" I pointed to an elderly man, bent with age, walking along the sidewalk.

"Yeah, what about him?"

The air was charged, as if a thunderstorm was near. "That's one of my patients." It was the first time I had seen a patient outside the prison. "I'm sorry. It was just weird for me to see a patient out on the street."

"I thought all your patients are locked up, Mom!" Dane said from the backseat.

"They mostly are, honey. This old man was just released. He finished his sentence and was placed in that home." Saying it brought tears to my eyes.

"What'd he do, Mom?" Dane leaned forward.

"You know I can't tell you. Anyway, he's a free man now. It just gave me a start to see him out of the prison setting, that's all."

"Mom, none of those guys will ever come and get us, will they?"

"No, of course not. That's why we have an unlisted phone number. You never have to worry, you hear me?" No other mother was likely to be having a discussion about released prisoners and her children's safety on a day when the forsythia shrubs bloomed and children already wore shorts to school.

"That won't do much good. Anybody can find anyone they want just by one click of the mouse," Caleigh said. "I suppose you've heard about the Internet, Mom."

"Don't worry, sweetheart. I've taken all the precautions necessary to make sure we're safe. Besides, when my patients are discharged, they generally go back to the prison they came from to finish out their sentences."

Before we knew it, we were at Dane's school and the conversation was forgotten.

"Bye, Mom!" Dane called as he climbed out of the car. He wore jeans and a jacket even though the day promised to be in the seventies. "I love you!"

"You too, sweetheart. See you tonight." I said, unable to shake off the strange sensation of seeing Finn on the street.

CHAPTER TWENTY

J OSIE! WAIT UP!"
Josie strode across the parking lot with her arms pumping at her
side, almost power walking to the prison entrance. She stopped and
turned around. "Hey, girl. How was your weekend?"

We fell into step together. "Fantastic. I have some big news!"

"What's up? Hey, did you ever hear back from the police about
who slashed your tires? No clues?" she asked.

Since Christmas, I had done my best to avoid Bud Anderson and
his smirks. The way he looked at me still made my skin crawl. The last
thing I wanted was to be reminded of the incident. "No. I'm thinking it
was a prank or something," I said, waving to the inmates. They were
already planting seeds in the vegetable garden. Some watched Josie and
me more than they actually worked.

"That's a pretty serious prank. You never called the cops?"

"I did, but I don't think it's high on their list of priorities. I filed a
police report, and the insurance company paid for new tires so I'm gonna
put the whole matter to rest. Do you really think it was Anderson?"

"I wouldn't put it past him. I told you I saw him there." Josie's nostrils flared. "And you know what a jerk he is."

"Anyway, I have a little surprise for the kids . . . Isn't it a beautiful
day? I can't remember such a warm early spring." The maple trees surrounding the prison were budding, robins twittered, and I finally felt at
ease.

"Yeah, you already said that. Come on, spill. What's the surprise?
Don't tell me you're pregnant! Is that what all this happiness and spring
fever is about?"

"Josie! Why would you even think such a thing?" I pretended to
swat her with her briefcase although the idea was not unpleasant.

"Well, I don't think Anderson was sitting outside Alex's watching
you two play cards . . ." she said.

"Very funny. And no, I'm not pregnant. But we are going to have
a new addition to the family."

"Oh, boy, here it comes." Josie looked at her watch. "We'd better
hurry. I have to clock in at eight sharp. What's the big news?"

"We're getting a puppy! Alex has a colleague at work who has a litter of King Charles spaniels. You know those cute little dogs with the floppy ears that are kind of brown and white spotted? One of those."

"First he's moving in, then the ring, and now you're getting a dog? What next?" Josie shook her head. "Oh, shit, don't look now, but there he is."

My disappointment over Josie's reaction stung. "What is it you have against Alex?"

"I'm talking about Anderson. There he is." She motioned to the other side of the parking lot. Bud was heading toward us. He noticed us watching him and hung his head.

"Anyway, I don't have anything against Alex," Josie said. "Call it a vibe or something. I'm not superstitious. Maybe it's my ex-cop instinct but something feels off. I'm sorry but that's just the way I feel. I hope you'll prove me totally wrong on this."

"What do you mean 'a vibe'? You're scaring me!"

"I dunno, like you're somehow not right for each other," she said as we arrived at the sallyport, took our shoes off and placed our bags on the conveyer belt. "I'm just looking out for you. You free for lunch today?"

"Yeah, I'm free for lunch. I have to say, I think you're wrong. Anyway, how about twelve-ish? Hey, I forgot to tell you. I saw Finn Koski on the street outside Oakwood Manor this morning. I guess he was taking a walk, but it was weird seeing one of our patients outside dressed in street clothes."

"Thank God Mr. Koski's harmless. Imagine seeing one of the other guys on the outside. That would not only be weird, it'd be downright scary. Twelve is good. See you then," Josie said before she strode down the hall to her unit.

The morning passed quickly. Tyrell Perkins was as stable as he had been for the past twenty years. I wrote my monthly note and signed off on his sleeping medication. Emanuel was stable enough that he was in the general ward population and allowed to walk to my office unaccompanied by a corrections officer. I was finishing the last of my notes when the phone jangled.

"Dr. Rendeau."

The line was silent. "Hello? Hello?"

"You don't know me," a woman's soft voice said. "I'm Alex's wife and I'm calling you to tell you to stay away from him."

"What? Who is this?" I demanded.

"I told you. Alex's wife. Angela Sawyer. I know you've been seeing him, but I'm telling you to stay away. He's married."

What the hell? Alex is divorced. The shock of this statement barely registered before there was a knock at my door. Emanuel was there for his session.

"I'm sorry, but I really have to go." I hung up the phone. I had no desire to delve into Alex's marital status with Angela Sawyer.

"Come in," I called. But instead of Emanuel, it was Bud Anderson who stood at the door. He stepped inside my office, and shut the door behind him. My heart was still pounding from the call I had just received. What the hell was going on here?

"Can I help you, Officer Anderson?" I asked, my finger on the alarm button.

"Well, yeah," Anderson said, his shoulders sagging. "I wanted to apologize for that little misunderstanding a couple of months ago. I've given it a lot of thought and I realize I was way out of line."

"I've put it behind me, and I suggest you do too," I said coldly. "Now, if there's nothing else, I have work to do."

"I just wanted to say I'm sorry," he said, before turning to leave.

"Wait a minute. There is one thing I'd like to know. What you were doing outside of Alex's house? Someone slashed my tires. You wouldn't have any idea who that might be, would you?" I looked at Bud pointedly.

"I have no idea what you're talking about, Doc. I didn't slash anybody's tires, that's for sure. I just wanted to make sure we're on the same page. I know your friend reported the incident to the warden but, I swear, it was just a misunderstanding."

I hoped to have time to pick up the phone and call Alex before my next session but the sound of a sharp rap on the door soon echoed through the office. "Come in," I called, my voice vibrating with an edgy weariness. It was Emanuel. "Please excuse me, officer, I have a session now," I said to Bud, wondering why I was becoming so unhinged.

"Sure, just didn't want any hard feelings between us." My heart was still galloping in my chest when he closed the door.

"Please sit down, Emanuel. How have you been feeling? I know that sounds like kind of a loaded question, coming from a shrink."

Emanuel sat down and placed a package bound in brown paper on the floor next to him. "Is that guy bothering you or something, Doctor? I don't want to get in trouble here but he's a jerk."

"I wouldn't let him hear you calling him that." I couldn't get Angela's phone call out of my mind. "But I think I know what you mean. Emanuel, I notice you have a package with you. Do you mind if I ask what's in it?"

"You better watch out for him. There's a name for guys like him on the street and it ain't officer. This," he pointed to the package, "is something for you."

"That's very sweet. Everything going okay on the unit, Emanuel? Are you sleeping? Eating okay? We had a major breakthrough when we talked about what happened the night of the crash."

"Yeah." He looked down at his hands, fingers were knotted together. "Yeah, I'm okay. I deserve what I got. If it wasn't for me. . ." Tears rolled down his cheeks. "Marisol and Mariangelie would still be here."

I settled back in my chair. There was nothing to say. "I know you didn't mean for it to happen. I have to tell you that in light of your improvement, we'll be transferring you back to prison in Puerto Rico ASAP. A marshal and possibly Josie Garrett will be accompanying you back."

"When do I go?" Emanuel looked down at his lap. "Sure I can't stay here a little longer? You have no idea what a Puerto Rican prison is like."

"I'm sorry but you're no longer psychotic," I said matter-of-factly. "I have to wait to get the orders from the warden and Josie has to arrange air transport. I'll let you know as soon as I know anything."

"Well, thanks for all you've done." He stood, offered his hand and handed me the package. It was a thick white paper rolled into a tube. "I drew it for you."

"It's beautiful. When did you do this?" It was an intricately shaded beach scene with an ocean, swaying palms and a setting sun in the background, done in pastel. "I won't be able to take it home. Prison regulations, but I'd love to hang it up in my office."

He flushed with pride. "I can mat and frame it for you if you like it. What color mat do you want?"

"How about lavender or pink to pick up on some of the colors you've drawn in the sky? That really was very sweet of you." It was the first gift I had received from an inmate and I was deeply touched by it.

"I'll see what colors they have in the art room. I wanted to thank you again for what you've done." He looked away as if embarrassed.

"Emanuel?" After the experience with Finn, I realized no one was necessarily happy to leave the hospital, especially if they were being transferred to a real prison.

He turned to look at me. "Yeah, Doc?"

"Thank you." And with that, I picked up my bag and my lunch and walked Emanuel to the dayroom. From there I continued to the cafeteria where Josie was already waiting.

"I just had the strangest phone call," I told her.

"You okay?" Josie asked. "You look pale, even for a *gringa*."

"I guess I'm a little shaken. Alex's ex-wife called claiming to still be married to him."

"Bastard. I knew it," Josie exclaimed.

"Josie! What is it you have against him? I don't believe a word of it. Alex wouldn't lie to me about something like that."

* * *

IT HAD STARTED OUT A BEAUTIFUL DAY, but a grim, cold rain drooled and trickled down the windows as I drove home. I had decided to wait to talk to Alex in person about the phone call. Somehow, Angela had managed to ruin my happiness at picking out a puppy with Alex.

Torrents of water ran down the street and swirled into the gutters. Dane had a Cub Scout meeting after school and Caleigh was staying late for a play rehearsal. I tried to remember if the children had worn jackets that morning. The rain was still coming as I dashed inside to an empty house, put down my purse and turned on the local news. Within minutes, Alex's car pulled in the driveway and he stood at the door wiping stray droplets from his nose.

"Let's go," I said gruffly, raincoat and umbrella in hand.

"Is something wrong?"

"I'll tell you when we get in the car." I scrambled to open the umbrella but the wind blew it inside out. Alex took it from me and managed to wrestle it open and hold it over our heads as he walked me to the passenger side of the car.

He got in and asked, "What's the matter, Grace?"

I hugged myself to warm my wind-chilled body. "Angela called me today," I said stonily.

"What? What are you talking about?"

"I'm talking about your ex-wife. Or is she your wife? Calling me at work!"

"I don't know what you mean." He looked at me with a level gaze. "I told you Angela and I are divorced. Do I have to get out our divorce decree to show you?"

"No. I mean, are you really divorced? Alex, I'm sorry. I was just so rattled to get that call at work. I don't know what's the matter with me."

"Yes, I'm divorced. I told you that. What did she say? I wonder how she got your number." He reached for my hand.

One look at his face and I knew I should have trusted him. "She said I'd better stay away from you and that she was your wife!" Repeating Angela's words upset me all over again.

"How could you even have thought that was true?" Alex demanded. "I told you she never got over it."

"I know. I'm sorry. How does she even know about me? Do you think she found out we're engaged?" I twirled the ring around my finger.

"I have no idea. Do you want me to call her and tell her to mind her own business?"

"No, that'll just add fuel to the fire. Let's try to forget about Angela and enjoy picking out our first puppy together, okay? I want to put the drama of your ex-wife behind us."

"Anything you say."

* * *

THE SMELL OF URINE-SOAKED PAPERS and rawhide chews hit us head on as soon as the thin, fortyish Professor Stephen Colberg opened the door.

Stephen wore smudged wire-rimmed glasses, had hunched shoulders and a puppy in each hand. "Here you go, buddy," he said, thrusting a brown-and-white-spotted pup into Alex's arms. "And here's one for you." He handed me a warm, sleepy pup with a pudgy belly and soft ears.

"Oh . . . oh, she's adorable." I held the warm, fuzzy body to my face. The pup woke and licked my cheek, wagging her stubby tail. Her little pink tongue licked my chin, her tongue as scratchy as sandpaper. "Oh, Alex . . . can we put them down and see what they do?" The adorable puppies made me forget about Angela Sawyer's crazy phone call.

"That one's a character!" Alex held a puppy. "Ugh!" the puppy piddled on him and I burst out laughing.

He put the pup down, and it waddled back to the litter where its siblings were hungrily nursing and squirmed in to get to a teat. "Look at yours, Grace, she's tiny but she's smart. Look at the way she maneuvers in there to edge the others out!"

"Any one you like is yours," Stephen offered. "There are two males and three females. They've all taken to puppy chow and water but they still like to get a sip from mama when they can."

"Oh, look, sweetie, I think she's saying, 'Pick me!'" The tiny female spaniel waddled back to me. "What do you think about her?" I picked up the squirming pup and held her up to Alex.

"I think she's perfect. I picked up some puppy supplies today. She's ready to go, right?"

"She's all yours," Stephen agreed.

The trip home was eventful with a whining puppy in the backseat, who barked a tiny bark and chewed at one of her many toys.

"Close your eyes, kids," Alex said when we got home, as excited as a child himself. "Your mom and I have a surprise for you. Ready? Open!" He pulled the puppy out from behind his back.

"Mom! It's a puppy!" Dane buried his nose in the puppy's neck. "Who's it for?"

"It's for you, buddy," Alex answered. "You and Caleigh."

Dane jumped into Alex's arms. "I love you, Alex! Thanks! Is it a boy or a girl?"

"She's a female. Caleigh, what do you think, honey? Do you have a name you'd like to give her?" I asked.

"Yeah, how about 'Hope'? I think she looks like hope."

"No! I want to call it Tyrannasaurus Rex," Dane suggested.

"No way! Thanks, Mom. Thanks, Alex," Caleigh said, sitting down with Dane on the floor. The puppy burrowed like a mole between them. "Come here, Sketcher," she called. "Come see your new sister!"

"I guess we can call it Hope," Dane grumbled.

"She's female, so I think Hope would suit her fine." Alex met my gaze from across the room and smiled. After the storm and Angela's upsetting phone call, everything was finally falling into place.

* * *

THE FOLLOWING WEEKEND Dane climbed into my bed with Hope. I woke up to the puppy's warm tongue licking my face. "Morning, Mommy!"

"Morning, Dane." I had to laugh. "Did you take Hope out yet?"

"Not yet. Is today the day Alex is coming to live with us?"

"Yes, it is." I sat up in bed. "You okay with that?" It was a big day for all of us.

"I guess so. Do you think he'll come to see my tee ball games?" Dane's eyes lit up.

My sweet boy. I hugged him tight. "I'm sure he will. Maybe we'll bring Hope too. Now, take her out before she pees in the bed!"

* * *

ALEX FINISHED UNPACKING the last of the boxes and hung his suits in my closet. The house was built long before walk-in closets were a common feature and although I had tried to make room, the closet was crammed. "Maybe we can do some remodeling in the fall. What do you think? At least to get more closet space. Maybe an addition with a bigger bedroom and closet and an office for you, if you'd like."

"Sure. We'll look into it after the trip, hon."

"I think the kids are doing well," I said, hanging up his shirts. "I told them we'd have a little talk after lunch to set some ground rules, okay?" I emptied out a couple of drawers for Alex's underwear and socks. "I want to be sure they know that when I'm not here, you're the adult in charge."

"Great. Let's take it slow though. I don't want them to think I'm trying to take Matt's place." Alex folded his tee shirts and put them away.

"That's what I love about you." I kissed him. "What did I ever do to deserve you?"

"I'm the lucky one, baby," Alex replied.

I hugged him and said, "I'm gonna go start lunch. I'll call you when it's ready," still unable to believe my life had finally turned around.

CHAPTER TWENTY-ONE

INDONESIA

L ATE AUGUST AND THE MORNING promised record heat for Minnesota again. We were next in line. "Can you believe we're finally on our way?" My itinerary made a perfect fan and I used it to dispel the heat. Each of us had a suitcase of medical supplies, clothing for a week, and a carry-on with computers and books. "I'm so excited!"

Alex wiped away a trickle of perspiration from his forehead. "At least we're early. Look at the line now!" A line of passengers snaked around the ropes behind us at the Minneapolis St. Paul International Airport. "This humidity is good preparation for Indonesia. It's supposed to be about one-hundred degrees Fahrenheit everyday this week."

"Oh, it can't be that bad, can it? I have a hat and sunscreen along. We'll be fine."

We passed through security screening and settled ourselves in at the gate. Half an hour later, we were boarding the short commuter flight to Chicago. My knowledge of internal medicine was spotty. I hoped I still remembered enough to be able to help in case they didn't have a pressing need for a psychiatrist.

Time passed quickly and before we knew it, the captain announced we would be leaving on time. A few more hours and we would be on a flight to South Korea. I lowered myself into the window seat and dug in my carry-on for a dog-eared mystery novel and a guidebook of Indonesia. Alex stowed his carry-on in the overhead bin and took his seat by the aisle, his knees at straight angles. "It's twelve hours from Chicago to Seoul," he announced. "I hope there's more leg room than this on the next flight."

"Poor baby. Want me to massage your knees?"

"Uhm, that feels good. After that, it's another six hours to Denpasar Airport in Bali. We'll be spending the first night in Bali rather than bumping along for a three- to four-hour bus ride to the village. All in all, it's a two-day trip. Thanks for being such a good sport and coming with me."

"I wouldn't miss it," I said and I meant it. We needed time alone together. "I hope the kids will be okay. It's the first time I've left them since Matt died."

"They seem to get along well with their grandparents. Don't worry, sweetheart. They'll have fun. And I'm sure their grandparents will enjoy spoiling them for a week."

"You're right. But it has been a lot for them to adjust to, with you moving in and the engagement and all. Hey, look at this. The guide-book says most people in rural villages go to a local healer for almost everything. Especially mental health conditions."

"I think you'll have your work cut out for you." Alex stretched his legs as far as he could and opened his book. "Ready to be busy? The couple of times I've gone overseas, it's been tough but more rewarding than any-thing I've ever done." He beamed. "It's really a life-changing experience."

"I can't wait. I hope I can help. Can you imagine? This is the first time I've been this far away from home. I'm probably worrying for noth-ing but I just can't shake this funny feeling something's wrong."

"The kids seemed to be fine with the trip and it's been going better than I expected these last few months, don't you think?" Alex said, flipping through his book. "I think you're worrying about nothing," he said, kissing me on the nose.

"I'm so glad they've taken to you like they have." I buckled my seatbelt, opened my mystery novel and resolved to put my worries be-hind me. "There's just so much to think about. Tell me about Bali. It sounds like a dream."

* * *

TWO DAYS LATER, IN PROBOLINGGO, eight degrees from the equator, the scorching sun burned through my cotton shirt. My hair was pulled back and I wiped my neck with a bandana. Alex's eyes were shaded by a wide-brimmed straw hat. Sweat flooded the dirty channels on his sun-burned skin. I took a long sip of water. It was dry season and as we walked to the village school, clouds of dust rose from a tangle of bicycle taxis, mopeds, and buses on the red-dirt road.

We trudged along the narrow shoulder. "Look at those muscles!" The rickshaw drivers' thigh and calf muscles bulged. "Can you imagine peddling those three-wheeled bicycles in this heat?" I held the bandanna to my nose and coughed. My eyes watered from the black exhaust fumes in the air.

Mopeds wove in front of the buses on the narrow road, sounding like the buzzing of Minnesota's cicada. "My god, do you suppose they ever get hit?" Alex asked, watching children dart in and out of traffic.

"I'd be terrified if that was Caleigh or Dane running across the road like that. I've just taken for granted how lucky we are," I said as we walked, swaddled in the oppressive heat, toward the public school where the clinic was held. Local children called out, "Hello, Missus! *Siapa namamu? Apa kabar?*" laughing at our confusion.

"My name is Grace." I tried to enunciate clearly and smile, hoping "*apa kabar*" meant what I thought it did. The crowd of slight, dark-haired, smiling children followed us into a small cement courtyard outside the school. It appeared to be a treeless open-air waiting room with hundreds of people already there, fanning themselves in the heat. The morning sun cast their shadows onto a cracked cement pavement with scraggly wilted yellow weeds poking through. Torn nets hung limply from rusty hoops on the basketball court. The morning was cloudless and still and the sun remained merciless. "I wish the kids were here to see this. These children look so happy despite the hardships they face," I said to Alex.

Two smiling women dressed in colorful long-sleeved batik blouses and fashionable jeans greeted us at the door—teachers who would act as interpreters, medical assistants and pharmacists for the medical staff. Bu Husnul and Bu Uci, the school administrators, welcomed us to their school, SMA Negeri 1 Dringu. "In Indonesia, "Bu" was a sign of respect for women and "Pak" preceded men's names," they explained to us.

My cotton skirt swished between my legs as I walked through the tiled open-air courtyard to my classroom. Yesterday, I had made the mistake of wearing a sleeveless blouse and shorts when we had had a tour of the facility, providing a source of entertainment for the children, who stared, open-mouthed, at my freckles. Egged on by the others, several of the older children had giggled in embarrassment and asked if they could touch my arms. I was now dressed in a long-sleeved cotton shirt and modest knee-length skirt.

I was beginning to understand why they took three 'baths' a day here. It was so unbearably warm that I found myself looking forward to each bath. The previous night—my first night in my host family's home, I had stood naked in their tiled bathroom, throwing buckets of cold water over my shoulders. The bathroom was a damp tiled room where dirty water flowed from the open drain on the floor directly into the sewage channels running along the sides of the road. Now, I searched my pocket, and felt for the tiny roll of travel toilet paper I learned to carry with me. I had my doubts I would become accustomed to the squatty potty and the cleaning bucket in our week in Indonesia.

We made their way to our makeshift offices. "What do you suppose the patients think of the equipment and all our questions? Do you think they'll be disappointed to find we're nothing like the village healer?"

"We'll see. I hope we can be of some help," Alex said.

"Me too." I stepped into my classroom. None of the windows opened, so I left the door ajar in hopes of a breeze. Mangy cats sauntered in and out, indifferent to the lime-green lizards that scaled the classroom walls. I walked around the room looking at the brightly colored pictures hanging on the walls remembering Dane's drawings of dinosaurs and smiling suns.

With no patients to see yet, I went out to help with triage. The teachers took brief histories of the patients, complete with presenting problem, treatment and any follow-up required during the week the medical team was present. They then directed patients to one of the five clinics: me in Psychiatry, Alex in Infectious Diseases, Dr. Randy Sotomayor in General Medicine, Dr. Elizabeth Siecks in Pediatrics, and Dr. Colin Boyd in Orthopedics.

Although I saw no order in the registration process, the interpreters pointed out the patients had sorted themselves into the sickest and weakest being seen first. An equally stooped man helped an elderly woman, bent like a dry twig. Her body wracked with spasms of coughing through the door. One look into her milky eyes and I directed her to the one ophthalmologist who had joined us. It was shocking to discover that this woman and her husband, both wizened and weathered by a lifetime in the sun, were fifty years old.

My heart broke at the sight of the young mother who came next. The woman carried an infant wrapped around her chest in a colorful, woven sling. Her baby's hands were covered in dirty gloves so she could not scratch the red, excoriated skin, covered with flaky, silver-white patches on her limbs and torso. "Please go to classroom number two," the youngest of the teachers told the distraught young mother. "Next!" she called to the growing number of patients, some of whom had travelled for hours to see the first doctor many of them had ever visited.

An entire family: mother, father, grandmother, grandfather, two young sisters and a disheveled-looking teenage boy entered. "Please ask them who the patient is," I instructed the interpreter. The family all pointed with the thumbs of their right hands to the teenage boy. The gesture was almost comical. I asked the Indonesian teacher what this meant.

"People never point with any other finger, Doctor Grace. It's considered extremely rude to point with anything other than your thumbs," she whispered. "His name is Maide, which means second born. He is eighteen. They say he is possessed by bad spirits."

After a lengthy discussion, judging by the looks they gave me, I was convinced that the family believed they would have been better off bringing Maide to the village healer.

"They say he stays up all night and talks to bad spirits who have entered his head. He doesn't eat. He thinks he is an *imam*. They say it is very shameful to them."

He looked like a scared teenager, like so many of my patients back home. "How long has he believed himself to be an *imam*? Did he eat and sleep well prior to this? Has he been violent or unusually sad?" The father gave me a doubtful look.

"The mother says that this began after Ramadan last year. When the fasting ended, he never started eating again. He was accustomed to eating during the night before the sun came up and now has not been able to sleep. He is not violent but talks to spirits."

"Are there any other family members with psychological problems?" I fanned myself with the file. Poor kid, he's just a few years older than Caleigh. His parents appeared devastated. The father, whose hands were as dry and leathery as an old baseball glove, looked down. He replied quietly in Baha Indonesian.

"He says it was a great shame, but his brother became possessed at age twenty and never recovered. That is why he is so worried about his son," the interpreter said.

I picked up the file I had begun on the boy. It would be difficult for the family to understand psychosis was a symptom of an illness rather than evidence of being possessed. Based on the history and the boy's flat affect, I believed he might be psychotic. Probably the beginning of a major affective or bipolar disorder. "I'll give them some medicine that he is to take twice every day. I want him to come back in three days. I'd like to see him every three days, if possible, while I am here." I could provide enough medication to last a few months but then what? The young man's bleak future loomed before me.

The parents smiled hopefully. The father took out his camera, and spoke to the interpreter.

"He wants to know if you would please take a picture with the family. They have never seen anyone with red hair before," she said smiling.

At noon, we took a much-needed break. Large vats of rice, vegetables in a spicy green sauce and shiny red snappers grilled over coals were brought in by moped to the school. It was the first break Alex and I had had all morning. The smell of fish hung on the hot still air. We found seats at the table, covered by a colorful cloth and tried not to stare at the Indonesian staff eating with their hands. "Are there any forks?" I asked the interpreter.

"Yes, we brought some for the Americans," Bu Tutut replied. "Here, it's common to eat with your hands. It's not considered rude at all. Unless you use your left hand. NEVER do that!" she said. "In the bathroom, you use your left hand to clean yourself, since we do not use paper. That is why we have the water buckets. Never eat or touch anyone or shake anyone's hand with your left hand!" she repeated.

"Now you tell me!" I laughed, wondering how many rules of etiquette I had broken.

Chapter Twenty-Two

A WEEK LATER, I felt a part of the village in a way I hadn't anticipated. There was so much I wanted to tell Caleigh and Dane.
Alex and I walked along the now familiar, dusty road to school
and were greeted for the last time by the staff. Pak Naiman, the school
principal, asked solemnly what I thought of his country. "I have never
met nicer people," I reassured him. Indonesia was the fourth most
densely populated nation in the world. The standard of living was extremely modest by Western standards. An average salary was two to
three dollars per day, yet the people were more generous than any I
had ever met.

"We worried what you would think of Muslims," he said haltingly.
"Because, it's only a very few extremists who cause the problems in our
country and in the world."

My eyes filled with tears. That these warm, generous, people who
had opened up their homes and their hearts to us should have any
worry about what I, as an American, thought of them was deeply disturbing to me. Hoping to reassure him, I told him the tragic acts which
had been committed were the work of extremists and neither I, nor the
majority of Americans held this against them or any Muslim country.
Our eyes met and an understanding seemed to develop, which was
unimaginable to me just a week ago.

On the last day, the villagers brought candy, batik clothing, and
fresh fruit for the bus trip to Surabaya. "Eat the durian before you get
on the bus!" the senior teacher whispered. "It's not allowed on public
transportation," she said, pointing to a foot-long, oblong fruit with a
thick thorn-covered green husk.

Alex sniffed the fruit. "I can see why! What's it taste like?" The
odor was as strong and penetrating as a bad case of flatulence.

"It is banned in hotels because it smells like rotten onions but the
taste is like custard flavored with almonds. I'd be glad to keep it," the
teacher said, "so you don't have to worry about it."

That evening there was a shadow puppet theater or shadow play
production in the village the teachers insisted we see. Called *wayang*

kulit, it was a beautiful performance of puppets made from buffalo skin, with an Indonesian orchestra composed of bamboo xylophones, wooden chimes, gongs, and singers. The puppets were behind a thin cotton screen lit by a halogen lamp.

"Amazing how life-like these one-dimensional puppets are behind the screen. The shadows seem almost alive, the way they seem to run and fly, don't they? I wish we knew the story behind it! Oh, look, Alex! Now they're dancing!"

"Beautiful, aren't they?" he replied, his arm around my shoulder. He gave me a squeeze. "I can't wait to tell the kids about it. Maybe we can make one at home. Not as artistic as this but I bet Dane would like to string up a curtain and light a couple of lanterns and put on a shadow play."

"You're so good with them. We're so lucky to have you in our lives."

The next morning, the bus swerved along narrow crater-filled roads, passing vehicles on both sides. White-knuckled, I clutched Alex's arm each time the driver swerved in front of another bus or truck. It appeared we were bound for a head-on collision every time we rounded a curve. Three hours later, we stepped off at the airport, dusty, dirty, and shaken.

"Just think, in an hour we'll be in paradise." Alex collected our luggage. "We're staying at Alam Indah in Bali. Thank goodness they'll have someone picking us up at the airport."

An hour later, we checked into a traditional Balinese hotel. The outdoor lobby was surrounded by palms, ferns, and flowering shrubs whose fragrance hung heavy on the humid air. Offerings of flower petals, incense, and fruit were laid out in small, woven bamboo trays around the perimeter. The hotel clerk needed only to shake a fly swatter at the comical monkeys who roamed the grounds to shoo them away.

We sat at a round bamboo table, finally alone. "It's really been a whirlwind of activity since the engagement, hasn't it? I can't believe we're finally alone," I said. Alex took my hand and the young clerk returned. "Would you like coffee or tea, madam?" he asked. "We are serving tea right now with homemade cakes and scones."

"Apparently not for long," Alex said. "What do you want, Grace?"

"Mmmmm. The lemon tea and that pastry look good." The Indonesian pastry looked like carrot cake. "Oh, look, Alex! He's back." A monkey darted to the offering placed at the base of a nearby statue, unpeeled a small banana and stuffed it into his cheeks. The clerk got out the fly swatter and the monkey quickly ran off into the lush forest surrounding the hotel.

"I'll have the same," Alex said.

After our tea, I bathed in a large, luxurious bathtub, scrubbing until my skin was as smooth as the polished marble floors and counters. I dressed in a long cotton batik skirt and white blouse and sat outside on the veranda where Alex was waiting his turn to shower. The mesmerizing scent of incense burning hung in the air. "I promised the kids I'd call. It'll just be a few minutes. It should be about 8:00 a.m. there."

"Okay. I'll shower while you do that. Tell them we have all sorts of stories for them when we get back," he said before burying his nose in my long, wet hair. "You smell so good," he murmured. "Let me go before I get carried away!"

It took several minutes for the call to go through. "Hello? Hello?"

"Mommy!" Six-year-old Dane cried in a muffled voice.

"Dane, what is it? Is something wrong?" A raspy, scratching sound over the phone made it hard for her to hear. "I can't hear you sweetie. Are you okay?"

"Mommy, Hope is gone!" he cried.

"What do you mean? Have you and Grandma looked everywhere? Did she have her collar on?"

"Yes." Dane sobbed. "Here's Grandma."

"Dahlia? Is everything okay?" My heart rose to my chest. I was two thousand miles away and felt helpless to comfort my son. "What's happened?"

"The kids are okay, Grace, but I'm afraid Dane is right. We haven't seen the puppy since the day before yesterday. The kids were outside playing with her and I called them in for dinner. We left Hope in the yard for about fifteen minutes and when we went back out, she was gone. I'm so sorry, Grace! The kids are just heartbroken."

Dahlia said something inaudible to the kids before she returned to the phone. "Grace," she whispered. "There's something else I have to tell you."

"Dahlia, what is it? I can hardly hear you. Can you speak a little louder?" It sounded like Dahlia was crying on the other end. "Did you call the animal shelter? Maybe she wandered off and someone turned her in. Is Sktecher okay?"

"Sketcher is fine. He was asleep on the sofa the entire time. I called the shelter and the pound. We put up signs and have walked around the woods and driveway. We asked the neighbors. I feel terrible about this. That puppy just disappeared. But that's not what I want to tell you. Oh, this is so terrible." She lowered her voice. "There's something else . . ."

"What's wrong?"

"Oh, Grace, it's Caleigh . . . I'm so worried about her."

I inhaled sharply and feared the worst. "Caleigh? What's happened?"

Dahlia cleared her throat. "I think she's been cutting herself, Grace."

I wasn't sure I heard her correctly. "What did you say?"

"I can't be sure, but the day after the puppy disappeared, I noticed marks on her arms. Little ones scabbed over. Perfectly straight, like she'd made them herself. I went into her room to say good night and she was in pajama pants and a tank top. That's how I noticed them, cuts from her elbow to her shoulder."

"Did you ask her about it? Maybe she got scratched somehow." There were no words to nail it down. I knew there was something wrong.

"Of course I asked her! That was the strangest part. She put on her robe and pretended like there was nothing there. She didn't say she'd been scratching her arm, or been injured somehow, she just said it was nothing with this blank expression on her face. Oh, I feel like it's all my fault for not insisting they bring the puppy inside." Dahlia blew her nose with a loud honking sound.

"Tell the kids we'll be home the day after tomorrow. Thanks, for telling me. Don't worry, it's not your fault. Just keep an eye on her, okay?" I suddenly felt a foreboding chill in the tropical heat.

Alex came out of the shower, wrapped in a towel. "What happened?"

"I just had the strangest conversation with Dahlia. The puppy is missing, and worse, Dahlia thinks Caleigh's been cutting herself." I sat dumbly on the edge of a rattan chair. None of this made any sense.

"What? What do you mean, cutting herself?" he asked, sitting beside me, his face tight with anxiety. "We don't even know for sure, that's what's going on, sweetheart. Do you think we should fly home tomorrow?"

I gripped his hand. "No. It'd be a nightmare to try to change the tickets now. I know Dahlia and Stan are taking good care of them. It means so much to me that you would offer, but it's just one day more. Let's go out for dinner. Maybe things will look brighter tomorrow."

The sky was a sea of stars. We walked hand in hand along an illuminated boardwalk on the ocean. Dusk fell slowly, the waves and beach still lit by the sun's last rays. The cries of gulls shattered the silence and highlighted the worry I felt. Palm fronds curled curiously toward one another against the steadily darkening sky. "I just don't understand how Caleigh could be cutting herself or how a puppy could disappear. I'm so worried, Alex. Dahlia seems to think Caleigh might have started cutting because of the puppy but I've seen this a thousand times. It's usually in response to a deep-seated psychological pain. I wonder what could be bothering Caleigh this much?"

Gulls scavenged along the beach, flapping their wings like underwear hung out to dry on a windy day. The horizon was heavy, almost crushing the rolling waves underneath it. A few pleasure boats, scattered like white flags raced the rising tide. We walked ahead along the dusk-draped shore, the water coming up around our ankles and the waves lapping the shore. Sunlight danced on Alex's hair and the sea surged with what should have been laughter.

CHAPTER TWENTY-THREE

AFTER A TWENTY-EIGHT-HOUR FLIGHT, nothing had ever been as welcome as Minnesota's clear skies and green-checkered corn-fields. We circled the Minneapolis St Paul International Airport, and Alex took my hand, the engagement ring still awkward on my finger, and told me not to worry. We were landing into a new life as a family.

The plane shuddered to the ground and the captain announced the temperature in Minneapolis was a very pleasant eighty degrees. The local time was 11:00 a.m. I had been waiting for the announcement indicating that cell phone use was permitted and I anxiously called the children to tell them we were on our way home. No answer. That was strange. When I'd talked to them the other day they were heartbroken about Hope, but excited we were coming home. I made a mental note to put an ad in the paper and contact the animal shelter and pound again as soon as we got home.

It took longer for the passengers to deplane than it took to pour thick maple syrup out of a bottle. I listened to my voicemail. Dahlia had left a message saying she and Stan were going to church and out to brunch with some old neighbors but Caleigh and Dane preferred to stay home and wait for us. I called Dahlia's cell phone but got her voicemail. Maybe the kids had decided to go out with their grandparents after all.

Our luggage was circling the carousel by the time we got to the baggage claim. The shuttle to the Bloomington Park 'n' Fly was waiting. Alex smiled encouragingly, grateful everything was moving smoothly. Despite my exhaustion, I felt a shiver of pleasure at the prospect of Dane jumping into my arms and hearing about Caleigh and Dahlia's shopping trip to the Mall of America.

Within minutes we were heading south on Highway 52. I tried calling again, letting the phone ring six times before hanging up. "Alex, there's no answer. I know I'm silly to worry but something doesn't feel right."

Alex attempted a wrinkled smile and reached for my hand. "Are you worried about what Dahlia said about Caleigh?"

"Yeah, and the fact that they're not answering the phone."

"Maybe they're outside. It is a beautiful summer day. Try not to worry. I'm sure we'll get everything straightened out once we get home. If Caleigh really is cutting herself, we'll get her into therapy, maybe go as a family."

It wasn't like them to not answer the phone but Alex tried to convince me we'd get home and there would be a perfectly logical explanation. He was right. The children had both seemed to adjust to the idea of us getting married. Still, I tried calling again, picturing the hollow ring of the phone in the empty house.

An hour later, the wheels of the jeep crunched on the rocky driveway. The newspaper lay in its flimsy plastic sheath on the sidewalk. The green shutters, the front porch and tire swing, all as familiar to me as my right hand, looked strangely foreign. I pushed open the heavy kitchen door, inhaled the smell of home and rushed into the house. "Caleigh! Dane! We're home."

I was greeted by silence and the smell of something wrong. The house was empty, the children's books and toys scattered about the living room floor. Sketcher did not rush at me, wagging his tail, nor did Dane run jumping into my arms. The breakfast dishes sat on the table, runny egg yolk dried on the plates. Half-filled glasses of juice stood waiting to be finished.

Sketcher barked from his kennel and I was irrationally relieved, as if he could tell me where the children were. I opened the door to the back porch and ran outside, catching myself before spilling headlong into the grass. The gate to the pen was closed and when I opened it, Sketcher jumped on me, wagging his tail, wild with excitement. He licked my hands and cocked his head at me, whimpering.

"What is it, boy? Come on, Sketcher, let's get inside."

My eye was drawn to a sheet of paper on the kitchen counter I hadn't noticed earlier. It was folded into quarters. I fumbled with the stiff, heavy sheet of paper thinking it was a note from the kids.

The bold printed letters were in stark contrast to its brightness. YOUR CHILDREN ARE GONE. THIS IS WHAT YOU DESERVE. I'LL BE IN TOUCH.

"Oh, God!" My fingers were numb as they clenched the creased white paper. A sob swelled in my throat and erupted in a strangled cry. "Alex!" I screamed.

"Grace, what is it?" he called from the landing, a suitcase in each hand. He rushed downstairs and I pointed dumbly at the note.

"What is this?" he demanded.

I rose and sprinted up the stairs, two steps at a time. I flung the door open to Caleigh's room. The bed was unmade and clothes were strewn over the floor. The room resembled a gothic cathedral. Candles and incense burners sat on the desk, dripping wax had dried on the ceramic candleholders we had made together at Color Me Mine. The faint woodsy odor of sandalwood lingered in the air. It was almost reassuring to see her room in the same state it had always been in.

I raced to Dane's room and opened his door. He was the most responsible six-year-old I had ever known. His room was as tidy as always.

I flung the bathroom door open. Toothbrushes and hairbrushes lined up matter-of-factly along the sink. I leaned against the wall. The sound of my breath could have qualified for a prank phone caller's as I forced it in and out of my lungs.

I looked out the window, remembering back to a tornado scare we'd had last summer. The light had scattered, turning the sky green. The tornado sirens had wailed and I'd quickly filled the bathtub with pillows and blankets from my bed and yelled for the children to take cover. Through the small, rectangular window, we could see willow branches flowing like silvery locks of hair in the wind. An eerie calm settled before hail hammered the roof top and winds licked the shingles. A strange train-like whistling noise filled the air.

We were holed up with Sketcher in the downstairs bathroom for the duration of the storm. I had read *Harry Potter* aloud to the kids and encouraged Dane to think of it more as a slumber party than a potential disaster.

I barreled downstairs. "We have to call Dahlia! Where's my phone?" My eyes darted frantically around the room.

"Sweetheart, here." Alex picked it up from the cluttered counter and I inexplicably blanked. I looked at the phone and all I saw was the random flicker of snow on an empty TV screen. I couldn't remember the number I had called just that morning and had called several times a week for years.

I frantically pressed speed dial and hoped Dahlia would answer. The phone rang three times before Dahlia greeted me. "Grace! Welcome home!"

"Are the children with you?" I spit, my mouth a lint trap.

"What are you saying?" Dahlia asked calmly. "Stan and I are home. We met the Hendricksons for brunch after church this morning. Caleigh told us she and Dane would be fine for an hour or two, so we left around ten."

There was a sickening sense of foreboding crawling in my gut. "Were they okay when you left?"

"Yes, I made them breakfast and Caleigh said she'd clean up afterwards. They wanted to stay home and wait for you. She said she watches Dane all the time. Oh, my God, what's wrong?"

My heart pounded dully in my chest. "I got home and the kids were gone. Dahlia, the kids are gone!"

"What do you mean they're gone? Did you call the police?" She had begun to shriek. "Grace!"

"I'm calling them right now." Alex was already running out the door. I had a crazy, irrational thought my in-laws must have had something to do with this. "There's a note, Dahlia. I was hoping maybe there was a misunderstanding and you had the kids."

"We'll be right over," my mother-in-law said before the line went dead.

"Grace, did you call the police?" Alex demanded. "Grace!" Alex shook me. "Call the police! I'm going outside to look for them."

"I'm doing that now!" I trembled violently as I picked up the phone and dialed 911. Alex was already running out the door.

"Operator. What is your emergency?"

"My children are gone!" I screamed into the phone. "I came home and they're gone." I began to cry, loud sobs I could not control. "There's a note!"

"Ma'am, please calm down," the dispatcher said. "What does the note say?"

I gasped for air. The words stuck in my throat. "'Your children are gone. This is what you deserve. I'll be in touch,'" I finally whispered, certain I would remember it for the rest of my life.

"Ma'am? I'm sending someone right over. What's your address?"

"Five sixty-five Spring Road." My harsh, shrill voice was unrecognizable to me. "Hurry!" My voice was frozen in a scream.

"It'll just be a few minutes," the dispatcher assured me. "What are the names and ages of the children?"

"Caleigh Rendeau. She's thirteen and Dane Rendeau. He's only six years old." I swayed as I walked to the living room, hoping Alex would burst in with the children, and it would all have been some sort of bizarre joke. Alex rushed into the room with Sketcher on his heels. He shook his head and jammed his hands into his pockets.

"I went all around the yard and into the path they like to walk on in the woods. There has to be a logical explanation for this."

I nodded mutely and sat stone-faced, my arms wrapped around me. I felt shell-shocked as I sat staring at the wooden-plank floor.

"What did Dahlia say?" Alex sat down next to me. "Grace! What did she say?"

The coffee I drank on the flight rose to my throat. "They don't have the children. They're coming right over. Oh. God, I'm gonna throw up!" I ran to the bathroom with Alex following. The sound of muffled sobs and retching filled my ears. When I emerged, Alex brought me back to wash my face. My eyes were almost swollen shut.

CHAPTER TWENTY-FOUR

MY FEET PAWED THE FLOOR like a caged animal's. I hung up the phone after calling every one of Caleigh's friends. No one had heard from her since yesterday. The last contact had been a text from Caleigh to Brianna Kohl at 7:00 p.m. last night, which said, GOT THE CUTEST STUFF FOR SCHOOL. The nearest neighbors hadn't seen the children since yesterday when they drove by with their grandparents on their way to the Mall of America.

Police cruisers wailed in the distance and shortly afterwards pulled into our driveway. Sketcher's deep resonant bark announced their arrival and I was at the door before they had a chance to ring the bell. Detectives Rose Donnelly and Bill Meyers, the last people I could have imagined meeting that morning, stood at the door. Sketcher stood by me, his fur bristling, and growled a low, throaty, ominous growl.

"Alex, for God's sake! Can you lock him in the kitchen?" I said, immediately sorry for snapping.

The officers filed in one by one entering the living room. Detective Donnelly was a buxom, no-nonsense sort of woman with sharply defined features. She was dressed in a bilious green suit.

Detective Meyers was bland-faced with sparse jet-black hair, parted above his left ear. He was dressed in conservative gray slacks and a checkered blazer with a button-down shirt underneath. His shoulders were covered in a blanket of dandruff. "When did you first notice your children were missing, ma'am?" he asked.

I almost laughed at the absurdity of the question. *My children are missing.* It was a phrase from a nightmare. The conversational equivalent of a Salvatore Dali painting. The patterns in the living room rug began to crawl snake-like along the floor. The house was so still it seemed as though it were breathing on its own. I crumpled onto the sofa and looked up to see the detectives exchanging a look that frightened me.

"Are you the father?" Donnelly asked Alex.

"No. I'm Grace's fiancé, Alex Sawyer," he said. "We became engaged a month ago."

My heart rolled over. I was tired and disoriented after two days of travel, unable to remember if it was 1:00 p.m. or 1:00 a.m. I struggled to remember what Meyers had just asked me. "About ten minutes ago," I finally said. Was it jet lag or a bad dream I had walked into? "I just got home from a medical mission trip to Indonesia with Alex. I'm a psychiatrist. My former in-laws, Stan and Dahlia Rendeau, stayed here with the children while we were away. I talked to them yesterday and told them I would see them today. When I got home, they were gone."

"Have you called your in-laws, ma'am? Have you checked to see if there is anything missing?" Meyers asked. "Do your children have cell phones?"

"Yes, I called. Dahlia and Stan are on their way over." My vision blurred. I must have blacked out because moments later, Detective Donnelly was shaking me and holding a glass of water to my lips, jerking me back into consciousness.

"Dr. Rendeau, snap out of it," she barked.

I looked at her wordlessly, feeling something between desperation and terror. Why hadn't I been able to keep my children as safe as I had during that tornado warning? I looked to see Alex's lips forming my name but I couldn't piece together what he was saying.

"Grace, please. Try to pull yourself together." I finally heard him say. "We'll find them. We tried calling her daughter's phone," he said to Meyers, "but she didn't pick up. Caleigh always picks up if her mother calls."

"Dr. Rendeau, I understand you work with inmates. Is that correct? Has anyone made any threats against you lately? Has anyone been released who might have motive for harming you or your children? Have the children ever talked about running away from home?" Donnelly seemed impatient. The barrage of questions was as rapid as gunfire.

"Of course not! They're very happy, well-adjusted children. We have a great relationship," I insisted, summoning all my strength to think logically. "At the prison, we plan discharge very carefully. Most times the patients go back to their families or if the families are unwilling to take them, Josie Garrett, our social worker, finds halfway housing for them. It's never been a problem. My number and address are unlisted."

"Do you have Ms. Garrett's number, ma'am?"

"It's stored in my phone. Alex, where did I put it?"

"Here it is, Grace." Alex handed it to me and I gave Detective Donnelly the number and then sank to the table. My breath came out in rapid, painful bursts. Sketcher nudged me and put his head in my lap. I walked to the window and placed my forehead against the cool, clear glass.

"Ma'am? Ma'am. Has everything been going all right at home?" Donnelly asked, dialing Josie's number. "No answer." Her voice registered somewhere in the back of my mind along with the screech of tires on the drive. I stumbled to the door and my in-laws burst into the house.

"Oh, Grace." Dahlia took my face into her thin-skinned, speckled hands. Her carefully made-up eyes were veined with red. "I fixed breakfast when they got up. We went to church and then brunch with the Hendricksons. They wanted to stay so they'd be home to see you when you got back."

"These are my in-laws, Dr. and Mrs. Rendeau," I said to the detectives, the nightmare becoming more real by the minute.

Donnelly nodded. "What time was that, ma'am?" She had the manner of a crabby waiter.

"Around ten o'colock." Dahlia looked at me helplessly. She looked like linens soaked in bleach.

"Dr. Rendeau, what time did you arrive home?" the detective asked.

"Around 12:30."

"We've got an Amber Alert called in," Detective Meyers said. "Get someone to talk to the neighbors to see if they saw anything," he instructed Donnelly. "Whoever has them has a window of possibly two to two and a half hours. Don't touch anything, anyone. We'll call in the team to dust for prints. And I'll bring the note in for analysis. Are you sure nothing is missing from the house, Dr. Rendeau?"

"What note?" Stan asked. He was a tall, thin man with a full head of silver hair and hooded blue eyes that reminded me of Matt every time I looked at him. He still had the steady hands and gaze that had stood him well during his long career as a cardiac surgeon at Mayo.

The detectives had already bagged the note as evidence. The words were indelibly imprinted on my heart. "It says, 'Your children are gone. This is what you deserve. I'll be in touch,'" I whispered.

Dahlia gasped. Stan turned to the window but not before he could erase the pained expression on his normally composed features. "Officer! The puppy is missing. But that happened several days ago," he said.

Donnelly raised her eyebrows. "Your puppy is missing?"

"We have, I mean we had a new King Charles spaniel puppy and shortly after I left on my trip, the kids left her outside with Sketcher while they came in to eat dinner and the dog disappeared," I said. "They were heartbroken. I don't understand what happened since she had already been trained to avoid the invisible fence."

"The dog never turned up?" Detective Donnelly jotted something down in her notebook. "Where was the children's father during all of this?"

"The children's father is dead," Dahlia said icily.

"I promised once I got home I would put an ad in the paper and contact the local shelters, and maybe put up signs. What the hell is this? Go out and find them! While we're standing here talking about the puppy, my kids are out there somewhere. Do something!" Terror hovered over the room like a bad odor. I had an almost irresistible impulse to throw something at Detective Donnelly.

"Calm down, ma'am. We've called in an Amber Alert. If it wasn't important, we wouldn't be asking you these questions. Do you have a picture of the children? Age, height, weight, hair and eye color, any identifying marks?" Detective Donnelly asked the questions as though she had them memorized. "How long has the father been dead?"

Dahlia still wore her heartache on her sleeve. "Please. My son died two years ago of cancer." We all reached into our wallets for school pictures. "Give her the ones on the piano, Grace," Dahlia suggested, blotting under her eyes with a wadded up tissue. "You can really tell what they look like from those. Just like Matt."

"I have their fingerprints too," I said numbly. "It's the sort of thing no mother ever thinks she'll need but last year there was a 'Stay Safe' program at the local elementary school. They provided finger printing to anyone who wanted it so I have Dane's and Caleigh's finger prints on a card upstairs." My mouth quivered and my voice broke.

A framed photo of Caleigh looking directly into the camera, a half-smile on her face sat on the polished surface of the old upright piano. "Caleigh's thirteen. One hundred pounds, and about this tall." I held my hand up to my nose. "Blue eyes and white-blonde hair. She has a half-moon shaped scar over her left eyebrow." I picked up Dane's picture and could hardly speak. "Dane is six. He loves dinosaurs. He is about four feet tall, and weighs seventy pounds. He has reddish hair, the same color as mine and green eyes. Freckles. He's missing his front tooth. Oh, God!"

Alex wrapped his arms around me, and I sobbed into his shoulder. Dahlia and Stan sat down on the other side of the sofa. "Don't worry, honey, they'll find them," Stan said. My former father-in-law took my hand. I desperately needed to believe this to make my world feel orderly again.

"Any idea what they were wearing today, Mrs. Rendeau?" Detective Donnelly asked Dahlia abruptly.

Dahlia Rendeau, dressed for Sunday services, remembered exactly what they were wearing. "Caleigh had on dark jeans, a long-sleeved yellow top and orange flip-flops. Dane was wearing khaki shorts and his red shirt with a T-Rex on the front. Sneakers and socks. Right, Stan?"

"You got me," Stan shook his head. All I remember is that they were hungry. We made 'em breakfast but it doesn't look as though they ate much of it." He gestured toward the plates of eggs and toast on the table.

"Did anything out of the ordinary happen in the week you were with the children?" Donnelly asked.

"Let's see." Stan filled his pipe. Light reflected off the gleaming dome of his skull. "There were quite a few annoying hang-up calls. Caleigh said it'd been happening a lot lately."

"We'll get phone records of all incoming and out-going phone calls from the phone company," the detective replied. "Anything else you can think of?"

"Well, the puppy. We were only inside for a couple of minutes. I decided to go back out and get the puppy while Dahlia served the children their dinner. There wasn't hide nor hair of her to be seen. But I thought maybe I saw a car drive away, way off in the distance."

The air in the room seemed to still. Meyers asked, "Did you get the make or model of the car?"

"It was too far away. The only reason I even noticed it was because we're so far out here you don't see a lot of cars pass by, especially later on in the day. This was about six-thirty at night. All I saw was a cloud of dust as it drove away."

"I don't know if this has any relevance to what's happened . . ." Dahlia hesitated.

"We need to know everything. Even something you may think has no relevance could be important, ma'am," Meyers encouraged her. "Now why don't you sit down and tell us what it is."

"Well, I went into Caleigh's room to say good-night and she had these small scabbed-over cuts up and down her left arm. I had just seen a show on TV about teenage girls cutting themselves, and that was the first thing I thought of. Especially because she was so secretive about it. She pulled on her robe and refused to tell me what had happened. She said it was nothing."

"We'll keep that in mind. Dr. Rendeau. Has your daughter cut herself before? She have any psychological problems?"

"No! Absolutely not. Dahlia told me over the phone while I was in Indonesia and that was the first time I knew about it." I felt myself deflating like a flat tire. A creeping sense of guilt shuddered through me as I wondered if I'd missed anything else over the past several months.

"Grace, I'm going to make some coffee. Would you like some, detectives?" Dahlia asked. Stan followed his wife into the kitchen.

"That'd be great, ma'am," Meyers answered. "Cream and sugar for me. We're going to need a list of all her friends, Dr. Rendeau."

"I called the ones I know. The others should be in her phone. Oh, my god. Her phone is gone. She must have it with her."

"We'll see if we can track it," Meyers said. "If you give me a list of her friends, we'll be able to get their numbers. We'll have someone interview them."

Detective Donnelly got off the phone and said, "Ms. Garrett didn't answer. I left a message to call the RPD. Dr. Rendeau, if you talk to her, have her call me ASAP. I'll also call the warden at the prison to see if anything out of the ordinary has happened."

"I'd like to get the Hendricksons' number," Detective Donnelly said as Dahlia and Stan came into the room with steaming mugs of coffee and handed them to the detectives.

Despite the dull thud behind my eyes that told me I should drink it, I shook my head and refused the coffee Dahlia placed in front of me.

"You can't possibly think we have anything to do with this, young lady," Dahlia said, giving the detective a dirty look.

"Just covering all the bases, ma'am," Donnelly replied. "I'd like you come down to the station for finger printing, too, if you don't mind. We'll need a sample of everyone's handwriting as well."

"Detective, my in-laws love the children. They would never do anything to harm them," I insisted.

"Again, ma'am, just doing my job. I'd like you both to provide handwriting samples, if you don't mind," the detective informed us.

"We were on a plane! How can you even suggest Alex or I had anything to do with this?" I had tried to keep myself together but a rising panic, as dark and ominous as a sea in winter, threatened to consume me.

Alex attempted to calm me. "Grace, she has to do this. Please."

"In cases like this it's usually family members, ex-care givers, ex-spouses, and so on who take the children. I'm not accusing you, ma'am, just trying to get to the bottom of this. We'll contact the feds, and they'll be in to set up a command center and distribute the children's pictures nationally. The crime scene people will be in to dust for prints and luminol for blood. We're bringing in the K-9 units now, and we've called in the state troopers who'll expand the survey of our mapped coverage area with additional ground and air searches. The department's helicopters do an air-land search to come up with any infra-red sightings in open fields and such."

"Oh, God, do you mean . . . ?" A reeling sensation pulled me away from any semblance of rational thought.

"Not necessarily, ma'am. Just don't want to miss anything," Meyers interjected, as gently as if he were talking to a child. "Oh, and Dr. Rendeau, we're gonna put a tap on your phone in case there are any ransom calls made. Try to keep 'em on the line as long as possible. I have to warn you there'll probably be prank calls to the station made by people saying they want to confess. All of 'em nuts, in it for the attention."

"Can you think of anyone else who would want to take your children?" Detective Donnelly asked bluntly. "Would they have gone to stay with a friend? Were they upset when you left them?"

I shook my head. "No! They were fine. Otherwise, I never would have gone." The words blurred. It felt like I was seeing the world through a pair of cheap reading glasses.

"They were fine," Dahlia repeated, wiping her eyes. "They were looking forward to seeing their mother. They would never have run away. We just went school shopping!"

CHAPTER TWENTY-FIVE

I T LOOKS LIKE THAT'S THEM," Donnelly said when the doorbell chimed. I opened the door to see a gray van, the color of dead skin, outside with ROCHESTER POLICE DEPARTMENT in small letters on the side. Two officers, looking no older than college students dressed in gray RPD tee shirts and jeans stood at the door with a pair of floppy-eared bloodhounds. Behind them, a line of police cruisers screeched into the driveway.

"I'll stay outside with Cagney and Lacey while you guys dust," the taller man said. He identified himself as Josh Warren.

A solid-looking woman with short bleached-blonde hair and a craggy face strode to the door, carrying a small black case. She wore a neutral gray suit and a headset. "Amber Medina." She extended her hand. "And this is Detective Berg," she gestured to a tall young man who looked as though he might have been an underwear model in another life. "Mind if we come in?"

The room began to fill like church on Sunday. Officers Medina and Miles Berg brushed past me. Berg's shoes gleamed so I could almost see my reflection in them. The living room was soon filled with somber looking officers with phones and notepads. The detectives greeted Donnelly and Meyers and donned gloves. "We'll start upstairs. That okay with you, ma'am?"

"They'll get your prints," Donnelly explained to Dahlia and Stan. "And yours." She looked pointedly at Alex and me. "To have on file in case a different print turns up today."

"We got some good matches with the prints you provided, ma'am," Detective Medina said, coming down the stairs. "Several other good prints I'm assuming are yours." She gestured to us. "Two that are clear but unidentified. Trace amounts of blood in the bathroom."

I gasped, tasting the coppery bitterness of it in my mouth.

"Now this could be nothing. They were just trace amounts. Do you know the children's blood types, Dr. Rendeau?"

Yes, they're both A positive."

The second crime scene investigator, Amber Medina, followed with a clear plastic evidence bag. "This is probably the source of the blood," she said, pointing to a shiny razor blade with evidence of blood on it. "I found this in your daughter's room." A sheen of sweat shone on her upper lip.

The air was buzzing with activity. I bought Caleigh pink safety razors when she recently started shaving her legs, and had warned her to be careful. I had no idea where Caleigh would have gotten a straight-edge razor blade.

"The finger prints have to be ours," Stan said. "My wife and I stayed here this past week."

"We'll check that out now, if you don't mind," Medina told Stan. "If you'll come this way, please." He led Stan and Dahlia to the table.

"Warren, you can bring the K9s in now," she instructed the detective a few minutes later. "There are no unidentified prints. Ma'am, do you have something the victims have used recently to give Lacey a scent?"

I raced upstairs, took Caleigh's pink robe from the hook on the back of her door and then picked up Dane's dinosaur pajama top from where it lay under his pillow. Caleigh's robe smelled of her coconut-mango body lotion and Dane's had his own distinct little boy fragrance.

The dog sniffed each item, and Medina gave her a command. She found the scents throughout the house and sat at the front door. The officers let Lacey out and she ran to the driveway and sat down. "She's trained to find the freshest scent, ma'am," Warren explained. "Where the victims last were. Looks like it was here. They must have gotten into a car."

My worst nightmare had just come true. My children had gotten into a car with a stranger.

"One more thing," Detective Donnelly said as we stood there. "Was the note specifically addressed to you, Dr. Rendeau?"

"Well, no, but I assumed . . ." I looked at Alex. "Could it have been meant for you?" I asked. Alex's face had gone as white as a wedding cake. Our lives had inexorably careened out of control. Children, it seemed, went missing all the time. I stood on the tree-choked driveway looking down the road at an imaginary car with my children. My legs buckled underneath me and Alex wrapped his arm around me to steady me. A painful clarity sliced through me like a shard of glass. Maybe it had been too soon for us to think about getting married. I shouldn't have gone on that trip.

When Alex spoke, it was with a tremor in his voice. "Come on, sweetheart, let's go inside. The police will know what to do."

RPD police cruisers and FBI agents swarmed the driveway. Helicopters grumbled overhead. There was a loud knock on the door. I opened it to a thick-necked man, who looked to be about forty-five was stocky, rumpled and red-faced. A man who had seen too much to be shocked by anything introduced himself as FBI Agent Hector Rivera. He had closely cropped graying hair and a no-nonsense demeanor. A command center was being set up at Fire Station 4 on Forty-first Street. He would be in charge of the investigation. "I'd like to ask you a few questions, ma'am." He covered his mouth and coughed explosively. He had as much personality as a paper cup. "Can we sit down somewhere private?"

"Yes, of course. Alex, can you come over here?" Alex was being questioned by the police in the other room.

"Just you, ma'am, if you don't mind. Agent Northrup will be interviewing Dr. Sawyer."

Agent Rivera and I entered the dining room where we could have some privacy from the din outside. Sketcher barked at the K9 Unit scouring the woods behind the house. Agent Rivera asked the same questions the officers had asked me earlier. I couldn't help but notice he had a peculiar facial twitch. His head jerked to the left every minute or so. I felt a ridiculous compulsion to find out why. "Mind telling me about your trip?" he asked.

My throat tightened. "My fiancé and I were on a medical mission to Indonesia. We stayed an extra day in Bali." A napkin left over from our last family dinner sat on the dining room table and I dabbed at my eyes with it. "I couldn't believe we were finally on our way. Alex and I left with two suitcases of medical supplies, clothing for a week, and our computers."

"What day was this?" Rivera asked.

"Last Saturday. God, I wish I'd come home one day sooner. I had been a little worried about the kids the entire time. It was the first time I'd left them since my husband died."

"Sorry to hear that, ma'am. How long has it been?" He jotted notes as we spoke.

"Two years." I wiped my nose with my sleeve.

"How well do you know Mr. Sawyer?" Rivera asked.

"We're engaged! He's a doctor, a good man!" It was as though I were speaking into an unfeeling void.

"How long have you known Doctor Sawyer?" Rivera reiterated. "Did he and your children get along well?"

"Of course they did! You don't think . . ."

"I don't think anything at all, ma'am. Just trying to get the facts. Does Dr. Sawyer live here with you and your children? Any problems between them?"

"No! Well, they were a little upset when I first told them, but we worked it out. Alex loves them. He would never do anything to hurt them. Besides, he was with me in Indonesia!" As I spoke, I realized I was tearing the napkin into pieces. His facial tic was driving me crazy. "The note was here when we arrived."

"And he was with you the entire time? What'd the note say?" The agent took out a handkerchief, wiped his forehead and grimaced. "Who found it?"

"Haven't you seen it? It said, 'Your children are gone. This is what you deserve. I'll be in touch.' I found the note." I clenched my teeth together.

"Have you or your fiancé had any disagreements with anyone lately?"

"No! I haven't and Alex hasn't mentioned anything. What does that have to do with anything?"

Rivera looked at me as though I was holding something back. "What about the grandparents? Are they your parents or your husband's parents?"

"Stan and Dahlia are Matt's parents. They're devastated by this."

"Did the kids ever talk about running away?"

"No! The kids seemed to be fine with the trip. The last couple of months have been going better than I expected." I began to have an uneasy sense of being considered a suspect. I wanted to scream.

"Better than you expected? In what way do you mean?"

I hesitated. "I told you. They were angry at first. I mean, they'd lost their father and you know, it was a little threatening for them to see me involved with someone else. But Alex was really good with them. By the time he moved in, we already felt like a family. Everything was going fine! I spoke to the kids a couple of times during the trip and then two nights before we left, I had a disturbing conversation with Dahlia."

"Dahlia?" He jotted her name in his notebook. "What's the last name?"

"Rendeau. She's the children's grandmother. My late husband's mother. She and her husband stayed here with them. I remember it took several minutes for the call to go through and when I finally got through, Dane sounded like he'd been crying. I asked him what was wrong but there was such a raspy scratching sound, I could hardly hear him. I finally heard him say, 'Mommy, Hope is gone.'" My voice was barely under control.

Rivera waited for a moment, examined his fingernails and tore at a cuticle. "Who's Hope?" he asked.

I winced. "Hope is our puppy. Dahlia got on the line and said she'd disappeared the previous day. It was awful. I was two thousand miles away and I couldn't even comfort my son."

There was a pause. "Did they ever find the dog?" he asked brusquely.

There was no trace of compassion in his eyes. Not for me, not for the children, not even for a missing puppy. I was engulfed by panic and realized I didn't need someone smoldering with emotion. I needed someone who took his job seriously and whose actions were dictated by logic and reason. "I don't think so. I got home today and . . ." My voice quivered before it broke. "Dahlia told me on the phone they hadn't seen the puppy since the day before yesterday. The kids were outside playing with her and she called them in for dinner. They left Hope in the yard for about fifteen minutes and when they went back out, she was gone. The kids were heartbroken."

Rivera glanced at his watch. "Was this what disturbed you?"

"That and . . ."

"Ma'am? Was there something else about the conversation that disturbed you?" He clicked his pen repeatedly.

"It sounded like Dahlia was saying something about breakfast to the kids before she returned to the phone. Then she whispered there was something else she had to tell me. I could hardly hear her. She was crying on the other end. I thought maybe Sketcher, our retriever, was missing too."

"What did she say, Dr. Rendeau?" Rivera removed his glasses and looked at me thoughtfully.

"She said Sketcher was fine. He was asleep on the sofa the entire time. She had called the pound to see if they'd picked up any dogs matching Hope's description. They put up signs and walked around the woods, asked the neighbors . . . she felt terrible."

Rivera resumed clicking his pen again. The world seemed to spin on a different axis.

"Then Dahlia said she thought Caleigh had been cutting herself."

"Your daughter was cutting herself? What did she mean by that?" Agent Rivera scratched his head and wrote something down in his notebook. "How long has this been going on?"

"I don't know." I stiffened, feeling as though I should have known. "That was the first I had heard about it. Dahlia said she noticed marks on Caleigh's arms the day after the puppy disappeared. Little ones scabbed over. Perfectly straight. Dahlia had gone into her room to say good night and she was in pajama pants and a tank top. That's how she noticed them." Time felt as though it had been suspended, the way I'd felt when I fell out of my favorite tree as a child. "There were no words to nail it down. I knew then there was something wrong."

"Did Mrs. Rendeau ask what the marks were?"

"That was the strangest part. Dahlia said Caleigh put on her robe and pretended like there was nothing there. She didn't say she'd been scratching her arm, or been injured somehow. She said it was nothing with a blank expression on her face. I think Dahlia thought it was a reaction to the puppy being missing. Caleigh loved that puppy."

"I'd like to see your itinerary. Where you stayed and your ticket information," Rivera said abruptly. "And your passport." His head jerked to the left again.

"Agent, while you're looking at my ticket information, my children are out there somewhere!" I had been gritting my teeth and my jaw began to ache.

"Ma'am, we have ten agents plus the Rochester Police on this case. We have road blockades set up. Your phone has been tapped. We have people searching a twenty-mile radius of your house. We're looking at all calls made and sent from your house. We're questioning your in-laws, neighbors, co-workers and working with the prison department to see if there's any connection to an inmate. We're checking the registry for any sex-offenders who might have recently moved into the area."

"Right. I'm sorry." Harsh afternoon light flooded the room. I wanted to close my eyes and pretend none of this was happening. "Ask me anything."

There was a brisk knock at the door. A youngish woman with acne-scarred skin and tortoise-frame glasses came into the room. She was tall and as sharp as a ferret in a rabbit hole. She slouched in an effort to make herself look smaller. "Rivera, we're linked. Just wanted to let you know."

"What the hell does that mean?" I interjected.

"It's a computer program that systemizes criminal investigations throughout the country," he explained to me. "Thanks, Sellnow. Let me know if you come up with anything at all." She backed out of the room and Rivera asked, "How long did you say you and Dr. Sawyer have been engaged?"

It was like a fresh wound opening every time I was forced to explain. "A couple of months." The words fell like stones on the table. It was growing warmer in the house. I mopped the sweat off my brow and wondered why Caleigh and Dane had not had the air conditioning on.

Rivera continued to jot notes. "Were the children in the habit of staying home alone? Is anything missing from the house, ma'am?"

"It was only for a couple of hours! Caleigh is almost fourteen. They occasionally stay home by themselves for short periods. Everything seems to be here. We haven't touched anything. The breakfast dishes were on the table and it looks like they hadn't finished eating . . ." My voice had become anxious and high-pitched. Sketcher whined at the door. "The only thing out of the ordinary that happened was the puppy disappearing. Do you think this has anything to do with the kidnapping? They looked everywhere but she never turned up."

"Your father-in-law didn't see anything out of the ordinary? Did they check with the neighbors to see if the pup had wandered over there?"

"Our nearest neighbors are a couple of acres away, Agent. It was only a few minutes. She was a small puppy. She couldn't have gotten that far so quickly. We have an invisible fence and she had her collar on. She was trained not to go near it. Stan said he thought he saw a car down the road which is a little unusual since we're so isolated here." I covered my face with my hands. "Would you excuse me for a moment?" I went into the bathroom for a tissue. The skin around my nostrils had been rubbed raw. My eyes were red and waterlogged from crying. I was teetering on the verge of hysteria.

"Just a few more questions," the agent said when I returned, more gently than I felt I deserved. "I'm sure you know, ma'am, the first few hours in cases like this are crucial to the investigation. Does your daughter have any other psychological issues that would make you think she'd deliberately run away? Have you had any threats made against you by any of your patients?"

"My daughter may have been cutting herself but she would never run away. And then there's Dane . . . Where would they go? I have an elderly patient, named Finn Koski, who was recently released to a halfway house. He wasn't happy about it and I think he blamed me, but there was nothing I could do about it. Josie Garrett, the prison social worker, found him the placement because his family refused to take him in. I saw him one day when I drove by. You know, somebody almost ran into me that day, trying to cut in front of me. I had to slam on the brakes to keep from hitting them. I'd forgotten all about it."

"Okay, Finn Koski. How do you spell that? Anybody else come to mind?"

"Another patient was transferred to the Metropolitan Detention Center in Guaynabo, Puerto Rico. He escaped shortly after he got there. He was escorted by Josie and a marshal. Emanuel Venegas. He had a major affective disorder, and a depressed mood. Psychotic, actually. But over the course of several months, he improved and was transferred to prison to complete his sentence."

"Has he been recaptured?"

"Not as far as I know but I've been gone a week. But surely you don't think he'd come all the way back . . ."

"We can't say for certain what a mental patient would do so we can't rule him out. Can you think of anyone else who might have a grudge against you or Dr. Sawyer?" Agent Rivera sat back in his chair and drummed his fingers along the table.

I shut my eyes and tired to think. "Bud Anderson," I opened my eyes and said. "He's an officer at the prison. He tried to force himself onto me at a Christmas party and I rejected him. Kneed him in the genitals, actually. He was pretty angry."

"Bud Anderson? What's his full name?"

A sense of impending doom pounded like a bass drum. "I think it's Walter. At least that's what his badge says. One night when I was at Alex's, and my in-laws had the kids for the weekend, someone slashed my tires. Josie, my friend, the social worker, said she saw Anderson in his truck and it looked like he was taking pictures of Alex's townhouse. I'm embarrassed to say it, Agent, but we were making love and forgot to close the drapes. I don't know what, if anything, he saw."

"Anyone you know been behaving strangely? Threatened you?"

"Alex's ex-wife called me after she found out we were engaged and told me I'd be sorry, but I chalked that up to jealousy. Alex says she never really got over their divorce. I never heard from her after that one phone call."

"I'd like to talk to your fiancé about this. If anything at all comes to mind, call me," Agent Rivera shut his notebook and put away his pen. "Anything at all, no matter how unimportant it might seem."

CHAPTER TWENTY-SIX

SEPTEMBER 2012

BUD ANDERSON

THE NEWSPAPER WAS SPREAD out over my belly as I lay on the couch, trying to catch a wink before my goddamn three to eleven shift. In a few hours, I'd be heading to the prison. The Sunday visit with Mom and Dad had me running in and out of the bathroom all morning, the way visits with them always do. I slugged another mouthful of Maalox and fell into a nightmare. It was warm that day. For some reason, the sun on my arms and the visit to Mom and Dad's house reminded me of the county fair. It wasn't something I ever thought about so maybe I was dreaming.

I rose with a little boy's anticipation of the day ahead. The curtains were threadbare and faded by summer. Dappled sunlight spilled onto the wide floorboards, the cracked green paint crumbled in flakes. I lay in bed and savored the warmth of a summer morning. I had pushed the twin bed against the wall so I could look at my heroes—you know, the sports posters every kid has in his room. I pictured them talking to me about power, about the ability to face opponents without fear, to resist attack and be tough. These guys, the ones who could slam a ninety-mile-per-hour pitch or had the lightning speed of a running back carrying the pigskin to the end zone, were my heroes. I wanted to slam-dunk. A slam-dunk that would make everything all right again.

I pulled on my tee shirt and shorts and my sister yelled at me to hurry.

We rolled the windows down, the wind hot against our faces. All we could talk about were the animals, the cotton candy, and the midway. Dad was a strong, strapping foreman at the Seneca Foods Plant next to the fairgrounds. He pointed out the water tower, shaped like a sixty-foot ear of corn, storing 50,000 gallons of water. "Seven million nine hundred thousand acres of corn planted that year alone," he said proudly.

We had arrived and Dad paid the admission. A woman with a triangular face and a large tattoo on her arm took the money and handed over our tickets. Inside, vendors hawked lemonade and cheese curds. On the midway, old carnies with nicotine-stained teeth, egged us on to try our hands at winning cheap souvenirs.

The sun was high. Hot, dry dust rose to coat our faces. Streaks of dirt mixed with sweat drew crooked lines in my sister's elbow creases. Dad bought cotton candy. I took one bite before dropping it.

"What the hell, Buddy?" Dad swore. "I paid good money for that." Right then I knew something bad was going to happen.

In the 4H tents, my sister laughed about the large floppy-eared rabbits nibbling feed pellets. Dad bought a handful and lifted her up so she could feed them. I breathed in the smells. The dusty, green smell of hay, the manure, the horses' sweat. They whinnied in their stalls, thrilling me when I walked by.

Dad carried Sharon on his shoulders and Mom and I struggled to keep pace. Everywhere there were sounds. "Buy your corn-on-the-cob, corn-dogs, cornbread, corn muffins, corn pudding. Corn Carnival in Mankato coming up next!"

Mom was ridiculously dressed in bright yellow pants and high heels. She looked like a canary let out of its cage, confused about which way to go. I stayed with her, carrying the goldfish I had won in a plastic bag. "For crissakes, can't you keep up?" Dad snapped. "I haven't got all day here." I pleaded with her to hurry.

At home, I shut his eyes and covered my ears to the shouts behind their bedroom door. I was hungry and my belly full of dread, when he yelled, "No matter what I do, you're never happy."

Mommy came out of the room, stony faced as Dad slammed the front door shut and threw our battered old suitcase into the pickup. He turned and nodded to me. I stood at the front door crying. "Daddy, no, don't go!"

* * *

A KNOCK AT THE DOOR which sounded like it had been going on for a while woke me.

"Bud Anderson?" a man and a woman flashing police badges were standing on the cement step. "I'm Detective Meyers. This is Detective Donnelly." A tall man in a checked sport jacket with dandruff on the shoulders pointed to a middle-aged woman with a pinched face and a surly manner. "Mind if we come in?"

"What's going on?" I shook myself awake and wished there wasn't an empty six-pack by the couch and that the house didn't look so run-down.

"Just a friendly chat, that's all." They edged their way in through the crowded hallway. "Moving somewhere?" Donnelly asked, skirting around the boxes stacked three feet high on the floor.

"Just moved in. Haven't had a chance to unpack yet." I cleared the sofa of newspapers and paper plates. "Have a seat. What's this all about?"

"We have a few questions we'd like to ask you, pertaining to the disappearance of the children of one of your co-workers," Detective Meyers said. His pistol glared from its holster.

"I don't know what the hell you're talking about."

"Not so quick there, buddy. Did you know Dr. Grace Rendeau's children have been reported missing?" Detective Donnelly asked, looking directly at me.

"How the fuck would I know that? I've had a few days off."

"Do you mind telling us what you did during those few days off?" she asked in a more accusatory tone than was called for.

It was getting stuffy in the small living room. "Actually, yes, I do mind." I stood and opened a window. Without my boots on and without the orthotic, I limped a little. That bitch, Grace, must have given my name to the cops.

"We could bring you down to the station, if you'd prefer." Donnelly crossed her arms over her chest, cool and composed.

"Fuck. Okay. Anything you want to ask me, you can ask me right here." I wiped my forehead with the back of my hand, a gesture which had caused Donnelly to raise her eyebrows. "This is crazy! You think I have something to do with those kids being missing?"

"Mr. Anderson, where were you on Sunday, August twenty-sixth?" Detective Meyers asked.

"I was home. I made lunch. Went out to do a little fishing."

"What time was this?" Donnelly looked to be inspecting her fingernails.

Sharp-nosed little terrier bitch. "Around twelve."

"Anybody see you?"

"How the hell do I know? I have a canoe. After I ate, I put it in the truck, took it over to the Zumbro River, got in and spent a couple of hours communing with nature."

"Then where did you go?" Donnelly barked.

"I didn't want to go home. I wanted to surprise my parents. My mother's eighty-years old, so I drove out to Red Wing. They had just gotten home from eating lunch at the old St. James Hotel. It was good to be with them so I stayed. I played video games in their basement. You can call and ask them. They'll tell you. I was on Xbox Live, logged in under my screen name, MilitaryMight, the whole time."

"We tried to call earlier. Why didn't you answer your phone Mr. Anderson?"

"I must have been on my way back. I left my phone at home. I realized it when I was halfway to Red Wing and didn't want to turn around and come back for it."

"Where was your car while you were visiting your parents?"

"My car was in their garage. Look, what is this? I have kids of my own. I'd never hurt anybody's kids. Here's my parents' number. Call them. They'll tell you I was there from Sunday afternoon at around 2:00 p.m. until today. I got home this afternoon and heard the news on the radio and the next thing I know I'm a suspect. I don't know what the fuck is happening here, but you've got the wrong guy. I've already told you everything I know."

"If you'll just give me that number, I'll certainly be calling. Probably paying a little visit too," Detective Donnelly said. "So, which is it? You didn't know anything about the Rendeau kids being missing or you did know? 'Cause it seems to me it's either one way or the other."

I gave her the number. "Jesus. My mother's eighty-years old. You're gonna give her a heart attack . . . I didn't know until I got home today."

The detective opened the door and stepped outside. Meyers sat on the couch. I reached in my pocket for a handkerchief and wiped a line of sweat dribbling down my cheek. I felt as though I had just farted in church. He didn't look like the kind of guy who wanted to chitchat about the weather. Detective Donnelly's voice drifted in from outside the screen door. "If you don't mind, ma'am, I'd like to ask you a few questions. Yes, ma'am, that's fine. Put your husband on the phone."

"So, when did this happen?" I finally asked Meyers. "I mean, Dr. Rendeau's kids. What happened?"

Meyers didn't seem to want to make conversation. He stared me in the eye. "Why don't you tell me?"

I took out my handkerchief out again and wiped my mouth. "I got nothin' to tell," I said deliberately.

The wind blew the screen door wide open and Donnelly's nasally voice ricocheted into the living room. "Hello, Mr. Anderson? This is Detective Donnelly from the Rochester Police Department speaking. Your son is here with me. I'd like a few words with you, if you don't mind. It's about your son, Bud Anderson. No, he's fine. I'm just checking on his whereabouts this morning. All morning? Thank you, sir. Good-bye."

She came into the house and avoided looking at me. "I understand there have been some hard feelings between you and Dr. Rendeau."

"Just a little misunderstanding, that's all," I answered with a nervous laugh.

"Care to let us in on this little misunderstanding?"

"I was drunk, okay? She's hot. I tried to kiss her and she kneed me in the nuts. Period. End of story." I knew they knew I was breathing faster.

Donnelly's eyes glinted like a dog's. "How'd you react to that, Anderson? Must've made you pretty angry, huh? A big strapping hunk like you to be rejected like that?"

"It happens. Look, I got over it. If it wasn't for that meddling dyke Garrett it would've been the end of the story." Why the hell didn't the landlord put in the freakin' AC when I asked him to?

"Can you think of anyone else who would want to take Dr. Rendeau's children?" Donnelly asked.

"Why don't you ask Garrett? She's a real bitch. Probably do anything to make it look like I had something to do with this."

"Mind if we take a look around?" Donnelly asked as she stood. Her gaze traveled around the room.

"Not at all. Go right ahead. I got nothin' to hide."

Fifteen minutes later, Donnelly said, "If anything comes to mind, give me a call," and slapped her card down on the table. "Don't leave town."

"We'll be checking with the gaming site, Anderson," Meyers said. He snorted. "You wouldn't be the first one who tried to pull the 'I was signed on' alibi. Get a subpoena for the site and the names of the gamers he supposedly played with to verify whether he was active or just logged on, will ya?" he said to Donnelly.

CHAPTER TWENTY-SEVEN

T HE LAYERS OF GOOSE DOWN were suffocating but all I wanted to do was lie there under the weight of my despair. *The Black Dog.* Churchill's name for his gloomy periods. I felt the black dog beside me, as faithful as any dog had ever been. The numbers on my alarm clock swam into view. Noon. Alex must have left for work hours ago. I had swallowed a sleeping pill sometime during the night and was still in a groggy state between sleeping and waking when the phone rang.

"Dr. Rendeau. Meyers here. I understand you have serious reason to believe Finn Koski threatened you in the last session before his discharge?"

"What?" I sat up straighter, still disoriented.

"I've been reading over your patient notes . . ."

"Aren't those confidential?" I was finding it difficult to follow any rational train of thought. It was as if the wheel spun around me but the hamster was dead.

"Dr. Rendeau, this is a criminal investigation. The records were subpoenaed. Koski made a threat against you. Unless the medical center wanted to block it, Warden Briscoe had no choice but to hand them over."

"Finn Koski is an elderly man who killed his wife in an act of mercy, Detective," I insisted and then gulped greedily from a glass of water on the night table. I felt as nauseous and hung-over as when I'd drank peach schnapps in college. I'd never been able to look at it again. "He was upset about being discharged, yes, but I didn't take it as threatening."

"I have Koski here saying, 'Congratulations. You must not know anything about halfway houses, young lady. Or about being unwanted. I'm sorry, but this is not the last you'll hear of me.' You didn't take this as a threat, Doctor?"

"No, I . . . I thought he was distraught at the time. I didn't take it as a threat or we wouldn't have released him. I guess working with psychiatric inmates has taught me something. I can distinguish real threats from run-of-the-mill bull, Detective."

"Just the same. I'm having him brought in for questioning right now."

"I'm quite sure he would never do anything to harm me or my children. I've seen him outside Oakwood Manor. Josie found him a job at a nursery. He's eighty-years old, for God's sake."

"The other lead we're following is Emanuel Venegas. He is a patient of yours, I believe?"

"Yes. He was transferred to Puerto Rico during the time I was away. He actually did make a threat, but it was against an FBI agent."

"He escaped days after being transferred to the Detention Center, and has not been recaptured to date."

"I heard. Josie brought him there with a marshal."

"She and Officer William Torres delivered Venegas to the Metropolitan Detention Center without incident by air charter with a flight crew, an armed lieutenant, a medical assistant and car escorts. Two days later, Juan Ríos Maldonado, an individual who worked for a company which had a contract to supply produce to the federal prison's kitchen, assisted him in breaking out during a shift change. The United States attorney for the District of Puerto Rico announced his escape."

Oh, God. At one point, he was psychotic, but he had been doing so well. He couldn't have come back. "Why would he come back here? As tight as airline security is these days, I can't see him going anywhere near an airport if he doesn't want to be recaptured."

The hangover from the sleeping meds began to dissipate as I pondered these developments. "Detective, isn't it true most children who are abducted know their abductors? I just don't see why Mr. Koski or Emanuel would have any reason to harm Caleigh and Dane."

"We're following every lead, Grace. These are dangerous men we're talking about. Anybody else ever threatened you that you can recall?"

"No!" I held my head in my hands and then dropped the phone and rushed to the bathroom. I retched until only copious amounts of acidic yellow bile splashed into the toilet. Cold sweat ran off my forehead as I dry heaved. I washed my face, my tears mixing with sweat.

Back in bed, I dialed Detective Meyers' number. "Detective, I'm sorry. I was sick. I just don't know how much longer I can take this."

The AC blew full blast and I shivered. "Detective, Dayna Light, a psychic, called my service and left a message saying she said she might be able to help. Dayna's a spiritualist, a psychic detective of sorts."

"Grace, listen to me before you say anything. We've received dozens of calls from so-called psychics," Meyers grumbled. "They've never provided any information we've been able to use in a case of missing persons. They're actually harmful because we have to waste a lot of police and volunteer effort and resources following up on their worthless 'clues.' She claims she 'sees things' have never been proven. She says she has psychic abilities but who's to say?"

"But what if she's right? What if this is the once-in-a-million chance she could provide some information?"

"I can't stop you from going, but just keep in mind what I've told you, okay? After the Elizabeth Smart case, the police got as many as nine thousand tips from people who called themselves psychics. It took a lot of police hours to respond to all these tips and in the end, I know it wasn't a psychic tip that helped nab the guy. It was someone who recognized Elizabeth on the street from seeing a report of the kidnapping on America's Most Wanted. I'd like for you to consider giving an interview, Grace. Get their faces out there."

"I can't even leave the house without reporters swarming me like barracudas, detective. But if you think it would help . . ."

"I do. I have someone on KTTC news who I'd like you to talk to, Grace. I want to get your children's faces out ASAP. Appeal to people's emotions. Someone may recognize them or see something odd. That's what usually happens, Grace. The FBI and U.S. Marshals service also announced a reward of up to $50,000 for information leading to the location of the children."

Meyers hung up and I sat listening to a dead phone before calling Dahlia. My mother-in-law answered on the first ring.

"Dahlia?"

"Oh, Grace. Is there anything new? Oh, Grace, you don't know how terrible Stan and I feel." She broke down and sobbed. "It's all my fault. If only I hadn't left them. I'll never forgive myself for this."

"Dahlia, listen. A psychic called me. She lives up in Stillwater. She said she might have some information. I want you to go with me. Her name is Dayna Light."

"Are you sure this is wise? You know I'll do anything to help but I don't know if you should get your hopes up by something like this."

I pictured Dahlia sitting and waiting for God to intervene. "Will you go with me or not? I'll call her and see when she's available."

Ten minutes later, I was on the phone with Dahlia again. "She'll see us at two. We'd better be on the move. Stillwater's at least an hour and a half away. She said to bring something personal, an item of clothing or something Dane and Caleigh have worn recently."

* * *

DO YOU REALLY THINK SHE CAN HELP?" Dahlia asked as we merged onto Highway 52 North. "I've heard the police have used psychics a few times but they say there's no proof their information is real. I just don't know about this. What if this comes from a dark place? What if it comes from Satan and his demons?"

"Oh, for God's sake, Dahlia. You can't really believe that, can you? Even if there's a chance in a million what she says is true, I have to try." I stroked Caleigh's bathrobe and Dane's pajama top. "I'm sorry. I know this is hard for you too."

Dahlia had aged in the few weeks since the children's disappearance. She sat and stared as impassively as a bus driver collecting tokens, but I could tell I had hurt her. Her eyes were downcast. She had her rosary beads in hand, and silently mouthed what I imagined were the sorrowful mysteries. Finally, she brought the crucifix to her lips and kissed it.

Life had pulled the rug out from both of us. Matt and I had planned our lives so carefully and now it had played the cruelest jokes imaginable on us. First, Matt's death and now this. I had lost my place in the life I had so carefully constructed. My illusion of control tumbled with each fallen brick.

Stillwater was a small town nestled in the bluffs of the St. Croix River, about twenty miles east of St. Paul. With only about 18,000 residents, it was quaint as a picture postcard. I wanted to shrink from my chaotic reality and howl like a wounded animal on the street. We turned onto Nelson Street, along the river and parked behind a two-story red-brick building. Santosha Studio was on the first floor of the picturesque building. Dayna's studio was the first door on the right.

A woman with silver-streaked hair, pulled into a waist-length braid greeted us. "Welcome, Grace. And this must be Mrs. Rendeau." The women shook hands firmly. Dayna's green eyes, watery behind thick, iron-rimmed glasses were as deep as a pool. Her long drop earrings had violet gemstones and dangled almost to her shoulders. Her skin was ivory satin. Her age was impossible to determine. She was dressed casually in a loose flowing fern-green skirt, long-sleeved white blousy top, and sandals.

"Won't you come in?" Her voice was breathy and soothing. I felt calmer than I had felt since the nightmare began.

"Go ahead, Grace. I'll be right here," Dahlia said, sitting down on a love seat in the waiting room. Bamboo shades were drawn in several windows, allowing filtered afternoon light to bathe the office.

"Are you sure you don't want to come in?" I asked Dahlia.

Whether it was because of her religious or personal beliefs, she refused. Natural wood-paned French windows were open to the outside air. A few moments in the sun might do Dahlia some good and if there was anything to this business, I couldn't risk Dahlia's skepticism scaring anybody off.

I entered the room and had a sudden impulse to take my shoes off and bury my feet into the lush thick-pile carpet. Instead, I lowered myself onto a cranberry-colored leather sofa. Several thriving potted plants and a gurgling aquarium provided a splash of color to the neutral tones of the walls and carpet. Expecting something out of a Stephen King novel, I was relieved to see bright tropical fish providing a welcome sense of normalcy. A table opposite the window, surrounded by four straight-backed chairs similar to those in the waiting room, looked out onto the street. I wondered but didn't dare ask if this was where Dayna held séances. There were no crystal balls or Ouija boards.

"I'm a medium. An intermediary between the world of the living and the world of the dead. I listen to the spirits of those who have passed and pass on any messages they want to send," Dayna said, sitting directly across from me. "May I have the items please?" She closed her eyes and the room seemed to turn inward.

"There has been a death," she said quietly without opening her eyes.

I gasped. The world revolved in rapid-fire revolutions, sucking the air right out of me. "It's a man, someone you loved very much," Dayna said, opening her eyes and looking at me. "Am I right?"

I nodded. My heart was a beating bruise. "My husband died two years ago."

"He died at home but had been away."

"Yes, he died at home after a nine-month illness. He was in the hospital frequently during the last few months," I whispered. The aquarium gurgled and I turned to look wondering if it was a sign of some sort.

"He wants you to know he is happy, and he wants you to be happy as well." The light in the room seemed to grow dimmer. I watched, mesmerized as Dayna's brows knit together. "I see a boy. A young child."

It was as though a boxer was sparring with the inside of my lungs. I couldn't breathe. I had hoped but really hadn't expected any contact with the supernatural. I grasped the armrest of the sofa and leaned forward, speechless.

"A girl. They are together, but it's cold and dark. No sound except for some sort of hissing noise."

"Are they okay? Do you see anyone with them?"

Dayna's foam-green eyes focused on me. She shook her head and seemed to return from a trance-like state. "That's all I could see. The images are like pictures. They flit very quickly across my mind. They are alive. I'm sorry I can't tell you more."

"Thank you! They're alive, I knew it! Dahlia!" I opened the door to the waiting room. "They're alive!"

An uncertain look passed between Dahlia and Dayna Light, but I paid no attention. "How about we stop for a cup of coffee before heading back?" Dahlia suggested. "I saw a place nearby called the Dock Café. The sign said they offer lunch and dinner."

"I can't wait to tell you what she said." I felt more optimistic than I had since the children were taken.

We sat at an outdoor table. The sun shone on the restaurant deck without a hint of forgiveness. Relieved to be in the shade of the large patio umbrella, I twisted my damp hair into a knot and secured it with a clip, less stylish than practical. Our seating afforded us a view of the river. There were several canoes passing by and a couple stepping off the dock onto a gondola. We ordered two coffees from a bosomy young woman with short, spiked, black hair.

As I was about to tell Dahlia what Dayna saw, my phone vibrated and I jumped. It was Detective Meyers.

"Grace? Meyers. I've got the interview lined up for the day after tomorrow, 5:00 p.m."

"Detective, I just saw Dayna Light. They're alive!" I said with a surge of optimism coursing through my veins.

Resignation echoed in his voice. "Don't get your hopes up, Grace. You can tell me all about it on Thursday. I'll pick you up. There are bound to be a lot of media around. Four thirty, okay?"

"I'll be ready. That was Detective Meyers," I told Dahlia. "We'll be on the news on Thursday. It's a good thing to get the children's faces out there, in case someone has missed all the fliers we've put up around town. Dahlia, Dayna connected with Matt!" I said with less excitement than I'd had before speaking to Meyers.

The older woman's hands flew to the crucifix at her throat. She made the sign of the cross over her heart and closed her eyes.

"Dahlia!" I went around the table and took her hand. "Here, take a sip of water. It's okay. He's fine. She told me she saw the death of a man I love very much and he wants us to know he's fine. I just don't know what to believe. How could Dayna have known about Matt's death?"

"Grace, I have to tell you the Bible gives us no reason to believe deceased loved ones can contact us." Dahlia breathed deeply. "What did she say about the children?"

A cold chill traveled through my body. "She saw them in some sort of cold, dark place with a hissing noise."

"Oh, no!" Dahlia picked up a napkin to wipe her eyes. "Does that mean . . ."

"No! She said it was a flitting image, but they're together and they're alive! I have to believe they're okay."

"Oh, Grace. I don't know what to believe. I need to talk to Father Tupper about this."

Dayna's startling revelations brought back the painful memories that being with Alex had all but erased. I stirred my coffee absently and stared at the young couple in the gondola. "Dahlia, we've never really talked about the last months of Matt's life. Would it upset you too much?" The quick pinprick of pain I always felt when thinking of Matt's death jabbed at me, although I knew the memories had begun to shrink. I was terrified to think someone I had once loved more than anyone could begin to fade like laundry on a line.

"No, sweetheart. I always thought it would be too painful for you to talk about." Dahlia smiled. "For as long as I could remember, Matt wanted to be a doctor. Stan and I were so proud when he got into the University of Minnesota Medical School."

"Do you remember the apartment he lived in, in Dinkytown, when he rotated at the University Hospital?" I laughed, the pain becoming more of a dull ache. "He had to share a bathroom with four female students and hated being late."

"I sure do. Once Matthew graduated, and he took the position at Mayo Clinic, his living situation improved dramatically."

"Yes, but the hour-and-a half trip between Rochester and Minneapolis was hell. It was so much easier once we got married."

"Matt was lucky to find someone like you. Stan and I have always loved you as a daughter, my dear." Dahlia covered my hand with her own.

"After that it was four years of residency training, and Caleigh was born." I remembered the day with perfect clarity. "It was one of the happiest days of my life. I still can't believe what happened. Matt's illness. We were so happy. After Dane was born, we really had it all." I remembered bringing the tiny bundle wrapped in blue blankets home. The pain of not having my children in my arms felt like the phantom limb pain amputees described. "I was so angry when Matt died."

"Do you want to talk about it, Grace?"

"A light snow had fallen that day. We went to the clinic and rode the elevator to the eighth floor. It was horrifying to think Matt was a patient there."

Dahlia sniffled. "Matt's care was so draining for you. Stan and I enjoyed the better days when we could take him for drives in the country, just like everyone else, enjoying life. Do you remember when we all went to the eagle center in Wabasha and saw the bald eagles over the Mississippi? Remember that tiny town, Stockholm, Wisconsin?" she laughed. "Population ninety-seven! We had coffee and fresh-baked pie. What was the name of that place? It was the best apple pie I'd ever eaten. The Stockholm Pie Company! That's it."

"Those are such bittersweet memories, aren't they? Later he began to dread the chemo. It was clear to me he wasn't going to make it when the cancer metastasized to his liver." Dahlia tugged her sweater on as the sun dipped below the horizon and a chill wind sprung up off the river. "His fingernails and toenails, his lips. They were all blue. The light in his eyes dimmed. The nausea and vomiting were so hard. He finally said he didn't think he could do it anymore." The memory brought him back as vividly as a slap.

"If it wasn't for my faith and for Stan, and you, and the kids, I don't know how I would've gotten through it." Dahlia reached for her crucifix again. "Are you cold, dear?"

"A little bit. Do you remember when we positioned his bed in front of the living room window so he could look out at winter one last time? I sat with him and held his hand and he seemed at peace. And then one afternoon it was over." The temperature was dropping and I hugged myself. "Afterwards, I felt so ashamed at how angry I was at him for leaving us."

"We've been through a lot, haven't we, sweetheart?" she asked.

"Dahlia?" I steeled myself. "We haven't talked about Alex. I know how hard this must be for you . . ."

Dahlia hugged me. "Alex is a good man, Grace. I see how happy he makes you. It's time for you to move on, dear. I know you'll get the children back and that you and Alex and the children will be able to rebuild your lives."

CHAPTER TWENTY-EIGHT

THE CEILING FAN WHIRLED lackadaisically overhead. I dabbed cotton balls soaked in calamine lotion on the weepy red rash on Alex's arms and legs. He had spent the day scouring the woods with volunteers who had banded together to search for Caleigh and Dane. The result was a bad case of poison ivy. The cool compresses seemed to ease his irritated skin as much as my guilt about everything that had gone wrong in our lives.

"She went into some kind of trance and then said they're alive," I said. "It's a good sign, don't you think?" Alex rolled down his sleeves and pants legs and held me close. I pulled away. "I'm gonna change, okay? Goodnight."

"Grace, I . . ."

We lay in bed in sweltering heat and I got up, not wanting to hear the rest. I went into the bathroom, and, in the mirror, saw a woman with lines of grief etched on her face, a woman heavy with sadness. Tired circles and a fine patchwork of lines surrounded her eyes. They were edged red with fatigue. I ran a brush through the tangles of my hair, which once glowed with fiery hues, but was now dry and flat. Gray shadows which looked like they had been shaded in with charcoal smudged my eyes.

Alex was already asleep and snoring softly when I stumbled back to bed. The room was unbearably warm and my chest heaved under my nightshirt. Unable to sleep, I opened the windows and padded quietly downstairs. I went into the kitchen for a glass of water and opened the lead-paneled glass doors of my chipped cabinets. I had never gotten around to having them refinished. My grandmother's delicate teacup collection sat behind those doors. I took one out and ran my fingers around the gold rim of the fragile china, missing Nana. They had been my mother's gift to me on my wedding day. Thank God, Nana was not here to see what had happened.

Alex was still snoring when I returned to lie beside him. My night-gown stuck to my back, my breasts were heavy underneath the sleeve-less cotton gown. The children were my last thought before I fell into a restless sleep.

I dreamed of them that night. After what seemed like hours, I sat up in bed, dazed and disoriented, and remembered with a pang they were gone. The next thing I knew, the first rays of sunrise streaked across the sky. I called the hospital to say I wouldn't be coming in to work yet. I asked about Josie but she hadn't retuned yet either. Strange that Josie hadn't called.

Another day went by without a word. How was it possible two children could disappear without a trace? That no one would have seen a thing? I pulled the sheet over my head to block the morning sun and remembered the solace I found in this house after Matt's death, even in the isolation of Minnesota's long, dark winters. Once Alex moved in, it had begun to feel like home. That happy family felt like a lifetime ago. Maybe it had been too much too soon to have Alex move in. I thought I'd been a good mother but perhaps I'd missed something. Certainly, I hadn't always been as patient or as understanding as I might have been.

The urge to stay in bed was almost unbearable but I knew I had to get up and do something. I dialed Detective Meyers's number but the call went directly to voicemail. Why had I imagined he would be in his office at six in the morning? I returned to bed and I as lay there in a dizzy, fitful sleep, I heard Caleigh's voice. "Caleigh!" I cried as I woke. Hope roared in my chest but after I'd run to her room, silence filled my ears. Was my mind playing tricks on me? A picture of Caleigh at age eight, in which she had a crooked part in her hair, and a pink scalp and sun-bleached pigtails, hung on the wall. A golden coating of freckles danced across her cheeks.

"Couldn't sleep?" Alex stood in the doorway.

I hastily put the picture down, not wanting to admit I'd heard Caleigh's voice. I told him I'd been preoccupied with my interview that afternoon and providing cold drinks and snacks for the tireless volun-teers. Alex promised to buy bottled water and snacks and then took me in his arms. "Sweetheart, are you sure you want me to go to work today? I'm sure I could wangle another week off under the circum-stances. Do you want me to be here with you?"

But there was nothing else he could do. His patients needed him too. "Why don't you hop in the shower and I'll make you some breakfast. You've barely eaten all week," he suggested.

The scalding water felt good against my skin. I lathered my hair and dragged my nails across my scalp, rinsed it and wrung out it out until it hurt. I stepped out of the shower, wrapped a towel around me and wrote the children's names in the mirror. Caleigh Rachel Rendeau. Dane Michael Rendeau. Soon, the smell of fresh coffee and sizzling bacon and the sound of Alex's voice calling me down to eat broke my reverie. An odor I would once have found delicious now threatened to make me sick. I descended the stairs in my ratty bathrobe to a table already set for breakfast.

"After the interview, why don't you try to get out today?" Alex asked. "Maybe take a walk with Sketcher? If there's any news, Detective Meyers can reach you on your cell."

A triangle of toast with butter and jam and bacon and eggs sat on my plate. Breakfast was achingly quiet without the children. The slimy yolk dripped off my fork onto the plate and I knew I wouldn't be able to eat it.

Alex pulled his sleeves down and scraped my uneaten breakfast into the trashcan. "I'm worried about leaving you here alone. Are you sure you don't want me to stay?"

But there was nothing he could do. Besides, I had Sketcher with me. There was a time when a day wasn't enough time to do all I had to do. After Alex kissed me good-bye at the door, I was left with the prospects of a long day of quiet and regret. I was fatigued and distracted, plagued by the unmoving silence. I had to force myself not to give in to the desire to go back to bed.

The interview was not for several hours. It was time to unpack. The shadow puppets Alex and I bought lay on top of our clothes. I closed the suitcase quickly, feeling as flat and dead as the shadow puppet.

Maybe Alex was right. It was time to get out of the house. At the bottom of my drawer was a pair of yoga pants which bagged at the knees and hung on me like wash on a clothesline. I had retrieved my yoga mat from the closet and tried to concentrate on my breath entering and leaving my body, to rise above the pain and focus on the healing energy of my breath and maybe even of the universe. In the worst times, my mat had been an oasis. In that moment, it was all I could do to be present and focus on the ocean-like waves and the sound of my breath. And pray.

Afterwards, I felt calmer than I had felt all week and thought I would attempt a trip to the grocery store. I opened the refrigerator and then closed it. I opened it again, the way Caleigh and Dane did, expecting new contents to magically materialize. With my grocery list in hand, I drove to the supermarket, marveling that life had managed to go on despite the children's abduction.

* * *

TRADER JOE'S WAS PAINFULLY COLD. A mother with two young children in her cart passed me as I stood in the entrance not sure of what to do. The younger child, a boy, smiled and waved. Bleary-eyed, I made my way through the refrigerated store gathering the necessities from an overwhelming number of choices. I shifted from one foot to the other in the checkout line and saw the headlines. *Doctor in Bali on Vacation While Children Are Abducted.*

"Hey, you forgot your groceries!" the cashier yelled as I staggered blindly to the door.

* * *

THE PHONE WAS RINGING when I arrived home. My hands shook too badly to open the door in time. The caller ID said Rochester Police Department. "Detective? It's Grace Rendeau." My heart rattled in my chest. "Have you heard something?"

"Just checking in. I'm sorry there is no news to report but I wanted to assure you I am working on this case twenty-four seven. You ready for the interview? They want you in the studio at four-thirty. I'll be there at four. They'll do it live on the five o'clock news."

"Will you come on with me?" I asked piteously.

"I can't answer any questions about the investigation. But I'll be there for moral support," Meyers assured me.

* * *

CANDY SUTHERLAND'S PLATINUM-colored hair wrapped around her head like a helmet. I couldn't help but picture an insect caught in the journalist's sticky web of hair. There was a line of peach-colored pancake makeup below her jaw. The make-up man wiped Candy's face with a powdery finish just before they went on the air. Everything about her was phony—from her solicitous manner to her artificial nails. She wore Manolos, a wasp-waisted Chanel suit and a Rolex.

"Good evening. I'm Candy Sutherland." She beamed toward the imaginary audience. "Tonight we have with us Dr. Grace Rendeau, whose children have been missing for almost a week. Dr. Rendeau, can you tell us when you first discovered your children were missing?" Pictures of a smiling Dane and Caleigh in the video monitor beamed through the studio. "Dr. Rendeau, when did you first discover your children missing?" the news anchor repeated, her smile beginning to fade.

I stared dumbly from the children's pictures to Candy's heavily lined glittering eyes. Bright lights shone on me and a warm flush crept up toward my face. My sweater chafed at my neck. I brought my hands to my neck and felt the red, raised surfaces of hives beginning to develop and wished I hadn't worn wool. "One week ago. I came home from a medical mission trip. My in-laws had been staying with them, but when I got home, they were gone." I dabbed at my eyes with a balled up tissue.

"Your in-laws had no clue where the children might be?" Candy looked first at me and then into the camera, pursing her lips. There was a fine web of lines at the corners of Candy's eyes. The lights buzzed.

"No. They'd gone to church. The children wanted to be home when I got home. When I got home, they were gone. Please, please if anyone out there has seen or knows anything about the whereabouts of my children, call the police and help to bring them home." My pressured speech hung over me like a guilty conscience.

"Thank you, Dr. Rendeau. If anyone has seen six-year-old Dane Rendeau, or thirteen-year-old Caleigh Rendeau, please call the number on your screen." Time-lapsed photographs of the children from toothless grinning infants to Caleigh's self-conscious smile as a sixth grader with braces flashed on the screen. "And now we go to Trevor Jorgenson. Trevor, can we expect this beautiful weather to continue?" Candy slid smoothly into the next segment and I was shown off the set, my tragedy already relegated to old news. The taste was as bitter as quinine.

"You did good, Grace," Meyers said afterwards. "Just the right amount of desperation to show what a caring and loving parent you are. Honestly, we're bound to get a lot of crank calls after this but we'll investigate every one. Somebody out there has to have seen something they may not even have known was significant at the time. Someone stopping at a rest stop or a gas station or for fast food with two kids. These pictures will jar somebody's memory."

Through the evening rush-hour drive home, the interview replayed itself over and over again in my head. I arrived home and went back to bed, until Alex's car pulled up the drive. "Is there any mail?" I asked, my hands tracing the creases from the bedcovers that were embedded in my forehead.

"No mail. Come on. Let's go out and get something to eat. You have to eat."

"What if the children come home and we're not there?"

"They'll call, Grace. The police will call."

* * *

THE OVERCOOKED HAMBURGERS and greasy fries did not settle well. Alex meant well but I had made up my mind. I no longer wanted to leave home for any reason. At home, Sketcher rubbed against my legs and whined. "You hungry, boy?" I scooped a cup of dry food out of the bag. Even Sketcher seemed listless. I brought him outside and sat on the front step while he watered the rhododendron. "If only you could talk, boy. I have a feeling you might be able to tell us something. Come on, let's get inside," I said to the dog and then checked the answering machine for messages and trudged back up to bed.

CHAPTER TWENTY-NINE

I WORKED HARD TO STAY BUSY. The city's streets exploded with Missing posters, many of which I had put up with Dahlia and Stan. I had never truly realized the magnitude of sadness the anonymous faces on Crime Stopper posters symbolized until they were my own children's faces. In the past two weeks, thousands of volunteers had put up fliers in gas stations and fast food restaurants throughout Minnesota. They even distributed them at yesterday's Twins game.

When there was nothing else I could do, I returned home to an empty house. I wanted to go for a run but couldn't quite force myself to do it. Instead, I sat on the porch, feeling like a gutted fish. The air was warm and heavy. A hummingbird fluttered between yellow and purple coneflowers, its tail feathers vibrating rapidly. Dane had been amazed, just last summer, to learn hummingbirds could fly backwards. He and Stan had made birdhouses while Caleigh picked wildflower bouquets and I sat outside watching.

The FBI and the K9 unit had combed the silent meadows and woods behind the house for days. The bloodhounds were given the scent of the kids' clothes but it led only to the middle of the driveway. It was still impossible for me to believe the children had gotten into a car with a stranger. Should I have emphasized the dangers of getting into a car with strangers even more than I did? Was there something I could have said that would have made a bigger impact on them?

The wind chimes tinkled a chilling lullaby. Orange streaks from the setting sun glinted on the meadow and emblazoned it with a sea of color. My eyes watered from the blooming ragweed and sagebrush. The scorching days of summer had collided with the shorter days of autumn.

A musky scent blew through the air reminding me of Dane on a summer night, just before his bath. The breeze rustled my own unwashed hair and the approaching chill wrapped around me. A school bus stopped down the road, its red flashing lights shining in the distance. I pictured the children's faces pressed against the windowpanes, and Dane climbing off the bus. The afternoon gloom slowly descended and, as the bus pulled away, Alex's car rounded the bend and pulled into the driveway. "You're out," he said, smiling, and then reached in the backseat for the groceries. He set the groceries down and kissed me. He told me he had gone to the bank to set up a reward for information leading to the children's safe return.

I shrank like a fine washable run through the dryer. A reward for information for a safe return sounded ominous. "Oh, Alex . . . I really have to get out of here. Run a little."

He picked up the groceries and pushed the door open with his foot. "Do you want me to go with you?"

"No, I need to be alone. You understand, right?"

"How about if I rustle up something for us to eat while you're gone?" he asked.

I gave him a weak smile and plugged my headphones into my iPod. Would I really be able to set one foot in front of the other? Would I ever enjoy eating again? I set off at a slow jogging pace to the end of the driveway. The glaring crime-scene tape and the reporters who had hung around like bats for the past two weeks were gone. Probably camped out at the latest tragedy. New tragedies seemed to happen every day when one was paying attention.

Brushing aside whip-thin branches, I left the road for my running trail. The five-mile loop passed a farm where I had marked the passage of seasons by the growth of a black-and-white spotted calf born last spring. Caleigh and I had often walked by to see the calf. The sunlight spilling through the canopy of leaves overhead highlighted my pain. My love of autumn was at odds with my grief.

Fresh deer scat and pale spore-coated fungi called dead man's fingers edged the path. Only the plodding of my feet against the softly yielding earth was audible. I slowed to cross a stream. In its center were large, slippery stones worn smooth by the river. An occasional jumping trout broke the silence. Striped snapping turtles sunned themselves on half-submerged logs, reminding me of our last outing to Quarry Hill Nature Center.

Turtles. A chill spread through my body as I remembered the outing and the woman Caleigh thought was following us. I needed to tell Meyers. I ran home, gasping for breath and asked Alex if anyone had called. I told him about the woman Caleigh and I had noticed outside the cave and later, at the cemetery.

"I don't think I remember her," he said slowly. "What'd she look like?"

"She wore a blue baseball cap and a red jacket but I never saw her face, or paid much attention to her. It was more a feeling," I said sheepishly.

"That's not much to go on, Grace," he said, draping his arm around my shoulders. "Why don't you wash up? I'll start dinner. You haven't eaten all week."

Alex had the news turned on high. Snippets of a news report about Caleigh and Dane's disappearance and the dreaded words, no leads, hammered away at me. I kicked off my running shoes, my despair negating any endorphins that might have been released by running. "I'm gonna shower, okay?" I called.

* * *

ALEX WAS BUTCHERING THE CHICKEN into pieces with a meat cleaver when I came down. He tossed romaine, fresh tomatoes and green peppers with oil and vinegar, poured wine into goblets and opened the sliding glass door to the deck. A bed of red drumstick alliums I once planted bloomed in the back yard. I asked if he minded if I dried my hair before we ate.

The phone rang while I blow-dried my hair. I turned off the hairdryer and heard Alex answer.

"Hello? Rendeau residence. Who is this? I'm a friend of Dr. Rendeau's."

There was a note of alarm in his voice. I dropped the hair dryer and ran downstairs. He paced on the deck, panicky. "Keep talking," I mouthed. He had to keep the caller on the phone long enough for the police to be able to trace the call. He flipped on speakerphone. The voice was loud and angry. "It's none of your fucking business who I am. Tell Grace the children are fine, but if she wants to see them again, you'll get out of her life now. And remember, the Lord is slow to anger and abounding in steadfast love, forgiving iniquity and transgression, but he will by no means clear the guilty, visiting the iniquity of the fathers on the children, to the third and the fourth generation."

"Who is this? Where are the kids?" Alex demanded. He was pale and obviously shaken.

I yanked the phone out of his hands. "Hello? Hello? Who is this?" The line had gone dead. "Alex, who was it? What did they say?"

"The voice was barely audible. You heard most of it, Grace. I couldn't even tell whether it was a man or a woman. What do you think that means, if you want to see the kids, I'd better be out of your life?" He sat down and put his head in his hands.

I was elated. I dialed the detective's number and told him they called!

"What did the caller say? Were you able to keep them talking?" Meyers asked.

"Alex answered. He kept them on as long as possible but when I got on they hung up. The caller said something about Alex getting out of my life if I want to see the kids again. Something about the sins of the fathers. That proves they've got the kids, doesn't it?"

"Was it a male or a female, Grace?"

"It was hard to tell because the voice was disguised and muffled. But if they called, that means we're getting closer!"

"Grace, don't get your hopes up. I'll see if we can trace the call. We've had a slew of calls at the station today from people wanting to confess. Another heap of calls from people who think they've seen the kids. We're following every credible lead. We're following up a couple of leads about sex offenders in the area who've just been released and doing background checks on everyone who calls in," Meyers said and added, "I need to see if we got that call," before hanging up.

He sounded exhausted. I could picture his features so clearly, as blurred and gray as my own.

"Detective Meyers is going to trace the call. It's hopeful, Alex, I know it is. It's not a sex offender. It's not," I said as much to myself as to him.

"Did you hear what the caller said? If you want to see the kids again, I need to be out of your life. What does that mean to you?" he asked in the silence that hung between us. "It's my fault."

The fear of losing Alex too, paralyzed me. I needed him. It was impossible to choose between him and my children. He was the stitching that had barely held me together. The thought of him leaving ripped apart the yawning wound that hadn't even begun to knit yet.

He walked over to me and drew me to him, every movement played out in torturously slow motion. He kissed my cheek and then my neck. He leaned his forehead against mine, touched noses with me, and grazed my lips with his. I tried to kiss him but he pulled back. "Are you sure?" he asked, his face older than I had ever seen it. I needed to feel something resembling normal, if only for a few minutes. Something that could take me beyond myself where I could cry not tears of despair, but tears of physical release. I felt weak at what I knew would come next. We left our dinner untouched and climbed the stairs to the bedroom. I looked at Alex and then looked away, shocked at the force of my desire for him.

He kissed me, touching every part of me, as he made love to me. For a few moments, I gave myself to pure physical release. Afterwards, he kissed my brow and smoothed my hair from my forehead. I turned away and returned to my own private hell.

We lay in silence. The phone rang, jangling my already frayed nerves. I hadn't dressed yet. I pulled the sheet over me and answered on the first ring. It was Meyers.

"We got the transcript of Alex's conversation with the caller," he said with a sense of urgency. "Does this mean anything to you? 'Keeping mercy for thousands, forgiving iniquity and transgression and sin, and that will by no means clear the guilty; visiting the iniquity of the fathers upon the children, and upon the children's children, unto the third and to the fourth generation'"

My hand flew to my mouth. "It sounds like a fanatic who's taking the Bible very literally. Someone who thinks I'm guilty of something."

* * *

IT WAS MIDNIGHT. My pencil scratched against the yellow legal pad. It was the only sound in the dimly lit room. Sleep was a fleeting thought, secondary to the lists I had begun to compile. Check lists detailing the mundane tasks that made up a day. #1 Brush teeth. #2 Shower. #3 Wash hair. #4 Eat. #5 Put up posters. Tonight I added #6. Call to make appointment with Dayna Light.

Alex snored softly beside me. I envied his ability to sleep. The following day he would be distracted by appointments and office hours ahead of him and I envied that too. I chewed the pink eraser and forced myself back to the task at hand. What to do tomorrow. How to fill the hours between awakening and when Alex returned home. Co-workers and neighbors still provided the occasional casserole and I was grateful for these kindnesses but they didn't bring the children back.

At 2:00 a.m. I slipped out of the bedroom and padded down the stairs to the kitchen. Sketcher stirred and yawned. I poured a bowl of cereal and cracked open a beer.

The extended and indefinite leave of absence from my job left me with nothing but time. Later that morning, after Alex left, I sat at the kitchen table, sipping lukewarm coffee and staring out the window. It was imperative I stopped moving through the days like an apparition and think clearly about who had reason to take the children.

Think, Grace. Who would have any reason at all to take them? Theories about who and why branched off like gnarled fingers. I pulled out the legal pad and jotted down: BUD ANDERSON. He resented me because I had rejected his sexual advance and reprimanded him about his treatment of Emanuel. He had followed me to Alex's apartment and for all I knew, had watched Alex and me making love. He may have slashed my tires. Yet he had come into my office and awkwardly apologized for our misunderstanding. According to the police, he had an alibi for the afternoon the kids were missing although none for Sunday morning. He agreed to have his house searched and the detectives found nothing.

Who else? I printed FINN KOSKI in block letters. It was like leading an octopus on a leash—so many theories. Finn was a long shot but he was angry about the discharge to the halfway house. Not only angry, but also crushed when his daughter refused to provide a home for him. Oakwood Manor was no place for an elderly man who had acted in compassion to fulfill a dying woman's last wish to die with dignity. It was impossible to believe he would be angry enough to seek revenge by taking the children. Would he even have the strength to overcome Caleigh?

My other patients remained behind bars, with the exception of Emanuel Venegas, who had escaped from the Guaynabo Detention Center in Puerto Rico. Warden Briscoe called early in the week to offer his sympathy and his help in doing whatever he could to help find the kids. He mentioned Venegas, along with another inmate named Roberto (a.k.a. "Tito") Gutierrez Garcia had apparently planned the escape knowing Venegas was to be transferred. What was the likelihood he would be able to get on a plane and return to Minnesota? FBI agents in Puerto Rico were searching for both of them.

Gutierrez Garcia! I knew I had heard the name before. It was Josie's last name.

Josie had once told me in Puerto Rico the maternal and paternal last names are used to differentiate from all the other Garcias and Gutierrezes on the island. Was Gutierrez Garcia a common combination of surnames in Puerto Rico?

There was no one else. There had been no ransom demands. Detective Meyers had said earlier that child abductions are often done by a family member or person known to the children. I still couldn't grasp the fact that someone I might know could do such an awful thing.

CHAPTER THIRTY

THE DAYS MELTED INTO ONE ANOTHER. Like a dripping candle, each began with a drip of memory and dried into a brittle clump of pain. The missing posters had clung to trees and bulletin boards for almost a month. There were still no leads. The worst scenario was becoming the most likely. There was a rhythm in my sadness, one not for the faint of heart.

That morning, I rinsed out my coffee mug cup and despite Alex's bullheadedness about Dayna I dialed her number. She answered on the first ring and I stammered that I needed to see her.

"Grace. I thought you might call. Matt has been trying to contact you. We have unfinished business, don't we?" she asked.

I gasped. "You saw him the first time I was there. I don't know how you knew about Matt but I'm going to trust you saw him. I need you to help me find my children. Does that sound crazy? Oh, God, I'm going crazy." Could it be my mind was constructing elaborate defense mechanisms to protect me from the horror of what had happened?

"You're not going crazy. I'm going to help you, Grace."

It was such a seductive idea to talk to Matt again. I couldn't help but be drawn in, caressed by the thought of what Dayna said was true. None of what Dayna had just professed sounded crazy to me. "I need to see you."

"Two o'clock?" she suggested.

"Two o'clock." After making the appointment, I climbed upstairs and, exhausted with the effort, searched through my closet for anything that still fit. My jeans had grown to be a size too large and my sweaters, baggy and shapeless.

Two hours later, I sat in the empty waiting room and picked up a copy of *Two Worlds Magazine*. It seems I had developed a strange sort of attention disorder. I was unable to focus on anything before my mind wandered down the familiar track and all its terrifying possibilities.

An elderly woman, leaning heavily on her cane, came out of Dayna's studio. Her lavender-tinted curls sprung tightly from a pinkish scalp. She carried a purse the size of Mary Poppins's magic carpetbag.

The woman beamed, her small blue eyes buried under a mass of wrinkles. Under any other circumstances, I might have suspected Dayna Light was a fraud but I had begun to believe she might be a last hope to many.

Dayna was dressed in fuchsia. A form fitting long-sleeved tee, black and fuchsia print flowing skirt, strappy leather sandals and her signature dangling gemstone earrings. The room was as soothing as I remembered it to be. The aquarium still gurgled in the corner and the plants still reached toward the slanted light coming through the wide slatted bamboo shades.

I brought Matt's powder blue Fair Isle sweater with me, the only piece of clothing I kept because it was his favorite. The soft sweater sat in my lap as warm and soft as a kitten.

Dayna drew the blinds, letting in softly filtered light and sat down opposite me. "Sometimes a spirit takes control of my voice and uses it to relay a message. Don't be alarmed. I have a feeling . . ." she murmured before breaking off suddenly.

My heart felt as though it might burst out of my chest and lie shuddering on the table between us. I caressed Matt's sweater and watched Dayna's eyelids flutter. Only the babbling aquarium and the occasional slosh of one of the neon-colored fish broke the silence. Dayna's face seemed to contort and change before my eyes. After several minutes, she murmured, "Grace," in a voice decidedly not her own.

"Matt?" It was clear that it was not Dayna who had spoken. I was too stunned to be frightened. "Matt?" I repeated. Her eyes rolled back in her head and she nodded. The hush in the room took on a life of its own as I waited for him to respond.

"What's wrong?" Dayna's voice asked.

It was as though a vortex of heat or light or energy passed through the room. Something I didn't understand. "The kids," I whispered, "are missing." They were the last words I had ever imagined saying to anyone, let alone Matt.

"Don't worry, Grace. I love you," Dayna said and then shook her head and opened her eyes. The energy in the room shifted and it became apparent he was gone.

It had been Matt speaking to me. "Where is he? Where are they?" I asked, almost as devastated as when he had left me the first time.

"Grace, I'm sorry. We connected but then the static made it impossible to continue. Possibly we can try again next week."

It took several minutes for me to compose myself enough to be able to stand. I took out my wallet and happily paid Dayna's exorbitant fee, refusing to let my worry about Alex's reaction destroy my last hope.

As I walked along Nelson Street, I taped more fliers onto the quaint lampposts and clung to the belief Matt was right and the children were alive. My children's faces stared back at me as if in encouragement. Stillwater was a Midwest suburb where the American dream could do nothing but come true. Through Matt, I felt I had found my answer.

* * *

RUSH-HOUR TRAFFIC FLOWED SMOOTHLY through Inver Grove Heights. This time a year ago, Caleigh and I had driven to the nearby Mall of America for school shopping. We had made a mother-daughter day of it and had dinner afterwards at Ruby Tuesday. The thought slammed me with a nausea as overwhelming as morning sickness. I thought about pulling over and throwing up, but instead, dug in my purse for a pack of spearmint gum. With one hand, I pulled off a stick and chewed until my jaw ached and the nausea subsided.

The session with Dayna reverberated in my head. Alex and my in-laws would think I was losing my mind, but I was certain it was Matt speaking to me. I debated whether to tell Alex. The feeling that Matt had been in the room was just so real. It had been comforting, actually, not at all frightening or eerie in the way I might have expected. The knowledge that the children were alive and safe gave me something hopeful to focus on. Matt would not lie to me about that.

Apple Valley, Cannon Falls, Zumbrota, and Pine Island passed by in a blur. Half an hour later, County Road 14 loomed on the horizon and I followed the familiar road home. It was well past five when I arrived. Alex sat on the front porch. "Where were you?" he demanded. "I've been worried sick." The heat was still oppressive although the late afternoon light fell in low rays across the porch. Sweat beaded on a half-empty bottle of beer beside him. There were two empty bottles strewn on the floor.

"Alex, I'm sorry. I left in a rush and forgot to leave a note. Honestly, I thought I'd be home before you got here." I wondered why I was always the one apologizing.

"Jesus! I thought something had happened to you. Why didn't you answer my calls or texts?"

"I went to Stillwater," I said feebly. "I turned my phone off."

"Again? Come on, Grace. I don't want you getting your hopes up going to some charlatan who could have gotten the information about Matt dying of cancer anywhere. You know, for a doctor, you're not being very intelligent about this."

"I know you don't, but I believe her. It sounds crazy but Matt's spirit took control of her voice and he spoke to me! He said they're okay and that he loves me and not to worry . . ."

Alex's fists clenched. "You can't possibly believe that . . ." he said, raising his voice. "How much did you pay her for this? Don't you see what she's trying to do, sweetheart? She's taking advantage of your heartbreak and telling you what you want to hear. She didn't tell you anything different from what she told you last time." He took a swig of beer and offered me the bottle. "I don't want you to be hurt by someone who is most likely a fake. Come on, sit down. Do you want me to get you a glass of wine?"

"No, I'm fine." I stood taller. "I know it sounds bizarre, but it was him, I swear it."

"After you went the first time, I did a little research on it. I didn't want to discourage you but I can't let you be fooled into thinking you're talking to a dead person. Grace, listen to me, there aren't any instances of psychics providing any information that's been more helpful than other information received in a case."

His reason fueled my anger like kindling. "How can you be so sure? Isn't it just possible, that maybe there is something out there that we . . . that you . . . don't understand, and apparently don't even want to understand?"

"Listen." He put his hands on my shoulders. Our failure to keep the children safe hung between us. "I'm sorry to discourage you but anybody can have a fifty percent hit or miss rate when guessing about a person's whereabouts. Psychics predict the body will be found in a shallow grave in a wooded area and believe me, I'm not saying this is true or that I believe it about Caleigh and Dane, but it is a common prediction. But think about it, when murder victims are found, it's usually in a shallow grave. What killer takes time to dig a deep grave? And yes, they're in wooded areas, because they have to be out of sight."

I paced like an angry guard dog. "You think they're dead, don't you?"

"Maybe . . ." he hesitated. "Maybe it's time to prepare for the possibility that we may not find them, sweetheart."

A flush rose like wildfire in my face. "Maybe that's what you want. You never really wanted to be their father anyway, did you?"

"How can you even say such a thing?" Alex demanded. "You know that's not true. I know you're upset, but what's going to help is what Meyers suggested. More television appearances and interviews, not some vague suggestions by a psychic. All she has to do is throw out a few ambiguous remarks, and then read your reactions. You want to believe her and she knows this. What did 'Matt' actually say?"

"He said I'm troubled and not to worry, they're okay." I suddenly understood my patients' reactions to similar efforts I had made to disengage them of their delusions and I vowed never to destroy anyone's hopes again. "I don't know why you're being so bullheaded about this."

"Don't you see what she's doing? That's exactly what you want to hear. 'That they're fine and not to worry,'" he said as gently as if he were talking to a child. "Why don't we hire a private investigator? We know they got into a car. Someone has to have seen two kids fitting their description at a gas station or a convenience store or a rest stop."

"I'm going inside. I don't want us to start keeping secrets from each other, but I'm sorry I told you what happened today." This latest development felt like a nightmare happening to someone else.

"I'm sorry, Grace. But I can't let you go on believing in something that's never been proven. I don't want to have to be on guard with you all the time. To be afraid to tell you what I think."

Fat tears slid down my cheeks. The exhilaration I'd felt leaving Dayna's seemed to deflate in one huge whoosh. Alex slipped his arms around my waist, but I pulled away. "I'm worried about the kids, but also about us. This would be horrible enough for an old married couple but we were just beginning our lives together . . ." I choked back tears. "Maybe it's better if we . . ."

"If we what? Separate?"

I stared at the meadow without a word.

"Grace, I love those kids," Alex said, "but I can't help believing this is somehow my fault."

"What do you mean your fault? It's nobody's fault. It's one of those god-awful things in life that there is no rational reason for. Damn it. Don't you think I blame myself too? What if I hadn't gone to Indonesia? They'd be home safe with me right now. Maybe it was just too soon for you to move in with us." I regretted it as soon as the words tumbled out of my mouth. "Alex! I'm sorry. I didn't mean . . . it's just that for so long, Dane and Caleigh and I were a family. They were like anchors to life for me, especially after Matt died . . ."

"You didn't mean it, Grace? That's the second time you mentioned it," he pointed out. "We can second-guess this all we want. And blame ourselves, but in the end, it's not gonna bring them back. Why don't we ask Meyers for recommendations for a private investigator? Or maybe I should leave for a while, just until things settle down."

From the look in Alex's eyes, I knew I had hurt him. "Alex, I'm sorry. I didn't mean—"

"I know." He looked as though he'd just been sucker-punched. "By the way, I forgot to tell you. I got home early and Josie was here." His eye twitched.

"Josie? She's back from Puerto Rico? What was she doing here?"

"I imagine she came to see you. She was walking around the house when I pulled up. She said she was worried about you and wanted to check in and that she knocked but no one answered. She thought you might be asleep or avoiding visitors so she went around the house and tried the back door."

"Oh. I wonder how her trip was. Alex, your eye is twitching again."

"I know." He rubbed his eye with the back of his hand. "She didn't mention the trip. She seemed in kind of a hurry to leave. I told her I'd let you know she stopped by. Sketcher was going crazy inside, barking. We talked for a few minutes out here. I've never seen Sketcher react like that before."

At the mention of his name, Sketcher lifted his head from the floor. "What's gotten into you, boy?" I scratched him behind his ears. "The stress must be getting to him too. I wonder if Melanie and the kids met her down there. Come to think of it, I wonder if she ever told her family she's gay."

"Who?" Alex looked bewildered. "Who's Melanie?"

"Her lover. She has a boy and a girl. I don't remember their names but they're about Caleigh and Dane's ages, give or take a couple of years. I wonder if they all went to Puerto Rico for a vacation."

"That's funny. We've been neighbors for five years and I've never seen anyone with her. Maybe they live apart or something." The nervous tic crept across his eyelid as he spoke.

"Josie never mentioned that but I guess it's possible. Anyway, I'm going in to shower." The door slammed behind me, harder than I had intended. "Alex?" I stuck my head out. "Have you heard anything from Angela lately?"

"No, thank God. She seems to have forgotten all about me. Which is fine with me, since I haven't given her a thought since this whole thing began. Why do you ask?"

"I know it's crazy . . . I'm probably being paranoid, but don't you think that's kind of strange? I mean, I know she's a nut case and all, but she was calling and texting you pretty regularly and now . . . you don't think she has anything to do with the kids' disappearance, do you?"

"Angela?" Alex was as incredulous as if I'd just announced the house was on fire.

"Yeah, I mean you told me she'd been calling you ever since the divorce that she didn't want. She desperately wanted a baby, the calls stopped around the time the kids went missing . . ."

"I think you're really grasping at straws here but, just for argument's sake, let's say she wanted a baby. Why would she take thirteen- and six-year-old children? It's more likely she finally got the message it's over between us and has been for a long time."

My voice rose and I shouted, "Well, since you're the voice of reason, you tell me, who has the kids." The look on his face broke my heart and I asked softly, "Alex, could you just humor me and call her? Just to see what she's been up to?"

"That's the last thing I want to do. I don't want to give her any encouragement. Do you know how long it's taken for her to stop calling me? Why don't we mention it to Meyers and Donnelly and see what they think? If they see any reason to suspect her, I'd rather they handle it, okay?"

"You're right. It's probably crazy," I admitted. "Please. For me. Call her. I'll tell Meyers. It's just a weird coincidence, that's all. And now, I'm going in to shower. Please, Alex? Call her?"

CHAPTER THIRTY-ONE

THE NEXT MORNING, an unfamiliar truck roared into the driveway. Through the space between the kitchen curtains, I saw Bud Anderson get out of his truck and limp toward the house. What could he want? I cinched my robe around me as a loud knock reverberated through the house and then I cracked the door open.

"I came to see if there is anything you need." He removed his hat and stomped mud off his boots. Rain ran in torrents down the driveway.

I nodded and backed into the house. "I need my children home." My voice was tinged with desperation. Sketcher lumbered to the door. The odor of wet dog assailed my nose. I grabbed his collar but the dog stood calmly by my side.

"I know. I've been searching since day one," he said. "The woods and lakes and rivers in this town are as familiar to me as the back of my hand. I've been hunting and fishing 'em since I was a kid."

"What are you trying to say, Officer Anderson?" Rain pattered on the porch roof. Over the din, I spoke louder than I normally would.

"After the search didn't turn up anything, I started at the volunteer command center every day after work, studying maps and thinking about other places where two kids could be hidden," he said.

"Do the police know you're doing this?"

"If you're asking me whether they gave their approval and crossed me off the suspect list, the answer is 'yes.' I have an alibi for the day your kids disappeared. The cops interviewed me and my parents and everything checked out. You didn't think I had anything to do with their disappearance, did you?"

The wind whipped through the porch. It was a struggle to keep the door ajar. "I'm sorry, I . . . would you like to come in, Officer Anderson?" I didn't want to turn away anyone who offered to help, especially someone with as much knowledge of the terrain as Anderson had.

"It's okay," he said noticing my reticence. "If anything happened to my kids, I wouldn't trust anybody either." His fingers burrowed into Sketcher's thick coat. "Sweet dog."

"He seems to like you. I was just about to have a cup of coffee. Can I get you some? You'd better come in out of this rain." Even though he had apologized, I was still guarded after the incident at the Christmas party.

"If you're sure it's no trouble. I came to see if there's anything I can do." He removed his rain-soaked jacket and wiped his boots on the mat. The stench of his cologne followed him in. I took his jacket and hung it on a peg in the mudroom. "Sorry about the mess." Bud gestured at the muddy footprints on the floor.

"It's okay. Sit down. You know, there is something that's been bothering me." I took a deep breath. "Josie told me a while ago that she saw you outside Alex's house one night when I was there. With a camera. She thought you might have been taking pictures of me. Someone slashed my tires that same night. I need to ask if it was you." I looked directly at him, not sure what I expected him to say.

"You think I slashed your tires?" Bud snorted. "No way. I admit I was there one night. It was just after my wife left me. I was wrong. I shouldn't have followed you, but I never took any pictures . . . I'm embarrassed to even tell you this . . ."

"Go on." I crossed my arms over my chest. Sketcher whimpered at my side.

Bud flushed a deep crimson. "I was stupid enough to believe there might be something between us. It was crazy, I know, but I swear I didn't slash your tires and I sure as hell didn't take any pictures."

"Or follow Alex and me here? Somebody tried to run us off the road, for God's sake." A clap of thunder made us both jump.

"No! I swear on my mother's life. It wasn't me. I may have acted like a jerk to you at the Christmas party and followed you that day, but I had nothing to do with any of that other shit. I saw you were with another guy and I left."

I had been a psychiatrist for over ten years and believed I had developed a sixth sense of when people were lying. There was nothing defensive or angry about Bud's manner. No physical signs that would show anything but his telling the truth. I needed his help and I decided to trust my gut instinct and believe him. The house grew dark. "Looks like a big one rolling in," Bud said. "Do you have flashlights and candles case the power goes out?"

The kitchen drawers were crammed with the detritus of our lives. Old report cards, birthday candles, notepads, and pencils. Batteries long past their expiration dates. I searched for matches and then for the candles on the utility room shelf. Bud had gotten up and stood behind me. The sound of his breath filled the small laundry room.

"I can get them," I snapped. The thought that maybe I shouldn't have let him in entered my mind. "What were you doing at Alex's house that night, with a camera?"

"Is that what you've been thinking? That I'm a fuckin' pervert? Is that what the bitch, excuse me, Josie Garrett told you? She's always had it in for me. She came down, asked me what I was doing there and I left. Period. No camera. Listen, I'm in a custody battle for my kids. I'm trying to get joint custody."

"I'm sorry, I didn't know." I wondered what that had to do with anything.

"It was clear you and your boyfriend were an item, and I accepted it," he continued. "I couldn't do anything to mess up that or my custody case. I guess it was just wishful thinking that a classy, well-educated woman like you would ever look twice at me. Hell, I even . . ."

The wind and rain rattled the windows. "You even?"

"It's nothing. I just thought for a while that you might get tired of your boyfriend . . ."

Lightning flashed in the sky, heralding a storm, but the power hadn't gone out yet. I turned and regarded him warily. "I love Alex. But, thanks for telling me, Officer." I poured two mugs full of coffee and brought them to the table. "Cream and sugar? You didn't see anything unusual that night did you?"

"Bud, remember? Just sugar. Hell, when I left, your tires were just fine." He wrapped his hands around the mug. His broad shoulders strained the fabric of his uniform. Another clap of thunder shook the house. Sketcher whined and paced around the table.

"Bud. So who could have slashed them? Who followed us home? Who took the kids? I can't help thinking there's some connection." I stirred the bitter coffee, deep in thought, as I admitted, "You've helped me more than you realize. I was so sure it was you who had slashed the tires and followed me home that night."

Bud shook his head. "I swear it wasn't me. I want to help any way I can. I keep thinking what if those were my kids."

"If you'll excuse me, I want to call Detective Meyers. These events are really starting to seem like they're tied together. Thanks for coming by."

The rubber soles of Bud's army boots thumped on the hardwood floor as he walked to the door. "Remember, anything I can do, let me know."

His truck pulled away and I shivered. Fall had come early. The days were getting cooler and already a damp chill suffused the air. I paused at the door, thinking about what he had said. The tires, the near car accident. It seemed clearer to me now that those incidents must be in some way connected to the abduction. I stood at the window and punched in the number I knew by heart, hoping the children were not outside in the chill air. The windbreak at the edge of my property blocked my view of the neighbors' farm. Why had I moved to such an isolated location?

"Meyers here."

His voice had a reassuring familiarity which soothed me every time I heard it. "Detective, it's Grace Rendeau. I just had a visit from Bud Anderson. Remember I told you about him when you asked if there had been any problems with anybody at work?"

"Yeah, I remember. Donnelly and I interviewed him ourselves. What'd he want?"

"He said he was fishing that day and then went to visit his parents."

"Yup, that's right. Mr. and Mrs. Anderson validated his alibi. We were also able to verify that someone saw him on the Zumbro in his canoe that morning, fishing, just as he said he was. We subpoenaed the gaming site and the registered players for the time he said he was on, and it all pans out. Every moment of his day from ten o'clock on is accounted for."

"He said he's been assisting in the search and volunteering at the command center, manning the phones and studying aerial maps." As I spoke, Sketcher nudged me wanting to go outside. The worst of the storm seemed to be over. The sky was still half-dark with clouds but a rainbow suddenly appeared and spread across the sky.

"He's a good person to have in our corner, Grace. With his background in the Marines and the Minnesota National Guard, he's potentially a help. In 2009, he was deployed to Afghanistan and based out of

Kandahar Airfield. They provided evacuation services to patients and delivered over 200,000 gallons of fuel to the Marine's helicopter fleets. He was pretty badly injured in a crash. What'd he want?"

I hadn't known Bud was in the National Guard. "He came to offer his help. I asked him about the night I mentioned to you, when I was at Alex's and Josie found him outside taking pictures. I was so sure he was the one who had slashed my tires and followed Alex and me back to my house. But he swore it wasn't. And you know what, Detective? I believe him."

"It wasn't him outside Dr. Sawyer's house?" Meyers asked. A telephone rang in the background.

"No, he admitted to that. He said his wife had left him, and he acknowledged he had some notion of us getting together, but he swears he didn't slash the tires, take any pictures or follow us to my house that night. I wanted to tell you because I've been so focused on Bud Anderson as the one who did those things, but what if all these coincidences are tied up with the person who has the kids?"

"I'm gonna bring in Dr. Sorenson, Grace. She's a forensic psychologist we've worked with in the past to develop a profile of the type of person we're looking for. Why don't you come in first, though, and we'll go over what's happened so far?"

"Of course, I'll do anything." Sunlight poured in through the door as I hung up. I felt more optimistic now that one suspect had been eliminated.

CHAPTER THIRTY-TWO

THE POLICE STATION AT 10:00 a.m. was a busy place. The old red brick building smelled of dampness and must. I walked through the double paned glass doors and nodded to the police officer at the reception desk before climbing the stairs to Meyers's third floor office. Meyers looked as rumpled as his suit. There were several styrofoam cups with what looked like sludge in them on his desk. Stacks of papers and files cluttered the large surface.

"Have a seat." He pointed to one of two chairs directly across from the desk. Discolored Venetian blinds hung in the window casings. There was a water stain on the yellowing ceiling. "I wanted to keep you up to date on what's going on. A number of people have come forward offering various theories on the kids' whereabouts. I don't know if you've seen the tabloids . . ."

He seemed to notice how obviously I was appraising the state of his office. I averted my eyes from the chaos and told him I'd seen them. The rhythmic ticking of the clock and the whine of traffic outside broke the pressing silence. Meyers leaned back in his swivel chair and closed his eyes. "I have enough useless information and false leads to fill several file cabinets, but we're investigating everyone." He scratched his chin. He looked as though he hadn't shaved or showered that morning.

"Is anything new in the investigation?" The house was besieged the first week after the abduction since then, interest seemed to have dwindled.

He coughed and covered his mouth. Little had changed in the two days since I last spoke to him. His voice was gravelly. "Everybody and his mother have come forward with their theories on what happened."

"It's not as though they could have evaporated into thin air. The volunteers have given up, haven't they? There must be a new tragedy in the works." I hated how bitter I had become but I couldn't let Dane and Caleigh become a box of forgotten files. "Who would pilfer a child, Detective? I should've emphasized the dangers of talking to strangers more. Did I tell you I saw a documentary where an actor played an ice cream truck driver and every single kid got into the back of that truck when he offered free ice cream?"

"I saw it. Don't lose hope, Grace. We're combing the woods and nearby meadows, dragging the lakes. It's fall though and the weeds and brush are overgrown. It's difficult terrain to comb through."

"Dragging the lakes? Oh, God." I spit the gum out of my mouth, afraid I would vomit.

"Over there," Meyers gestured to the wastebasket. "It's routine, Grace. There is no reason to believe we would find anything, and we haven't. We're still searching nearby woods and fields. We're even checking the visitors' log at the prison. I'm not giving up on finding them alive," he insisted. "We're tracking down every caller, every lead, every possible sighting. He hesitated and I prepared for the worst. "Don't take this the wrong way, but it's not uncommon for the public to start to wonder about the parents' involvement in these types of situations. That's why I'd like for you to do a national interview."

"Oh, God. I don't know how anyone could ever think such a thing." Tears sprang to my eyes. "I've seen some of the rag sheets at the supermarket. How could anybody think we had anything to do with this? How can people buy such garbage? I feel guilty enough as it is about leaving the kids to go to Indonesia. Don't you think I go over and over this in my mind? What if we hadn't stayed the extra day? What if I hadn't gone? Besides, I already did the interview on KTTC and that didn't get us anywhere."

"I know you did the one with Candy Sutherland but the police media relations department has received a request from *Speak Up, America* for you to go on air with Tim Crawley from *American Life.* They want to do it this week."

I asked if he really thought it would help.

"People need to hear your side of the story. I'll be with you every step of the way. They'll broadcast the children's photos. I've sent them to the National Center for Missing and Exploited Children and to Most Wanted. The public needs to see you as a grieving mother right now, Grace. Just that fact and renewed publicity and getting the kids pictures on TV again may spark a memory for someone or even appeal to the burden of shame and guilt the perp may feel."

Meyers looked like he'd been through the ringer. I wondered when he'd slept last. "Thank you. You don't know how grateful I am for everything you've done. Are you married, Detective? It can't be easy on your family."

"Rosie's used to it. We have two kids of our own so she gets it. Okay, then. We've checked the alibis of a couple of names you gave as potential suspects."

I sat on the edge of my chair. "Go on."

"We checked with Oakwood Manor about your patient, Finn Koski. It seems he has a job at a nursery. The Sunday the kids went missing, he clocked in at 9:00 a.m. and didn't clock out until 3:00 p.m. We interviewed his supervisor," Meyers glanced at his notes, "Merv Jenkins, who says Finn was there the entire day. He remembers because it was a very busy day at the nursery and he was happy to have Koski's help. He didn't even leave for lunch."

"I'm glad he's doing well." I searched my bag for another stick of gum but came up instead with super-size tampons, my wallet, several ballpoint pens, a hairbrush, and finally one of Dane's size-six baseball socks. It had started out white and was now a dingy gray. I pulled the sock out of my bag and stared at it, thinking, of all things, that I needed to clean out my purse. "I never thought it was him," I said. "He was angry, but deep down, Finn's a decent guy. Detective, do you know what this is?" I held up Dane's sock.

He glanced at the sock and looked away. "Don't give up, Grace. The other person of interest we're still trying to find is Emanuel Venegas. We've been in touch with the FBI in Puerto Rico to let them know he's a person of interest in this case because of the connection between you and Venegas and the fact that he escaped. The police there have questioned Mayra Garcia Rodriguez about her son Roberto Gutierrez Garcia who escaped at the same time Venegas did."

"I don't know, Detective. I'm so confused." Something was wrong but I couldn't put my finger on what was bothering me. "His was a non-violent crime. The reason I saw him was because of mental health issues but I thought we parted on good terms. He never made any threats against me or my family. I don't know how he could have come back to hurt me. How could he have gotten on a plane?" I couldn't seem to stop talking.

"Apparently Roberto Gutierrez Garcia has been in and out of trouble since his older brother was shot down in a gang execution. He's been in a juvenile detention center and later in the federal prison for drug trafficking. I gotta warn you, the hills of Puerto Rico are pretty remote in places. A person could easily hide or be sheltered by family members and unless they're apprehended for another crime, they may go undiscovered for years."

Something still felt odd to me about Emanuel's escape.

"Just wanted to let you know the FBI is still looking for him. I've also gotten the report from Dr. Sorensen, our forensic psychologist. She mentioned the National Incidence Studies of Missing, Abducted, Runaway and Throwaway Children, or NISMART. Now I know you already know these statistics, but it's important to reiterate that fifty-three percent of the non-family abductions are committed by someone known to the victim: friends, neighbors, babysitters. Most of the perps are male and most of the victims are females between the ages of twelve and seventeen. The motive is sexual assault in seventy-seven percent of the cases."

With my eyes shut, I clamped down on my teeth, strangling my sobs. I still clutched the dirty sock in my hand.

"The Justice Department's Office of Juvenile and Delinquency prevention, or OJDP, did a similar study on child-abduction murders."

"Oh, God, what kind of monster are we dealing with?"

"I can stop here. Grace, listen to me. I want you to know I won't give up looking for them. Do you understand?"

I nodded. "What did Dr. Sorensen come up with for a preliminary profile?"

"The abductor is probably known to the children in this case because they were taken from home. There doesn't appear to have been a scuffle or any resistance from the lack of evidence at the scene. No blood. The perp had to have known you were away, and when your in-laws left. He or she must have gotten the children in the car willingly. Have you had any work done on the house, Grace? Anybody over to mow the lawn? Any repairmen the children may have gotten to know or wouldn't think much about letting into the house if they had some sort of excuse?"

I thought for a moment. Sunlight pooled in the room from one open set of blinds and I shifted position to avoid the rays. This meant whoever did this might have been watching us while I was completely oblivious to their evil presence. I'd been tripping over careless mistakes and it had cost me my children. "Nobody comes to mind," I said.

"We've checked out Dane's tee ball coach and Caleigh's soccer coach. You want me to draw the blinds?"

"No." My chest tightened. "Can I have a glass of water?"

"Yeah, help yourself. The cups are over there." He pointed to the water cooler and paper cups. "We've sent direct mailers to every mailbox in the county with their pictures and 'Help Bring Us Home,' as a caption."

The water helped soothe my throat.

"NISMART also says only five percent of stranger abductions take place in the victims' home or yard. So I think we can be fairly certain this is someone the children have had contact with." Meyers stood up and walked to the window. "The commonality of these abductors is that the initial contact is first made at home. It's usually a male with a prior criminal record, between the ages of twenty and thirty-nine. The perp usually has a legitimate reason for being where he was, like working at the house or delivering something. The good news is that in about eighty-five percent of cases the child or children are kept within fifty miles or even in the same town."

White flakes still blanketed the shoulders of Meyers's black suit, a little worse for wear than it had been when he first came to my door. I tried to focus on the good news, such as it was. Chances were the children were not far.

"That's the gist of it. Dr. Sorensen says the population of child molesters and abductors, which, by the way, comprise two completely different profiles, is too diverse to fit a single psychological profile, but there are a few things to consider."

"Such as?" The shifting sun jabbed at my eyes. I stood and dragged my chair a few feet to the right and wrangled with the sweater I'd hung on the back of the chair.

"At least ninety-five percent are men. Unmarried, with few friends. Losers, if you will. Outcasts. Someone with very disordered judgment. Almost no parent gives up on finding a missing child, as do police, neighbors or the media. So, they're inviting a lot of scrutiny."

"Why do they do it?" It was almost impossible to get the words out. I did and I didn't want to hear the answer.

"Most commonly, desire for sex with children, but again, it seems fairly certain we can rule that out because both of them were taken. A pedophile will usually be attracted to boys or girls, but not both. Other abductions are for monetary gain, and a third group is women who desperately want children, who may not be able to have children or who have miscarried. It's usually a pre-meditated crime involving infants though."

"Alex's ex-wife," I said to Meyers. "Angela. That has to be it. They've been divorced for two years but she called and texted Alex all that time but stopped right around the time the kids disappeared. I wanted so much to believe Alex when he said she wouldn't do such a thing, but now I just don't know . . ."

"Do you know the circumstances that led up to the divorce?" Meyers' ears perked up like a coonhound's on the hunt.

"Alex said she was desperate to have a baby. By then Alex knew the marriage was over and he just wanted out. He found that she'd stop using birth control without telling him and he filed for divorce. He had to wait a year to get it on the grounds of separation because she wouldn't agree to the divorce."

"Can you give me her full name and number? Do you know her address?" He was more animated than I'd ever seen him.

"Angela Sawyer. I don't know her address or phone number. Let me call Alex. Maybe he knows. But if it was Angela, that means they're safe! Don't you see , if a woman who wants children takes them to try to pass off or raise herself. That means she wouldn't hurt them! The psychic was right," I said confidently. "I knew she was."

"Grace, don't get your hopes up. That type of abduction is usually a pre-meditated crime involving infants."

CHAPTER THIRTY-THREE

AFTER WE LEARNED FRONT ROOMS such as ours had been used for funerals in the late nineteenth and early twentieth centuries, my home office became humorously known as the funeral parlor. Fittingly, I sat in the dark, as if staring at the body of a recently deceased loved one. I had painted the walls a soft robin's-egg blue, which was a symbol of renewal and rebirth, but even that did little to dispel the gloom in the room. The antique desk, armoire, books, and photos of the kids were as comforting as old friends. It was where I went when I wanted to be alone. The chair I'd rocked the children in as babies groaned in tune with the creaking of the floorboards. There had to be a clue somewhere.

Caleigh's room seemed the most likely to provide a clue. I searched under the mattress and under the bed. Thick, furry layers of dust rose in swirls causing me to sneeze several times. I ransacked her dresser drawers and desk. The police had taken her computer and her desktop was conspicuously bare.

In the online support group I had joined, many of the missing teens had met with online predators. In my heart, I could not believe my thirteen-year-old daughter had met anyone online and left with him.

And then I found them. Caleigh's diaries. Hidden behind the books on her bookshelf. Two small white journals with tiny locks that I had given her for her eleventh birthday which the police had obviously missed.

"Alex!" I burst into the room. "Wake up!" I turned on the light and shook his shoulder.

The bed moaned painfully as he bolted upright, the harsh light accentuating the shadows under his eyes.

"I found Caleigh's diaries. They were behind her books on the bookshelf!" It surprised me she was writing in the diary instead of keeping an online journal. I tucked my legs underneath me and thumbed to the most recent entries, feeling dirty at invading my daughter's privacy. I had no choice.

Alex rubbed his eyes. "What time is it?"

"It's 2:00 a.m. I'm sorry, I shouldn't have woken you. Go back to sleep."

He rubbed his shoulder. "Maybe you'd better hand them over to the police."

"I will but do you think I should read it? Oh, no . . ."

"What is it?" Alex sat up a little straighter. "Damn, this shoulder is really bothering me."

"Sorry. I didn't mean to shake it. Forget about your shoulder for a minute and listen, okay? Here, this is the second one. Listen to this. She wrote this after I told her you were moving in:

ALEX IS OKAY BUT I CAN'T STOP THINKING ABOUT WHAT'S GONNA HAPPEN TO DANE AND ME. AUBREY'S MOTHER GOT REMARRIED AND HER STEP-DAD IS A REAL JERK. I DON'T KNOW ALEX VERY WELL BUT WHAT IF HE STARTS TELLING US WHAT TO DO LIKE HE'S OUR DAD OR SOMETHING?

Alex shifted position and grimaced. "Did she write anything else?"

"Hmmm, let's see. Okay, here. The other one is from earlier, after Matt died. Oh, God, Alex . . . I wish I'd known how much pain she was in but she never said a word. I know she was upset but she was so angry, I just couldn't get through to her. Here she wrote:

MY DAD DIED TODAY. I wiped a tear from my eye. IT'S THE WORST DAY OF MY LIFE. I WISH I WERE DEAD.

"Poor kid. It's not your fault, Grace, how could you have known?"

"Shit."

"What?" Alex massaged his shoulder. "What did she say? Do you know where the heating pad is?"

"It's in the closet. This is where she talks about cutting herself. Listen to this:

AUBREY TOLD ME A BIG SECRET THAT I CAN'T TELL ANYONE. SHE CUTS HERSELF WITH A RAZOR AT NIGHT. SHE SAID IT MAKES HER FEEL GOOD, LIKE SHE'S LETTING SOME OF THE PAIN ABOUT HER PARENTS' DIVORCE OUT. I TRIED IT WHEN I TOOK A BATH TONIGHT AND SHE'S RIGHT. IT FELT GOOD. I DIDN'T GO TOO DEEP OR ANYTHING, JUST ENOUGH TO DRAW A TINY BIT OF BLOOD. I MADE ABOUT FOUR CUTS ON MY THIGH WHERE NO ONE WILL SEE THEM. THEY ARE LINED UP, STRAIGHT AS ARROWS. IT'S SORT OF A RE-MINDER OF HOW MUCH I MISS DADDY.

"Wow. So this has been going on for a while, huh?" Alex tried to put his good arm around me.

"Alex, how could I have missed this? I have to read more."

"Maybe that's enough for tonight, sweetheart. It's late. Why don't you try to get some sleep instead of torturing yourself like this?"

"I need to read this," I insisted and moved to the Queen Anne's chair. The standing lamp provided just enough light to read by. "You can go to sleep if you want. This is important."

"I didn't say it wasn't important. But anytime I say anything, you're ready to bite my head off. I just meant you should get some sleep and look at it tomorrow."

"I'm sorry, okay? It's just that I feel so bad about not even knowing what was going on in Caleigh's life. What kind of mother am I anyway?"

"You're a wonderful mother, you hear me? This is not your fault," Alex said, leaning back against the pillows.

"Yeah, but I'm a psychiatrist, Alex! How could I have not seen this? I could kick myself."

"She did write that she cut her thigh and how would you have seen that?" He got up and handed me the box of tissues from the night table. "Caleigh was pretty secretive about the whole thing. Is there anything that gives a clue about where they might be?"

"No, I don't think so. Oh, my god, listen to this!"

MOM HAD THE TALK WITH ME TONIGHT. SHE ACTUALLY BROUGHT A CUCUMBER INTO MY ROOM AND SHOWED ME HOW TO PUT A CONDOM ON IT. I THOUGHT I WOULD DIE!

"I remember that. That was your idea, not mine. Every time we bought cucumbers after that, Caleigh turned bright red."

"That's the way I did it in med school when I had to teach inner-city kids about using protection. It was kind of awkward. At least Dane doesn't want a hamster anymore. Every time he mentioned it, I thought about your med school job in the lab as a hamster ejaculator!"

"Hey, somebody had to do it. I made good money with that research. How else were we supposed to get hamster sperm samples? As soon as I walked in the door, they were ready to go at it!"

It felt strange to smile about anything again. My face hurt from the effort.

"Come on. Forget about hamsters and cucumbers. Let's try to get some sleep," Alex said, kissing me good night. "It's late."

"You're right. I'll read it in the morning. And then, I'll bring them in to Detective Meyers. Maybe he can get some information from them. I'm going to try calling Josie again too."

At five, I slipped on a fleece robe and padded softly down the stairs to start the coffee, Caleigh's diaries in hand. Might as well start at the beginning despite the misgivings I had about reading my daughter's private thoughts. With a mug of coffee in hand, I sat down on the living room sofa and pulled Caleigh's lilac checked comforter around me. The thin light of dawn did not provide much illumination, so I switched on a small table lamp. With Sketcher by my side, I began to read.

Much of what Caleigh wrote was about school and friends, and I skimmed quickly through this, smiling occasionally at a teenage girl's preoccupations with popularity and clothes. There were references to studying for exams and wanting to do well in school, and about a crush on a boy named Sam. It was a glimpse into an adolescent world of innocence and angst that I had all but forgotten, until I got to May.

WE WENT TO QUARRY HILL NATURE CENTER TODAY. THE CAVE AND THE CEMETERY WERE CREEPY BUT WHAT WAS REALLY CREEPY WAS THIS WOMAN FOLLOWING US.

A few weeks passed before she wrote about going to my unit picnic and meeting Josie.

I LIKED HER. SHE GAVE ME HER NUMBER AND WE'VE TEXTED A COUPLE OF TIMES.

I had forgotten about that day, a bright sunny day in early summer. Alex, the kids and I had gone. The warden had allowed the family to tour the facility and although the children hadn't been able to do so, they had enjoyed the picnic on the grounds and especially the food the inmates had prepared. A strange unease rose in my belly. Josie? Why the hell was Caleigh talking to Josie and why did they exchange phone numbers?

At that moment, Alex straggled down the stairs, still rubbing his shoulder. "You're up early. Hmmm. Coffee smells good."

"Help yourself. Poor Dahlia," I said to no one in particular. "Dahlia thought Caleigh began cutting because the puppy disappeared, but this had been going for over two years and I missed it. It's nothing she and Stan did. It had nothing to do with the puppy," I said, jumping up. "Alex! Did you call Angela? Caleigh mentioned that strange woman we saw at Quarry Hill. What if it was Angela?"

Alex came into the living room with his coffee and a blueberry muffin, and raised his eyebrows. "Grace, that doesn't make sense. That could have been anybody. I would've recognized her. Why would you think this woman might have been Angela? I thought you were going to mention it to Meyers." Alex's eye was twitching again.

"But you weren't around when she was. Don't you see? She could've ducked or turned whenever she saw you. There were a lot of people there that day. You wouldn't have noticed her if she stayed in the background. Besides, she was wearing a baseball cap."

"But why would Angela follow us around? What's Caleigh say about the woman?"

"Just that a strange woman followed us and she told Josie about it. I need to call Detective Meyers. I think it's time we had a talk with Angela. I mean she did call and text you and she did call me to tell me to stay away from you. She's crazy. I think the police should talk to her. Don't you think?"

Alex shrugged and took a sip of coffee.

"I'm going to call Josie, too. She has to be back from vacation by now. I had no idea that she and Caleigh were talking."

* * *

ALEX PACED IN THE STATION. "Fuck. I really don't want to see her again."

"Detective Meyers called and said they've interviewed her but still need to check out her alibi. It was decent of her to agree to talk to us." We sat in the dingy lobby. Angela Sawyer walked out of the detective's office toward us. I had been so hopeful that Angela was the answer but now I wasn't sure anymore.

Angela's gaze fell on Alex and it was obvious that she was still in love with him. Her eyes softened and her lips parted when she saw him. She was beautiful. Curvy, well dressed and well groomed. Her apricot-colored hair was shoulder length and expertly straightened and blow-dried, cascading like a waterfall around her shoulders. I tried to picture Angela in jeans and a baseball cap. This woman was wearing a business suit and heels and carrying a leather briefcase.

"Alex," Angela came over and took Alex's hand. "How are you?"

My nose wrinkled at the sickening smell of gardenias. Angela smiled, her lips swollen as if she'd been stung by bees. I peered at her, dissecting her image. Could this have been the woman Caleigh and I had seen at Quarry Hill Nature Center?

"Angela." Alex stood a little straighter. "This is Dr. Rendeau."

I tried to read his feelings about his ex-wife. Angela's smile faded. "Hello." She looked at me sideways and nodded curtly in my direction. Her narrow eyes were as sharp as a hawk's. "I'm sorry to hear about your children," she said before turning to Alex. "How've you been?" Alex rubbed his shoulder. As if on cue, Angela reached out and laid her manicured hand on it. "That shoulder's not acting up again, is it?"

Bitch. I felt like an imposter in front of this woman. Angela was professional, calm, and wearing expensive shoes. Her creamy breasts spilled out of the bustier she wore underneath her blouse. Alex was once in love with her. My children were missing and this woman was flirting with my fiancé. Detective Meyers had already told me that Angela said she was working the weekend the children went missing.

"I have to ask you a question," I said to Angela. She raised her plucked brows. "My daughter and I saw someone following us a few weeks ago, and I need to ask if it was you."

"You must be joking," Angela said coolly, turning to Alex. "Why in the world would I follow you?"

Her tone of condescension and the attempt to humiliate me in front of Alex made me want to slap her. "If you'll excuse me." I couldn't help myself. I ran outside. Alex called but I didn't stop. *He would've been better off with anybody but me,* I thought as tears stung my eyes. When I got to the car, Alex grabbed me by the hand.

"What the hell was that all about?"

"Why didn't you tell me she's beautiful and accomplished and everything I'm not?" I sobbed. "You would've been so much better off with her. She wouldn't have lost her children." Out of the corner of my eye, I saw Angela exit the revolving door of the station. She shielded her eyes with her hand at her forehead and smirked.

"Grace, stop this right now. I love you. Don't you get that? You, Grace. Not Angela." He kissed my eyelids and drew me closer. "I love you, okay?"

We watched Angela climb into her BMW and drive off. "Do you think she did it? She could be the woman Caleigh and I noticed lurking around the nature center."

"Honestly? No. She looks like she's pulled herself together and I really can't see her trudging around a nature center in the rain to follow us. What would be the point?" Alex wiped his forehead. "Do you think maybe it's just that you don't like Angela?"

"I don't know. Maybe she's trying to get back at you. Or at me for taking you away from her. Meyers told me some kidnappers have fantasies of being a parent. The kidnapper becomes confused with thinking they're doing something good for the child, like taking him or her out of a bad situation and giving them a wonderful life. And they begin to believe it. Sometimes the child doesn't even escape because he's become so dependent on the kidnapper for everything. Did you ever hear of Stockholm syndrome?"

"Yeah . . . Isn't that where the hostages felt empathy toward their captors and even defended them after they were freed?" Alex asked.

"Yeah. It's a form of traumatic bonding. Say a person threatens or abuses or intimidates you. The victim might still develop strong emotional ties because the abuser is the only one they have who is taking care of them in some sick way. It's an adaptive trait to align yourself with the captor. That's what happened in the Patty Hearst and the Jaycee Lee Dugard cases."

"Angela's pretty smart, Grace. I'm sure she could come up with a better scheme than that for getting back at me. One that doesn't involve two kids."

"I thought you said she really wanted a baby? Shit! We should've left the windows cracked. It's like a sauna in here." The car was an oven. "She looks evil enough to me to take someone else's kids, with those plumped-up lips and Botoxed forehead."

"Angela is much too self-centered to want to take on two kids. I really think her wanting a baby was just her way of trying to hang onto me. Come on. Let's get out of here." Alex started the car and turned on the air, full blast. "You didn't miss a thing, did you?"

"At least they're going to check out her alibi and keep her under surveillance if anything unusual comes up. I can't believe you ever loved that woman. Anyway, let's stop at Josie's okay? I want to see if she's home yet and ask her about Caleigh calling her. You could check if you have any mail while we're there."

"Sure, good idea. No more talk about Angela, okay?" Alex turned left onto Silver Lake Drive. We circled the lake and watched a squadron of geese flying overhead. When we pulled onto Churchill Lane, Alex pointed out that the FOR SALE sign was still up in front of his townhouse. "I guess the realtor hasn't sent anyone over to mow the lawn. Look at those weeds. Wonder how long it'll take for the town-house to sell. It's not too late, you know."

"Hmmm? Not too late for what, sweetie?"

"Grace, are you paying attention? You know, for me to move back here."

"Why on earth would you do that? It's not seeing that fucking Angela again is it?"

Alex laughed out loud. "You've got to be kidding. When I saw her today, I wondered what I ever saw in her in the first place. She has nothing on you. Believe me. I think it's the stress talking, Grace."

"Why would you say such a thing then? Did you just realize that maybe this is all too much for you? I know nothing has gone the way we planned . . ."

"Grace, stop. I said it because I was thinking that maybe if I was out of the picture, whoever has the kids would bring them home. Okay? I said it because I feel guilty that it seems to be about us in some way. I haven't been able to forget that crazy phone call. You know, the 'Where's your little Gracie? If she wants her children back, you'll be out of there,' one. I haven' been able to sleep since."

I put my hand on Alex's arm. "Listen to me. I love you. We're not going to let some lunatic drive us apart. I don't know if it would make any difference at all if you moved back or not, and I need you. I would seriously die if you left."

He parked in the driveway and took out his keys. "I'm going to check inside to make sure everything's okay. You're going to Josie's?"

"Yeah, that looks like her car. I think she's home. I'll meet you in about ten minutes, okay? You're going in to work today, right?"

"Yeah, I have a meeting. Meet you at the car in ten minutes," he said, kissing me.

CHAPTER THIRTY-FOUR

THE DRIVING RHYTHM OF CONGA beat behind the door. No one answered my knock. I knocked again, louder this time, rattling the doorknob. "It's me. Grace. Can you hear me?" After an interminable length of time, hollow footsteps tapped on a wooden floor. The door opened slowly.

"Josie! Where have you been?" I wanted to rush into Josie's arms and hug her but Josie took a step back. "You know about the kids, right?"

"Yeah, I'm sorry, Grace." Her voice was hard and raw. "I heard. I just got back. I was gonna call you today." There was something odd about the way Josie wouldn't meet my eyes.

"Can I come in? Where are Melanie and the kids?" I looked inside, expecting a mess. Surprisingly, the living room was tidy. There was nothing out of place. The sofa cushions were plump, no stray socks or toys or dirty dishes littered the floor. No suitcases or ticket jackets. My own house was always a mess when the kids were there. Too late, I realized I was thinking about them in past tense. I need to pull myself together. "Wow, you've really cleaned up quickly. I still haven't unpacked. You busy? Is that a new Civic outside?"

"Well . . ." Josie looked over her shoulder into the living room. It was painted a deep, dark red. "I just got home, but no, come in. They're out. That's Melanie's car. She's using mine. Has there been any word about the children?" She squeezed my arm. "You must be frantic. Do you want to sit down? Can I get you something to drink?"

"No word yet. I'm not giving up though. Josie, I need to ask you something. Why did you and Caleigh exchange phone numbers?"

Josie shrugged. "Why do you ask?"

"It's something I just found out and I'm wondering why you never mentioned it to me." I was ashamed at what I had missed and hurt that my daughter was confiding in Josie without my knowledge.

"We kind of hit it off at the picnic, and I thought maybe she and Melanie's daughter would enjoy hanging out. It wasn't a big secret, Grace."

The red walls were the color of blood. I sunk into the cushions and studied the artwork on the wall opposite me. A life size reproduction of Tamara de Lempika's painting, *The Dream*. Josie's eyes were fixed on it. It was not something I would want to live with every day. "I was at the station just now talking to Detective Meyers, he's the guy in charge of the investigation."

"Oh? Are you sure I can't get you something to drink?" Josie's eyes darted back and forth to the kitchen.

"No, thanks. I'm supposed to meet Alex outside in a couple of minutes. He has a meeting at work and we came in one car."

"How is he? And you? How are you holding up?"

"He's okay. He went back to work. I've taken some time off, but I'm going back part time on Monday. It's been three weeks and I need to do something to keep myself from going crazy. I just can't stay home by myself all day long anymore."

"I'm going back tomorrow too." There was an ashy, grayish quality to Josie's normally tanned olive complexion. "She's a beautiful woman, isn't she?" Josie asked, still staring at the painting.

"I'm not much of an art critic. But, yes, there is something really arresting about her. Something sensual."

"That was painted in 1927. She also modeled for a painting called *Beautiful Rafaela*. I have it in my bedroom. It shows a lot more than this one, so I didn't know if I should hang it in the living room." Josie laughed nervously. "Anyway, how are you and Alex doing? I mean with all the stress and everything . . ."

"We're okay. You had a long vacation, how come you're so pale? Didn't you and Melanie get to the beach at all when you were in Puerto Rico?"

Josie grunted something unintelligible.

"I'm sorry, what did you say?" I wondered why Josie wouldn't meet my gaze.

"I said I had a lot going on. The beach was the last thing on my mind," she said tersely, her eyes lost in the painting. "I bought my mother a house," she muttered. "In a suburb of San Juan."

"Josie! That's wonderful. This must mean so much to her."

"She deserves it. But even now she can't stop worrying . . ."

"What do you mean?"

"Nothing." Josie looked at me blankly. "I just meant that she's worrying about how we'll pay for it. She keeps it so clean I could eat off the floors." Josie smiled and said softly, "It's just what she's always wanted. Polished terrazzo floors, pastel walls and a huge crucifix in the living room." She wiped her eyes and fingered the small crucifix around her neck like a nun counting rosary beads.

"So, it wasn't much of a beach vacation, huh? I heard about Emanuel escaping. Any news about that?"

"Nope." Josie brushed lint off the sofa.

Her economy of words would have been surprising under any circumstances, considering how forthcoming Josie usually was but now it was shocking. Was it jet lag or fatigue from the trip that had Josie so irritable? Or maybe it was Emanuel's escape. Something was definitely wrong. "I heard he escaped with someone else. Who was this guy?" Maybe this ruined the vacation for her.

"I don't know, Grace. So, what happened at the station this morning?"

"Well, I found Caleigh's diaries and thought I should bring them in to Detective Meyers. The police interviewed Alex's ex-wife. Actually, would you mind getting me a glass of water? I am kind of thirsty."

"Sure." Josie went into the kitchen. Ice cubes clattered into a glass. I looked around the room again and pinpointed what had been bothering me all along. There was absolutely no clutter. No school pictures of Melanie's kids, or of anyone else, for that matter. Just the life-size painting of the nude. A strange painting to display with teenage children in the house.

Josie handed me the glass. "What's this about a diary? And Alex's ex-wife?"

I took a sip and swallowed hard. "When I was in Indonesia with Alex, my mother-in-law found little cuts on Caleigh's arms. She said Caleigh acted strange and didn't answer when Dahlia asked her about the cuts. She had just seen a program on cutting and was convinced Caleigh was doing it because our puppy disappeared . . ."

"Your puppy disappeared?" Josie lifted her brows. She had the unblinking eyes of a snake. "What's the ex-wife have to do with this? Are you really sure that she is an 'ex-wife'? She did call and say she was still married to the guy."

"Yes, I'm sure." Josie's dislike of Alex was beginning to irritate me. "Oh, Josie, there's so much I need to fill you in on but Alex is waiting. I need to drop him at the hospital. Can we talk later?"

She brushed her hair back and gave me a sidelong glance. "Sure, but what's this about a diary? What'd she write?"

"I wanted to ask you about that. She mentioned the cutting. Apparently, it's been going on since Matt died. I feel terrible. You know, working in the field and not realizing this was going on under my own nose."

Her lips narrowed. "Wow. What's up with that, Grace? I'm surprised you didn't see it. We see it all the time in the prison." A purplish vein fluttered at her temple.

"I know but it's different when it's your own kid. Plus, I was so happy the kids accepted Alex. I was thrilled with the engagement and the trip. Everything seemed to be finally falling into place. You can't imagine how I feel about this. Really. I feel horrible not to have seen it."

"It does seem like kind of a big thing to overlook." There wasn't a hint of sympathy in her eyes. "Remember I told you something about Alex moving in didn't seem right to me? I hate to ask you this, but are you sure Alex didn't have anything to do with this?"

"I can't believe you just said that." I was as dumbstruck as if she had slapped me. Maybe the loss of her own children had hardened her in a way I didn't understand.

"You know I'm only looking out for your own good," she muttered.

"I'm going to chalk it up to you being a friend and being concerned, but you are absolutely wrong. What's gotten into you anyway?"

She crossed her arms over her chest and said angrily, "You barely know the guy!"

"Believe me, nobody feels worse about this than I do, but Alex has absolutely nothing to do with it. He's been a rock."

"Hey, I'm just trying to look out for you." Josie flushed the color of her living room walls.

"Thanks but what I wanted to ask was whether you and Caleigh talked about her cutting? She mentioned it in her diary and honestly, I had no idea."

"Oh, she called me and texted me a couple of times. You know, it was the old 'my mother doesn't understand me' kind of thing. I was glad to help."

"I'm glad you were there for her when I obviously wasn't, but does that mean you knew about the cutting?"

Josie shrugged.

It suddenly became clear to me that Josie had known about it. "Didn't you think it was something you should have told me?" I asked, incredulous.

"She opened up to me and I didn't want to break her confidence, Grace."

"Yes, but she's my daughter."

"I'm sorry, Grace. I was just trying to help. What did the police say about the diary?"

"I don't know yet." I couldn't believe what Josie had just said. "They'll analyze it and send it to the forensic psychologist. I really have to go. Alex is waiting. I'll talk to you soon." I bumped into Josie's shoulder as we walked to the door. It was as sharp as a blade. "Have you lost weight?"

"No. I'm the same as ever. Still trying to run whenever I can. I'll see you Monday, okay?"

Alex was in the car with his eyes closed when I opened the door. "Sleepy?" I kissed him on the cheek.

"Mmm hmm. I took a pain reliever but this shoulder is killing me."

"Poor baby. We've been through a lot. No wonder your shoulder's acting up and you can't sleep."

"Mmmmm. That feels good," he said as I threaded my fingers around the knot in his shoulder. "Grace, is something wrong? Did you see Josie?"

"Yeah. At first I wondered if she was home, it took her so long to answer the door. She said she'd just gotten back and was going to call me today. She knew about the kids."

"Maybe she was asleep or something. We'd better get going. I need to be at the Infectious Diseases Symposium today. What's the matter? You look upset." Alex backed out of the driveway and turned his head gingerly.

"No, she was dressed. She knew about the kids. And she knew about Caleigh cutting."

"She knew about Caleigh's cutting?"

"Yeah," I looked down. "She said Caleigh had texted her but she didn't want to break her confidence and tell me."

"Wow. That's surprising. Why would she do that?"

"I don't know. It was poor judgment, don't you think?"

"Yeah, I do. I think she had a responsibility to tell you."

"Yeah, me too. I'm glad you don't think I'm overreacting to this. She looked terrible. I asked if she'd gone to the beach at all in Puerto Rico and she said something about having other things on her mind. I told you that the patient who she escorted to the prison there escaped, right?"

"Was that during the transfer or after he was already in the prison?" Alex asked, turning onto Rocky Creek Drive.

"Oh, afterwards, I think. He escaped with another inmate. It seems there was a plan with a kitchen staff member or something. They haven't been found yet as far as I know."

"That's funny. How could there be a plan to have your patient escape if no one knew he was being transferred back to Puerto Rico?"

"Well, the staff knew. I suppose there's some sort of underground information that gets around. You know inmates buy and sell cell phones and other contraband. Maybe Venegas somehow alerted this guy, Gutierrez he was returning, as soon as he heard."

Alex shook his head. "I worry about you, Grace, being in that job."

"I know. I've been thinking that . . . Now that the children are . . ."

"That what?" Alex prodded carefully.

"God, this is the second time today that I've caught myself thinking, 'now that the children aren't at home.' I can't lose hope but it's getting so frustrating. It's like some horrible evil has chosen us, maybe even watched us and changed our lives forever. I can't help but wonder if it has something to do with my job."

"I know, baby. But don't give up. We'll keep looking no matter what it takes."

"Anyway . . ." I wiped my eyes. There was no way Josie could be right about Alex having anything to do with this. "I've been thinking I might give notice at the prison and get another job. After what's happened, I just don't think I can be objective about working with people who have been convicted of the horrible sorts of crimes my patients have. Not now that I know how much the victims of those crimes suffer."

"I know what you mean. Yeah, they're paying for their crimes but an individual's or a family's life has been changed forever by one person's acts."

"I agree. There's a fellowship in Adolescent Psychiatry at Mayo I've been thinking about. After what I missed with Caleigh, maybe this is what I need to do. I was surprised by Josie's reaction though. I told her how horrible I felt about missing the signs and finding out from Caleigh's diary that she's been cutting herself for two years."

"What'd she say?"

"She said we see it all the time and I'd missed the signs. I thought she would be a little more sympathetic. I don't know, maybe she's hardened in some way after losing her kids. After she and Melanie got together, there were some problems with Melanie's kids too." The last thing I wanted to do was make Alex feel worse by mentioning what Josie said about him moving in.

"Who?" he asked absently.

"Melanie. I told you about her. Josie's lover. She and Josie are raising her two kids together."

"Grace, I told you before. Josie and I lived in the same town house community for five years. I've never seen anyone entering or leaving her house. I would have noticed if there were kids around. How old are they?"

"What? That's weird. Maybe you just missed them, that's all. I think they're about eleven and fourteen or so. I can't remember for sure."

"That place is as quiet as a tomb. You'd think with two kids, eleven and fourteen there'd be a bike outside or they'd throw a ball around in the yard or they'd come outside once in a while."

We passed the Kahler Inn and Suites and Alex pulled up in front of Mayo Clinic's Gonda Building on First Street Southwest. "Who knows? Maybe they're really quiet kids or something. It was weird though that there were no signs of kids in the townhouse. Who knows? Maybe Josie's a neat freak and their stuff is all in their rooms."

"Yeah, maybe," Alex replied noncommittally.

"I have this weird sense of something being off today. Maybe it was seeing Angela. She obviously still has feelings for you. I hope the police keep an eye on her. I feel like we're so close to an answer."

Alex leaned over to kiss me good-bye. "Call me and I'll pick you up tonight after work, okay?" I said.

"I will. We'll talk about it later, okay? How about a run before dinner?"

"Sure, a run will do me good."

"I'll give you a call when I'm done."

CHAPTER THIRTY-FIVE

THE SHARP SMELL OF PINE NEEDLES pierced the late night air. A full moon hung in the sky, glowing like an ivory pendant. Summer was slowly edging into fall. "I want us to have a few minutes to remember what it's like to feel normal again, with no talk about kidnapping or the children missing . . ." I broke off. My life had been pared down to the essentials: enough food to survive, water, sleep, and shelter. I barely remembered what it was like to have a thought that didn't take shape around the children's absence.

"Are you sure you can do this?" Alex reached across the Amish porch glider to take my hand. His palm was warm and dry and I clasped it gratefully. "You know we can talk about anything you want."

My own hands were as slick and clammy as mussels. I wiped them on my jeans. "We haven't really talked about our trip. Everything that happened afterward was so horrible."

"Unbelievable." Alex's voice was fraught with incredulity.

"There was so much I wanted to tell Caleigh and Dane about it. Do you remember that fruit the villagers brought for the bus trip back to Surabaya? Oh, my god, the durian! I laughed until tears ran down my cheeks. It really did smell like a bad case of flatulence!"

Alex smiled. "It's good to see you laugh again. Do you remember the shadow play production in the village? The performance of puppets behind that cotton screen? What was the name of it?"

"*Wayang kulit*. The puppets were made from buffalo skin. They were amazing. I fell in love with you all over again when you said you wanted to buy puppets and perform our own version of a shadow play with the kids."

Alex's arm was around my shoulder and he squeezed gently. "The shadows seemed almost lifelike, the way they seemed to move. Do you remember the offerings of flowers and incense that were laid out in bamboo trays every morning?"

"The monkeys who raided them for the fruit looked like little old men. Every time the clerk got out a fly swatter, they ran off into the bushes and as soon as his back was turned, they'd be back to eat the offerings. I wish the kids could have seen them . . ."

"Me too. Do you want to light some of the incense we brought back?" Alex asked.

I shrugged. I hadn't even unpacked them yet. "They're still in the suitcase."

"How about the coconut?" Alex asked. "I'll get it."

The incense filled the night with a fleeting memory of when everything seemed right in the world. "As worried as I was," he said, "the last night on the beach with you was amazing. The boardwalk and the sunset were spectacular."

"Oh, Alex. I was thinking of Caleigh again. Her long, shiny hair. How her arms and legs had been as suntanned and as spindly as a sandpiper's all summer. How could I not have known what was happening?" I wondered if I'd made a mistake in bringing Alex into our lives, and then ashamed, I pushed the thought away.

"As soon as we find them, we'll get treatment for her. For both of them. For all of us," Alex said diplomatically. "We will find them, you know."

I cast a grateful glance in his direction and struggled to put the thoughts of him being a mistake out of my mind. "I know. Let's talk about something else. It's already fall. That always meant an end to the laziness of summer and the thrill of school beginning for me. The kids' excitement about meeting their teachers brought it all back every year." We rocked slowly on the porch swing. "How about you?"

"Me too." He pulled me closer. "But for me, summer wasn't lazy. I grew up on a farm in Northern Minnesota and there was a lot to do. I was up at dawn with my dad planting or harvesting corn all spring and summer. I couldn't wait to get back to school!"

I wanted to lie down beside him and breathe in his woodsy smell. To be comforted by it. I just didn't know if it would ever be possible again. "You've never said much about that. I looked forward to it too, but more because summer was such a lonely place. I'm an only child and I didn't have a lot of friends. I've been so focused on school and my career and later, the kids, that I never really made any women friends. I guess that's why this thing with Josie bothers me so much. I thought of her as a friend. It really hurts, you know?"

"I know, sweetie." He intertwined his fingers through mine.

"It's nice to have a friend you can have lunch with and talk about things with . . . not that you're not terrific, but really, you didn't even notice Angela's shoes." He gave me a questioning look. "Hey, I'm kidding!"

"Was she wearing shoes?" he teased.

Pretending to slap him, I told him how much I had always loved fall. The smell of it, the leaves underfoot, the feeling of something just around the corner. Those dark nights just before winter when everything felt crisp and alive. Sometimes I'd pretend a blanket of stars covered the earth and the moon cast a spell.

"On Halloween, when Caleigh was young, she was so excited to get into her costume and go trick-or-treating that she could hardly eat. Dane is still like that. What I wouldn't give for them to be home . . ." I laid my head on Alex's shoulder. "You've been like a rock during this nightmare." I took in another deep breath, devouring his smell. The tears began before I could blink them away. "I guess I can't even make it an hour, huh? I just don't know if I can do this anymore. What if?" The unspoken words hovered like insects over our heads.

"Grace, don't." He tilted my face toward his. "Don't give up. We'll find them. Are you sure you're ready to go back to work on Monday?"

Time had hung as heavily as a woolen sweater left out in the rain. "Yeah, it's been three weeks. I can't stay home alone and wait by the phone another minute. I got permission to bring my cell phone into work so that Meyers can call me if there's any news. I'll apply to the Adolescent Psychiatry Fellowship for next year and hand in my resignation next summer."

"Maybe it will be good for you to get out of the house for a few hours each day," he said. "Come on. Let's go to bed. I'm beat."

* * *

THE FOLLOWING MONDAY when I walked through the parking lot, everything looked as it was supposed to. Inmates raked leaves inside the fenced-in areas. Officers and nurses walked by and chatted in small groups, lapsing into silence when they saw me. A nurse I knew waved awkwardly before hurrying away. It had been over four weeks since I

216

had last checked in at the sallyport, emptied my pockets, took off my shoes and passed through the metal detectors.

Josie was in the lobby removing her shoes when I got there. "Hey. I'm back." I had wondered if returning to work had been the right decision, but seeing Josie's face felt like winning at bingo.

"Hi." Josie stepped through the metal detector and slipped her shoes back on. She kept walking as I waited for the corrections officer to hand me the keys to the unit.

"Wait up!" I called, but she had gone on ahead.

The metal door into the psych unit was heavier than I remembered, and the unit darker and closer. A flickering sense of near panic rose in my chest. I counted my steps to the nurse's station, poured a cup of coffee and stole into my office. A pile of charts sat stacked on top of the desk. Renewing the long-standing medication orders would take all morning. By then, I hoped the panic would give a hint of subsiding.

It was almost noon before I finished writing medication orders for the new patients and saw the two most acute patients on the floor. They weren't too bad, considering it was a full moon. Tyrell Perkins was still there, and Emanuel and Finn were gone. For a few moments, I realized I had thought of something beside the abduction. The thin flat face of my watch said lunchtime and out of habit, I picked up the phone and dialed Josie's office. "Hey! I'm done for the morning. Want to meet in the cafeteria for lunch?"

"Sorry, Grace. I can't. I'm gonna go running."

"I'll go with you. I have my stuff in the car. I have a meeting at one, so I have an hour to tell you about Angela. The police are keeping her under surveillance."

"Can I take a rain check? I really feel like running alone today. I'm not up for company right now . . ." Josie's voice trailed off.

"Well, sure, another time then." Whatever. *What the fuck is wrong with her?* I sat at my desk and stared at the phone. The dial tone sounded a monotonous beep. I trudged to the cafeteria, hurt by Josie's disregard of my feelings. It had never been easy for me to make friends. I had always been the clinician, the academic living inside a textbook. Josie was a leap of faith. Someone who I thought understood and accepted me for who I was.

The cafeteria was filled with the hum of conversation. A line of nurses and corrections officers inched toward the counter. I picked out the most appetizing items on display: a salad and a diet soda, and swept my gaze across the room. Bud Anderson sat alone at a table by the window. He raised his head and motioned for me to join him. I wasn't sure if I was ready to join anyone. Conversations stopped as I walked to his table. My missing children and I had become the elephant in the room.

"Hi, Doc. How's it going? Any word yet?"

"Hi, uhm, Bud. Nope, no word yet. Do you mind if I sit down?"

He stood and pulled out a chair. "Glad to see you back."

"I want to thank you for the help you've been." I choked up despite the promise I had made to myself that morning. "I know you had a lot going on and yet you . . ."

"Don't worry about it. Glad to help. I know what it feels like to lose your kids."

"I've been so frantic about my situation that I never asked about what happened with your children. How's everything going?"

"The judge awarded custody to my ex-wife this week. I'll see my kids every other weekend." He looked down and stirred his coffee.

My stomach muscles tightened. "I'm sorry. Is there anything I can do to help?" We looked at one another and connected in a way I never would have thought possible.

"I dunno. My lawyer says we can appeal. We'll see. How're you doing? You hangin' in there?"

The salad and the rubbery hard-boiled boiled egg were impossible to swallow. "I'm trying." My stomach protested, and I pushed the salad away. Before I knew what was happening, I was blubbering, telling Bud Anderson about the fruitless tips, the reporters camped out on our doorstep, the tabloids' implications that Alex and I were to blame, and about meeting Angela, and Josie's odd behavior. My stomach went from protesting to feeling leaden.

Bud's face tightened. "I never liked that woman." He tried to arrange his features into banal lines.

Bud was an ex-marine not prone to emotional outbursts. Here was a man entirely different from the Bud Anderson who accosted me at the party. A man with feelings, with compassion and an understanding of suffering. He was the only staff member who had dared ask about the children. "Bud, what is it about Josie you don't like?"

"Just a feeling. I spent a lot of time around different people in the service and here in the prison. I can smell a rat a mile away," he said ominously. "She's rabid, Doc. Don't ask me how I know. I'm a hunter. I know a sick animal when I see one."

"Maybe you're mistaken," I suggested. "Josie's had a hard life."

"Yeah, maybe," he agreed, not very convincingly.

The afternoon lengthened and brought cooler air with it. At the end of the day, I walked back to the car, feeling a little satisfaction I had made it this far. Alex would be home late so I stopped at Joe's on the way home. Things between us had felt so strained lately I wanted to surprise him with dinner.

* * *

THE GROCERIES SAT ON THE FRONT SEAT. I pulled close to the mailbox and placed the day's mail alongside the chicken breasts, pasta salad, and sweet corn. From a distance, the house looked as forlorn as a never-worn bridal gown hanging in the closet. I lugged the groceries in and went back to the car for the mail. A thin white envelope with no stamp and my name printed on the face was stuffed between the bills.

My chest constricted as I unfolded the familiar white copy paper. I sat at the kitchen table, unable to breathe. Every nerve ending tingled.

IF YOU WANT TO SEE YOUR CHILDREN AGAIN, YOU WILL BRING $500,000 TO THE PLAYGROUND AT SILVER LAKE PARK AT MIDNIGHT ON FRIDAY, SEPTEMBER 21ST. COME ALONE OR YOU WILL NEVER SEE THEM AGAIN. NO POLICE.

The crisp white paper was stark against the dark tablecloth. The letters began to waver and the walls seemed to fold in on me. A strange sound came out of my mouth. Something between a sob and a scream. My phone in hand, I prayed, *Alex, pick up . . . Please pick up.*

I got his voicemail. Fuck. I called his office. "Dr. Sawyer's office," his nasal-voiced administrative assistant answered.

With a bubbling sense of panic, I said, "Ruth, it's Grace Rendeau. It's an emergency. Is Alex there?"

"Oh, Dr. Rendeau, how are you? I'm so sorry to hear about what's happened. I wrote your name down in our prayer circle at church."

"Thanks, and sorry to interrupt, but it's an emergency, Ruth. Could you put Alex on?"

"Oh, Dr. Sawyer left early today. Right after his last patient, about an hour ago."

"Did he say where he was going?" I struggled not to scream. "Was he making rounds in the hospital?"

"I don't think so. He took his briefcase and his coat. Said he'd see me tomorrow."

"Thanks, Ruth." I hung up, still staring at the note. I felt sick and small, like a child after too much candy. My throat constricted. My eyes were as coarse and gritty as sandpaper. Where the fuck was he? I went upstairs and splashed water on my face. No police. Should I get the money and go alone or should I tell Alex? I didn't have $500,000 but maybe between the two of us, we could come up with the money by Friday. I tried Alex's cell phone again. Nothing.

I was beginning to panic as I stood framed in the bathroom window, looking out onto the driveway. When Alex pulled up, my feet skimmed the stairs as I flew to meet him at the door. "Where have you been?" My voice was demanding, near hysterical. "I've been calling you for hours!" As soon as the words tumbled out, I saw it.

Alex stood at the door with a chocolate cake from my favorite bakery in one hand and a bouquet of wilting yellow roses in the other. "I wanted to surprise you after your first day back to work," he said sheepishly.

I pressed my cheek against his collarbone. His breath was laced with the smell of alcohol. An unnatural quiet settled between us. "Have you been drinking? Alex, there's been a ransom note," I said into his chest, furious he hadn't been here when I needed him.

"Grace, I'm sorry." He stumbled into the living room. "I stopped for one drink with Jason from work, and it just felt so good to be normal for a change that before I knew it, one drink turned into three."

"Jesus. I really can't believe you!" I snarled, more hurt by his explanation than by the fact that he'd been drinking. He wanted a normal life I might never be able to give him again.

The note was an incongruous seed of hope strewn in my path and I was determined to focus on that. Dinner was forgotten as we debated what to do. "I have to do it. I know it means they're still alive." I paced in the living room. "Don't you see? I could get them back."

"I don't want you going anywhere alone." Alex's voice was bone-dry. He turned away. In my peripheral vision, I saw him trawl the kitchen drawer for a corkscrew. "You don't know who these people are or what they might do to you. I need another drink. Do you want something?"

An awkward silence ensued. He was a man accustomed to getting his own way but now I despised him for it. I ran into the bathroom, not caring that he could hear me retching. "Do you think we could get a loan for that amount?" I asked when I came out.

"I don't know." Alex was having trouble opening the wine. His eyes were bloodshot. He took out a wine glass from the cabinet and dropped it, shattering it into sharp fragments. "Shit. Sorry. I'll get the broom."

"Forget the broom. Forget the fucking wine. Listen to me! I can't believe you're even thinking about wine at a time like this. Can we get a loan for $500,000?"

"Grace, you can't be serious. Call Meyers. He has to know."

I sat down, massaged my temples and stood again. "The note said NO POLICE. God, I can't sit still. What do you think?"

"Ransom notes always say that. What, the kidnappers will suggest you bring the police with you? I think you should call the police." Alex swept up the shards and reached for another glass. He sat down at the kitchen table, poured a brimful of white wine and said, "Today is Monday. The note said to have the money by Friday. That gives us plenty of time to think about this."

"It gives us time to cash our IRA's and take out a loan." I was both looking forward to and dreading Friday.

Alex rose from the table and walked over to where I stood. "I love you. I would do anything for you, but I think we should call the police. We have time to think about this, Grace. I want you to be safe," he whispered in my hair.

I had never needed anyone more desperately in my life but I pushed him away. "We have four days. I'll think about it. I'm just so afraid that if I tell Meyers, something will happen to them."

Alex went to the table and got a napkin to wipe my nose. He was breathing heavily. "I know, sweetheart. I just think he should know so that you're not in any danger. The police have experience in dealing with this sort of thing. They'll know what to do."

"I'm going to bed," I finally said. I understood that to Alex, I was everything, but to a woman with children, they were everything. That was the difference between us. "Maybe things will seem clearer in the morning. They're okay. I just have to believe that."

Alex kissed the top of my head. "You're right, it's late. Let's go upstairs. Are you going to go to work tomorrow?"

"I'd go absolutely crazy if I were here thinking about that note and what we should do all day. Maybe something will come to me at work."

When my head finally touched the pillow, I began to cry big heaving sobs. And then I decided to go to the bank alone.

CHAPTER THIRTY-SIX

JOSIE!" I burst into her office the next morning. "I got another note."
Josie sat at her desk, looking as tattered as old shoes in a flea market.
She whistled between her teeth. "You're kidding? What'd it say?"

"It was a ransom note. It asked for five-hundred thousand dollars by Friday."

"What are you going to do?" She stood and walked to the window in the sparsely furnished office. Sunlight burned through the bars and played up the highlights in her dark curly hair. There were greenish circles, like something swept in by a storm, smeared under her eyes.

"Oh, Josie. I know this brings up bad memories for you. Now I know what it must have been like for you to lose your kids."

Josie was trembling. I wasn't imagining it. "Yeah, it does. So, what are you going to do?" she asked, returning to her desk.

"I don't know. Alex wants to call the police."

"You're not gonna do that are you? If the note said no police it probably means no police." The note of warning in her voice was as spiked as a thorn.

"I don't know. I wish I did. I still have a few days to think about it. I'm gonna try to get some work done. I know this means they're okay. I feel so much better, just knowing that. Oh, Josie, I can't help feeling we're really close to finding them."

She smiled tightly. "Me, too."

"You want to meet in the cafeteria today for lunch?" I asked on my way out the door.

"Sorry, can't today. I have some errands to run. Maybe another time." She chewed her fingernail and looked away. "See ya, Grace."

Deep in thought as I walked back to my office, I didn't see Mr. Perkins until he spoke. "Mornin', Doc."

I jumped. Soapy water sloshed from his bucket onto the floor.

"Careful there that you don't slip. How's it going with you lately? You been gone a few weeks. Vacation?"

"No." I stepped cautiously around the puddle. "Thanks for asking. How are you doing, Mr. Perkins?" Time seemed to pass more slowly for me than for anyone around me, with the exception of Mr. Perkins. He mopped as carefully as if he were painting a portrait.

"Not too bad. Say, ya heard anything from old Finn?" he asked.

"As a matter of fact, I saw him the other day. He looked well. I hear he has a job in a nursery."

"Praise the Lord! I bet he's happy as a clam at high tide."

The expression gave me pause. Anything to take my mind off the ransom note. High tide was when clams were set free from the attentions of predators. It had more relevance to me than Mr. Perkins knew. "I hope so," I said, continuing to my office.

Time marched at a donkey's pace that morning. Progress notes were due but the words spun off at dizzying speeds every time I tried to think coherently. Just before noon, I was startled by a sharp rap at the door. It was Bud Anderson.

"How's it going today, Grace? Any news?"

"Come in, Bud. Do you have a minute? As a matter of fact, there has been some news."

He looked me hungrily. "A new lead?"

"If I tell you something, will you promise to keep it to yourself?" I studied Bud's face while he watched mine in turn. Could I trust him with something as important as this?

Bud loomed over me casting a shadow on my face. As if he had read my mind, he said, "You can count on me. I swear."

"There's been a ransom note." The room grew silent.

Bud brought his hand to his forehead and wiped away beads of perspiration. He sat down on the edge of the chair opposite my desk. "When?"

"Yesterday." I tapped my fingers on the desk out of sheer nervousness. "Can I really trust you?"

He leaned forward expectantly. "I swear on my grandmother's grave. What did it say?"

"It asked for five-hundred thousand dollars by Friday night." I was alternately elated and terrified. "No police. I have to go alone."

Bud whistled a long, long high-pitched sound. "You want me to go with you? I have a Beretta I can bring along." He began pacing the room.

"No! It said I need to go alone. I can't risk the kids or you or anyone else getting hurt. I probably shouldn't have told you."

"No, I'm glad you told me. Where's the drop off?"

"I can't tell you that. But thanks."

"If you change your mind, I'm here for you," he promised. "By the way, did you hear that Venegas was captured in Puerto Rico?"

The room shifted. "No. What happened? Where was he?"

"He was holed up with another inmate. The guy who escaped with him. Somebody named Gutierrez Garcia. They were at the asshole's mother's house. An old lady who's in a lot of trouble herself now."

I stood too quickly and grabbed hold of the edge of my desk, to keep from falling. "When did this happen?"

"Day before yesterday." He looked at me quizzically. "You okay?" I nodded in response and he continued, "I heard they took 'em down without any problem. They're back in Guaynabo's detention center. I sure as hell hope Venegas doesn't get sent back here again. What's wrong? You look like somebody just walked over your freakin' grave, Doc."

"Gutierrez Garcia." I realized why the name had stuck such a chord with me when Meyers mentioned it. "That's Josie's last name."

* * *

BUD

MY MOUTH WAS WATERING at the prospect of a burger and fries for lunch. I clocked out and as I walked to the truck, even though the sun was shining, I had a strange premonition. It was a nice Indian summer day. Every shade of red I knew and some I didn't know were on display. Tough break for what had happened to Grace. I felt for her.

Again, the feeling of something wrong crawled up my spine. My years in Afghanistan had taught me to trust my instincts and I listened to this one.

I saw her in the parking lot, with a backpack strapped to her back. She walked briskly to the bike trail and followed it behind the prison. I stayed a dozen yards behind but she never looked back. Eight-foot-tall bluestem perennials and blue lyme grass provided the camouflage I needed in case she turned around. She rounded a curve, nearing the pond. Again, I was in luck. The giant reed grass surrounding the pond was a perfect screen. Twelve feet tall, it provided the necessary cover.

She turned sharply and took an overgrown trail in the woods, turning back once to look when a twig I stepped on snapped and drew her attention. My summer uniform blended in with the gray-green Indian grass at the base of the trail and she kept going. From there on, I kept my distance. She wasn't difficult to trail. She stood out like a red flag.

The path climbed higher. There were bare spaces where volunteers had removed buckthorn. I tried to stay behind the tall oaks, in case she turned again. Dead leaves crackled under my feet but she was intent on where she was going and didn't turn again.

There was no real reason for following her except for her furtive manner and the feeling I had. I felt like a lightning rod absorbing strange charges in the air.

She walked quickly and although I was in pretty good shape, my breathing became labored. It was as if she'd walked the winding trail all her life. She followed it, without any hesitation, to the distant end of the nature center's wooded acreage. Bingo. There it was. A limestone cave around the bend, far from the trail. She unlocked the padlock on the metal gate. I heard the dog bark first. A small King Charles spaniel jumped on the her legs, wagging its tail.

Two children soon stepped out, shielding their eyes from the sun. From where I stood, the boy looked to be five or six years old, the girl, a teen. Their clothes were mud-stained, their faces gaunt and smudged the color of dust. The girl's hair was a long greasy strand of twine running down her back. The woman opened her backpack and took out sandwiches and juice and a bone for the dog.

My heart rattled in my chest. I knew who these children were. I took out my phone, praying I had a signal and called 911. She opened her backpack and took out a stack of clothes and a can of dog food. I hid behind a bush watching the children and the dog wolf down the food. They sat and talked and then the woman hugged them and locked them behind the gate. They waved good-bye and she started back down the trail. As soon as they were out of earshot, I wrestled her to the ground. "Fuckin' bitch," I said. "I should have known it was you."

She fought me with everything she had. Her nails were as sharp as daggers. She clawed my face. The blood and what she had done turned me into a mad dog. I wrestled the key away from her, threw her on the ground and pinned her arms under my knees. I grabbed a set of plastic restraints from my pocket with one hand. The training I had had in restraining inmates was a prize. I yanked her up by her hair, twisted her arms behind her back and snapped the cuffs on while she spit at me.

"Keep walking and don't make a sound," I told her. She was as strong as a wild cat, but her face was cold and empty. She kicked me in the knee and tried to squirm out of my grasp. "Fuckin' bitch." I shoved her and dragged her down the trail. Sirens shrieked in the distance and I knew the police would be waiting in the parking lot. I hoped Grace would be there too.

CHAPTER THIRTY-SEVEN

TIME TO GET BACK TO WORK. After eating a container of yogurt and some grapes, I sat at my desk, looking out at a beautiful fall day. The warden had given me permission to keep my phone in the office due to the special circumstances. I could have kissed him when my cell phone vibrated and I saw the caller I.D.

"Grace, it's Meyers. I need you to come outside now. I'm in the parking lot."

My heart leapt in my chest. "What is it, Detective?" I rose quickly and swayed on my feet. Adrenalin shot through my body like a drug. There was an urgency in his voice I hadn't heard before. "I think we've found the children, Grace," he said softly. "I want you to come outside now. I'll be waiting for you."

I asked if they were okay and hung up the phone before he could answer. I ran down the halls to the sallyport and threw my keys at the officer on duty, escaping through the front exit. Meyers and Donnelly sat in their unmarked car outside the entrance. I shot toward them. Donnelly got out of the car. "Get in the front," she said with a smile as she climbed in the back.

"Are they alive?" I held my breath. Everything, including the expressions on Meyers and Donnelly's faces, the sound of the siren, the blurred landscape, all seemed surreal.

"They're alive." Meyers put the lights and the siren on and we sped half a mile away to Quarry Hill Nature Center. For the first time in my life, I sobbed with happiness. It was an emotional release I had never known existed. I cried in the car until my body shook. We arrived at Quarry Hill Nature Center and Donnelly opened my door.

There were several haphazardly parked squad cars in the parking lot. A knot of excited students stood like a pack of young coyotes, pawing the asphalt. A routine field trip to the nature center had obviously taken an unexpected turn. Their two young teachers, dressed in jeans and sweatshirts, attempted to keep order. The excitement in the air was palpable.

"Where are they?" I didn't dare breathe. The three weeks the children had been missing were about to come to an end. I thanked God, and swore to myself that I would return to church.

My legs were rubbery. I looked at a squad car with several officers around it and was immediately stunned into silence. Josie stood handcuffed against the car. My tears dried on my face. A burly police officer with a buzz cut recited her Miranda rights as if in a bad crime drama. "Are you sure that you want to answer these questions, without the presence of a lawyer? You have the right to remain silent. Anything you say or do can and will be held against you in a court of law. You have the right to speak to an attorney. If you cannot afford an attorney, one will be appointed for you. Do you understand these rights as they have been read to you?"

Josie fixed the officer with a malevolent glare. Her eyes narrowed and glinted when she saw me. "Grace, tell them," she implored me. "I love you. I didn't do anything wrong. I love them."

"What's going on?" I shrieked.

Within moments, the sweetest sound I had ever heard filled the parking lot. It was the sound of my children crying, "Mommy! Mommy!" The sight of Caleigh and Dane rushing toward me, unharmed, from behind the squad car toward me was almost unbearably beautiful. I wanted to fall on my knees and thank God they were safe. I looked from their faces to Josie. Her dark eyes were heavily circled. She looked me in the eye. "I did what was best for them. I'm their mother now. Me!" The officer shoved her. "Alex doesn't deserve them or you. I do!" she screamed.

"I don't even know who you are!" I cried. I had gotten her completely wrong. I had trusted this ferocious, pitiful woman, and it had almost cost me everything.

"Ms. Garrett, do you or do you not understand your rights?" the officer said.

"Yes. I understand my fucking rights. And no, I do not want a lawyer," Josie snarled.

"You're barking up the wrong tree, Gutierrez," Bud yelled from the parking lot. "Put a sock in it."

"Bud!" I moaned. "What's going on? It was you who found them, wasn't it?"

He nodded as Caleigh walked slowly toward me, her eyes sunken in her thin, drawn face. Dane's face erupted in a wide smile as he jumped into my arms. "Josie found the puppy, Mom!" he said. I glanced at Bud and saw him wipe a tear from his eyes.

"Oh, my darlings." The children in my arms, I turned to Bud and wept with relief. "I don't know how I'll ever be able to thank you."

"Forget it. Following her was like shooting fish in a barrel." It was the first time I had ever seen him smile. "She led me right to them."

* * *

MEYERS TOLD ME LATER VENEGAS had escaped with Josie's brother, Roberto Gutierrez Garcia, aided by a kitchen worker named Humberto Rodriquez. Josie had contracted him to get her brother out of prison. She hadn't counted on Venegas and her brother knowing one another and escaping together. They were now both in custody in Puerto Rico. Meyers figured Josie finally sent the ransom note because she needed the money to pay Rodriquez, who was still at large and, word had it, was threatening to kill her mother.

Meyers also dug up records of a real estate transaction. As Josie told me, she had bought her mother a house four weeks ago and Meyers figured she needed the money to make payments. More shocking was the news that Josie lived alone. Melanie had left five years ago.

Between the loss of Melanie and her kids and Josie's own children, I believed Josie grieved the loss of two sets of children. She later confessed she had felt needed by Caleigh, who had begun to talk to her about the cutting and about her fears that once I married, they would pay second fiddle in my life.

* * *

I DON'T KNOW WHY it didn't set off an alarm in my head when you mentioned Melanie and her kids at Josie's," Alex said that night. "I guess I was so preoccupied with the children being gone and with how you were doing. I feel like such a fool."

I snuggled up to him in bed. We had just tucked the children into their beds after pizza and the movie, *Diary of a Wimpy Kid*, Dane's favorite.

"Do you remember when I told you I came home early and Josie was here?" Alex asked. "Caleigh said tonight that Josie had tried to get in to get them some clothes and a few things they had asked for. When

Sketcher began barking, I guess she was scared off. I'd never seen Sketcher act that way before. I let him out on the porch while we were talking and he circled her, snarling and baring his teeth. I'd never seen him do that. I wish I had paid more attention to his weird behavior. I could've saved us at least some of this pain."

"She fooled everybody, Alex. When I think of how I introduced her to the kids . . ."

"She must have been planning this for a while," he said.

"I'm not sure about that. What really seemed to be the turning point for Josie was when I told her I loved you. She was always so opposed to our relationship. I should have realized that was a clue."

"She functioned well for someone so disturbed," Alex said.

"She told me she'd been with Melanie and her children for ten years—ever since she got divorced and her husband moved to Wyoming with their daughters. You were right, with kids Caleigh and Dane's ages, there would have been a bike or a ball in the yard. They would have come outside, at least to go to school. It's my fault for not picking up on what you were trying to tell me and for not questioning Josie more about this so-called lover and children. And for not recognizing her feelings for me," I said softly. "When I think she made it all up, and I believed her . . ." My voice cracked. "I trusted her and invited her to my house to meet my children, and it was all a lie."

"You couldn't have known, sweetheart. Don't blame yourself. We have a long road ahead of us, but the important thing is they're safe and Josie will be put away for a very long time."

"I wonder how this will affect them. If I could only take it back." I edged closer to Alex.

"Listen, between the two of us and Dahlia and Stan, we'll make sure they know they're loved and safe. We'll get them help if they need it. I think being home with Sketcher and Hope and their family will be all it takes."

The End

EPILOGUE

I LEARNED LATER JOSIE had called the house on the morning Alex and I were due to arrive home and found out the children were alone. Josie came to the house and told the children she had seen Hope near the nature center. They went with her willingly.

That first night, in the cave, they were terrified. Dane cried all night. But Josie cared for them. She was the one who had taken Hope. The puppy stayed with the children. Josie came two or three times each day and took the children and Hope for short walks. Anything they asked for, she brought, except, of course, what they needed most—me. It was only later that Caleigh realized Josie was the woman we had seen following us at Quarry Hill.

After Officer Anderson found them, Caleigh and Dane tried to pretend everything was fine for my sake, but nothing was really ever the same after that. A bond had developed between Josie and the children. They didn't want to hurt me any more than I had already been hurt but they had begun to trust Josie. When the police put Josie in the squad car, I saw the tears of divided loyalties in their eyes. It was the Stockholm syndrome, the bond that develops between a kidnapper and his or her hostages, but it was painful nonetheless.

They know now that the loss they felt when Josie left our lives was normal. They had bonded in a way nobody can really ever understand. Dane was young and seemed to recover quickly, but for years, Caleigh suffered from flashbacks and debilitating anxiety.

As irrational as it seemed, they loved her. Josie did a terrible thing. She told them Alex and I didn't want them anymore. She said she would raise my children and love them the way they deserved to be loved. Some days she told them she would convince me to leave Alex, who never deserved me or us, according to Josie, and they would raise us together. The only thing my children balked at was calling her Mommy.

Later, people made judgments. They asked why the children hadn't tried to escape while on walks. What they didn't realize was Caleigh and Dane were children and after a while, Josie was their only connection to love and security.

I lost a trusted friend and almost lost my children. I still wonder if it will ever be possible to wash away the stains of betrayal.

Grace Rendeau